IN THE SHRUBBERY

A perfect feel-good read from one of
Britain's best-loved authors

Constable Nick Mystery Book 15

NICHOLAS RHEA

JOFFE BOOKS

Revised edition 2020
Joffe Books, London
www.joffebooks.com

© Nicholas Rhea, 1995, 2020
First published in Great Britain 1995

This book is a work of fiction. Names, characters, businesses, organisations, places and events are either the product of the author's imagination or are used fictitiously. Any resemblance to actual persons, living or dead, events or locales is entirely coincidental. The spelling used is British English except where fidelity to the author's rendering of accent or dialect supersedes this. The right of Nicholas Rhea to be identified as author of this work has been asserted by him in accordance with the Copyright, Designs and Patents Act 1988.

Cover credit: Colin Williamson
www.colinwilliamsonprints.com

Join our mailing list and become one of 1,000s of readers enjoying free Kindle crime thriller, detective, mystery, and romance books and new releases. Receive your first bargain book this month!

www.joffebooks.com

We love to hear from our readers! Please email any feedback you have to: feedback@joffebooks.com

ISBN: 978-1-78931-649-0

CHAPTER I

"If you could see my legs when I took my boots off!"
CHARLES DICKENS, 1812–70

There had never been a murder in Aidensfield. I contemplated that happy statistic as I gazed from the kitchen window one beautiful spring morning while waiting for the kettle to boil. I wanted to make a cup of coffee, and as I beheld the seemingly endless but incredibly tranquil moorland views with the kettle's temperature rising, I realised how fortunate I was to be a constable in such a place. The hard-working kettle was the noisiest object in my blissful world that morning.

I presided over a landscape which seemed to rest in eternal peace, a true retreat from the pressures of the world, lightyears away from violent human death. At such a time, it was possible to believe that no other living thing existed upon those moors and, had that been true, there would have been no crime and no vexing social problems. But life did exist out there. Problems did occur and crimes were committed. Seldom were they vicious, however; they comprised, in the main, petty crime and minor vandalism. These nuisances did not require the majesty of the courts to appease the victims;

the victims relied instead upon the common sense of the village constable and the wishes of the public.

But murder was not among those crimes although during my brief time as the village constable at Aidensfield, I had dealt with several sudden deaths. They included traffic fatalities, accidental shootings, drownings and even suicides but never a murder. Not that I would ever be allowed to deal with a case of murder. That would be the duty of teams of CID officers led by Detective Superintendent Gregory Galvin from my own Force Headquarters, inevitably nicknamed The Horse because of his initials, GG. The investigation of a murder in the North Riding of Yorkshire would not, however, be the responsibility of New Scotland Yard as some fiction writers would lead us to believe; every police force investigates the murders which occur within its boundaries. As the incumbent constable, however, I would have a role to play if a murder or any other serious crime, like rape, was committed on my beat.

It would be a minor role and might involve house-to-house enquiries or acting as liaison officer between the teams of investigators and the local population. But it was an academic question — there was no murder at Aidensfield. Even though it was my ambition, and the ambition of many police officers both in uniform and in the CID to arrest a murderer, I did not wish such a crime to manifest itself upon my peaceful rural patch. We can all do without murder.

I think my reflective mood arose because I was experiencing one of those times when nothing seemed to be happening. Over the past few days, there had been no traffic accidents to deal with, no major enquiries to concern me, no minor outbreaks of crime — in fact, very little had happened during the past month.

Boredom was threatening and I had reached the stage where it would be nice if something really exciting did occur. Then, as the kettle came to the boil, my musings were interrupted by a telephone call. Dashing into my office, I picked up the receiver.

"Aidensfield Police," I announced. "PC Rhea speaking."

"It's Sergeant Blaketon, Rhea," said the familiar voice. "I'm ringing to see if you are alive! There's been a deathly hush from Aidensfield of late, so what's happening on your patch these days?"

"Nothing, Sergeant," I responded, somewhat puzzled by his question. "It's all very quiet, all under control. Why do you ask?"

"Why do I ask, Rhea? I'll tell you why. I've received no offence reports from you for the past three weeks, no arrests chalked up against your name, no reports of suspicious goings-on, no evidence of police activity — damn all, in fact. So what are you doing, Rhea? Are you doing any work or are you gazing across the moors like The Thinker? You can't tell me that Aidensfield is a part of heaven where nothing nasty, evil or wrong ever happens. Surely some motorist has failed to insure his car or is driving around with defective brakes? Surely some pub landlord is serving under-age drinkers or allowing consumption of intoxicants after permitted hours!"

"Not on my patch, Sergeant," I retorted with confidence. "This beat is well conducted, we're all law-abiding citizens in these parts."

"So what are you doing today? It's Saturday, the day villains go hunting for victims. So are you letting secret law-breakers offend while you ignore them? Are you letting Claude Jeremiah Greengrass run riot?"

"Not at all, Sergeant . . ." I began. But he interrupted me.

"I'll bet Claude Jeremiah Greengrass isn't one of your goody-goodies! He and his cronies will be up to no good, mark my words. Shouldn't you be out there, patrolling your patch, checking cars for offences, stopping and questioning suspicious people, investigating crime, asking questions, making your presence felt, feeling a few collars? Preventing the nefarious activities of the Greengrasses of this world?"

"If offences are committed, Sergeant, you may be sure that I shall take the necessary action. I'm not on duty now because I'm working a late turn today; I'll be doing a patrol of Aidensfield, Crampton and Elsinby after lunch, checking a few stock registers, visiting a few pubs, asking a few questions about the activities of Claude Jeremiah Greengrass and his cronies, and tonight there's a big function at Elsinby Hall."

"I was going to remind you about that, Rhea. We don't want Viscount Elsinby thinking we've forgotten his party. You'll be on hand, I suppose, parking cars, preventing obstruction and annoyance, keeping the noise of revellers to a minimum, making sure there's no drunken driving or acts of vandalism. We never did get that "Halt — Major Road Ahead" sign back after Lord Ashfordly's son's birthday party and we never did find out what really happened to that Belisha beacon in Ashfordly High Street. So, I trust you will not shirk from stopping any blue-blooded offenders and dealing with them with the customary fairness of the constabulary. I hope you will not be deterred because they are of noble birth or occupy high positions of authority or esteem?"

"Sergeant," I said. "A lot of tonight's guests will be staying at the Hall over the weekend but if they do commit any offences, they will be dealt with. I can assure you of that!"

"Well, you can't tell me that offences are not being committed, Rhea, even on Aidensfield beat, so I shall expect a report of some kind before the end of today's duty. Somebody somewhere on Aidensfield beat will be offending behind your back!"

"Very good, Sergeant," I smiled, replacing the handset without any intention of reducing my well-ordered patch to a police state.

Sergeant Blaketon's outburst was a clear indication that he was bored too, but I wasn't going to be bullied into becoming an authoritarian police officer just for the sake of entering a few impressive statistics in our record books. The world, the nation and the North Riding of Yorkshire Constabulary had enough living examples of that kind of police officer and I had no intention of adding to their numbers.

I returned to the kitchen for my coffee. Being a Saturday, Mary had gone shopping with a friend; they'd gone to York because our four children were staying with their grandparents and would be away overnight. But for me, there was work to do. My duty this afternoon would be from 3pm until 11pm with a refreshment break in the middle. Tomorrow, Sunday, I would work a welcome day shift from 9am until 5pm. Tonight's late shift was not the most social of working routines although, compared with some Saturday nights, it meant an early finish. Working odd hours was part of my job and I never grumbled — one benefit from this kind of shift was that it gave me the morning off.

This was useful because I had some rubbish to clear from the garden. Having enjoyed my coffee I went outside to begin work on the borders. Some of the shrubs had overgrown and would have to be cut back before the spring growth really started. I should be able to complete those tasks before lunch and so I went into the shed for some gardening tools.

* * *

After lunch, I dressed in my uniform to begin a patrol in my official minivan. My first call was at Elsinby Estate Office where I wanted a chat with Bill Blades. Bill was Viscount Elsinby's estate manager and our work often coincided — especially when poachers trespassed upon the parkland in pursuit of pheasants or roamed across the moors after grouse. Of the local poaching fraternity however, Claude Jeremiah Greengrass was allowed to take game and rabbits from the Elsinby Estate — he was able to visit the estate without restriction. I never understood the reason for this but Claude often claimed that he and the Viscount's father were old mates, pals from the past, comrades in arms during the Second World War. Most of us ignored those boasts but the Earl of Thackerston, the Viscount's father, did have a soft spot for Claude. No one really knew why.

So far as this afternoon's meeting was concerned, however, it arose from a wish expressed by the Earl of Thackerston.

The Earl lived in Chelsea but had announced his intention to hold tonight's party at Elsinby Hall. That had been agreed by the Viscount, even though such a large gathering would involve all kinds of extra work and the expense of additional staff.

As the village constable upon whose patch the Hall stood, Bill Blades had contacted me with a request that I supervise the car parking and attend to matters such as gate-crashers and general security of the premises. Although this kind of work might not be considered part of a police constable's duties, it was in fact a useful exercise in local police/public relations and so I had agreed. When I arrived at the estate office behind Elsinby Hall, Bill settled me in a chair and asked his secretary, Alison Colburn, to provide us with tea. Then he gave me a list of invited guests and the names of all the staff who would be on duty.

"It's really a fairly modest gathering of friends and family of the Earl," Bill explained as we enjoyed our tea. "Lord Thackerston is a widower and he's celebrating his 60th birthday tonight. His birthday's on Sunday. He's always said he wanted to do this at the family seat, and so Viscount Victor agreed."

"So the guests are really those of Lord Thackerston, rather than those of his son?" I sought confirmation of this.

"Yes, there's a mixture of family and friends, some from a distance and some from the towns and villages nearby, with a few being friends of both the Viscount and His Lordship, but in the main, the guests are those of Lord Thackerston."

"It's good of Viscount Victor to allow this," I commented.

"I doubt if he had much alternative!" smiled Bill. "You might know that when the Countess died, Lord Thackerston decided to move out of the family home at Elsinby Hall and hand it over to his son, Victor, who bears the title of Viscount Elsinby.

"He was given the job of running the estate and maintaining the house, not the easiest of tasks for a man in his early twenties because of the expenses of paying staff, maintaining the house and running the business of the estate. His Lordship was relieved when his son took over — he virtually retired to his London home, occupying himself with his investments, his occasional attendance at the House of Lords, his varied business interests and a somewhat hectic social life."

"So the house and the estate don't belong to Viscount Victor?" I asked. Most of the local people called him Viscount Victor.

"Not yet. He's merely custodian until his father decides what to do about it; his father retains a strong interest and influence upon the estate. If things go as one assumes, the property will be passed to the eldest son — Viscount Victor — that's how it's always been in the past and the Earl is a stickler for tradition. But Victor can't pass it to his children because he hasn't any and, worse still, can't produce any. There's a rumour the Earl is going to announce radical changes at the party, but I think it is just a rumour, probably set off by the Earl himself to make sure the family turns up! The Earl's a lively character, Nick, he's got lots of business interests and Viscount Victor has been running the estate for ten years now. To be honest, it's not making enough money and I do know there are worries, among the tenants especially, that some of our farms might have to be sold off and that jobs will go. You can see why tonight's gathering is so important. Mind, the Earl has never made any public complaints about the way the estate is functioning — he's still getting a useful income from it and he knows Victor is doing his best in very difficult times."

"So what's the programme for tonight's rave-up?" My official duties were to be outside the premises. I had no responsibility for what happened inside, unless, of course, someone entered illegally or committed a crime. Outside the main gate on the public road, I could be regarded as fulfilling the conventional duties of a police officer in a public place, checking cars, maintaining the flow of traffic, preventing obstruction, deterring crime.

"Some of the guests will be staying on the premises; we can sleep twenty people in the house without difficulty," Bill told me. "The majority of the residents will arrive this afternoon but there will be some late comers, there always is. We've also invited people from the locality and they will be arriving just before the reception. Extra staff are being brought from the village — there's a three-piece orchestra too, they're playing for dancing after dinner. All those people — the orchestra, staff and guests — have been given invitations which bear their names. On previous occasions, people have tried to gate-crash, pretending to be a member of staff or musician or some such thing, and so I would ask you, Nick, when you arrive this evening, to ensure that everyone who comes through the gates is a *bona fide* visitor. The Earl has expressed a particular desire that no gate-crashers be allowed in, hence your presence. So, Nick, if you could be on the main gate from 6pm onwards, we should be most grateful."

"Of course, I'll make sure there are no unauthorised entries."

"Thanks. Most of the guests will be in the Hall before 8pm when they sit down to dinner. Once they're in, you might patrol the grounds, at your discretion, to ensure continuing security. I know that's not your responsibility, but the show of a uniformed presence could be advantageous. Some of the temporary staff will leave at 10pm when I shall lock the gates. We'll then see to our own security."

"And your staff will check any incomers who arrive before six?" He nodded and I went on, "The fact that many of them are sleeping on the premises is a relief. It removes some of the worries about drunken driving and noise from departing cars."

Bill smiled. "Our local guests and our staff won't be noisy when they leave, they've often been warned about not making unnecessary noise, especially when passing through Elsinby village in the early hours, but I don't think there'll be any problems. Now, Nick, there'll be refreshments for you when you require them. You know where to find the kitchen?"

I assured him that I knew my way around the premises, but nonetheless, we then executed a tour of the Hall and grounds to refresh my memory of the layout, particularly the car parking area, the entrances and exits for the party guests, the rooms being used during the evening and the private areas of the huge house. I was told that the responsibility for tonight's reception and welfare of the guests rested upon the butler, Johnson, and so I was introduced to him. He'd been with the family for five years but I'd never met him formally, although I had seen him in action. Johnson, a thickset man with a good head of dark hair, was in his late fifties and was always immaculate in his black tails and white shirt.

He always wore white gloves too. He had a bad leg, however and for mobility relied upon a heavy black walking stick as he moved around the house. With this in his left hand to support his weight, and moving it in unison with his left leg, he could progress around the house at a remarkably swift pace, even while balancing a tray of full wine glasses upon the palm of his right hand. He overcame his slight handicap with speed and skill although sometimes he appeared to be out of breath. He was always on hand, always available to do the bidding of his master. There were times he was like a wraith, appearing from nowhere only seconds before his attendance was required. It was an uncanny anticipatory ability.

His stick was unusual too; he rejected the conventional walking stick with its curved handle and slender lines in favour of one fashioned in heavy gnarled black wood, a handmade product of the blackthorn shrub. The stick had a thick, heavy elongated knob at the top while its shank looked as if the timber from which it was made had never been properly finished — it looked as if the thin branches had merely been lopped off to leave lumpy, irregular knots upon the stem. The blackthorn grew wild in the Hall grounds, just one of many trees and shrubs which produced white blossom throughout the year. I knew that this shrub was also used to make the traditional Irish cudgel known as the shillelagh but in Yorkshire, many countryfolk made walking sticks from this dark, tough wood.

In the entrance hall, oak panelled with its array of family portraits, there was a giant hallstand in which stood hundreds of similar walking sticks, a prized collection I was told.

There was a stick fashioned from every species of tree on the estate — a stick of ash, a beautiful one in hazel with a fox's head, sycamore, rowan, apple and more, with several chunky black ones made from the Estate's flourishing blackthorns. This unusual collection dated to the time of the great grandfather of the present Viscount — he'd wanted sticks leaving in every convenient part of the house because he was always forgetting where he'd left the one he was currently using. He'd walk a few yards, and then demand a stick before going any further — so dozens had been made especially for him. Now most of them occupied pride of place in the entrance hall although there were others in odd corners about the building — one or two in the library, others in the dining room, some on the landing upstairs or in the lounge, some beside the beautiful white grand piano in the stairwell, and there were even some in the morning room. Even some walls had walking sticks upon them, arranged in attractive displays which were proudly shown to visitors.

While I toured the house, work for the celebrations was being finalised under Johnson's supervision and the massive south-facing lounge was being cleared of furniture, the carpet being lifted for dancing. At either side of the lounge, separated from it by thick double doors, were (to the east) the book-lined library, comfortably furnished with tables and chairs, and to the west the bright and airy morning room for those who did not wish to dance or tolerate the music. There was also a white-painted conservatory beyond the library; its outer door opened onto a small patio not far from the fountain which bubbled near the renowned White Shrubbery of Elsinby. There was also a sundial close to the fountain, near a south-facing stone bench.

Even now, the garden was rich with white flowers. The shrubs, trees and garden plants, both wild and cultivated, were all playing their part in this famous display of white and by a careful selection of garden plants, that display would continue throughout the coming months. The *cerastium tomestoga* was particularly spectacular during the whole year. Near the entrance were clumps of blackthorn, thorny and dangerous but now covered with a thick covering of white blossom whose scent filled the air. Horse chestnut, hawthorn, white lilac, rowan, whitebeam, wayfaring tree and others would add their blooms to the spectacular display of white.

Indeed, the family name of the owners of this estate was Whitlock which came from this custom of encouraging white blossoms and upon each of the two main gateposts stood a large rabbit, carved from stone and painted white. The family legend said that so long as white rabbits occupied the grounds, the Whitlock dynasty would thrive.

Bill escorted me to all the ground-floor rooms, including the north wing which housed the gun room, the butler's sitting room, Viscount Elsinby's secretary's office and a small TV room for use by the domestic staff who lived in. There were six of them and they occupied flats near the estate office, which was behind the main body of the hall, nicely out of sight from the family rooms. The approach was across the spacious yard which would be utilised as a car park tonight and the entrance to that was via a stone archway, over which stood a block containing the billiards room, the table tennis room and the clock tower.

The estate office in which Bill and Alison worked lay at the western extremity of the yard while the gardener's cottage stood beside the yard. This afternoon, the gardener, Charlie Hirst, was signposting various parts of the garden for the incoming visitors and ensuring that the entire garden and grounds were in peak condition for the weekend — he was busy with those chores as I went about my perambulation. One of his problems was the fountain — the flow was spasmodic probably because an inlet valve was blocked, and Viscount Victor had insisted the water flowed smoothly, without interruption, during the night's festivities. It had to be floodlit too.

I could see that Charlie was worried about all this and bade him good afternoon as I passed by; the circular artificial pond in which the fountain stood amidst a forest of broad-leaved water plants, seemed to be in peak condition but I was no expert on troublesome waterworks so I left him to his task. Although some flowers were not yet in bloom there was a colourful display in many parts, with the garden, the famous White Shrubbery and all the borders having been tidied and trimmed during the week to give a clean and manicured effect.

As I completed my tour, I thought that ordinary people would pay handsomely to see the house and its treasures, especially the astonishing display of white blossoms, but Elsinby Hall was not open to the public. It remained a private house, with the possible exception of the occasional open day for the Red Cross or a charity garden fete arranged by one or other of the village clubs or organisations.

I would study the list of guests in the comfort of my office at home but upon leaving the Hall, the first person I encountered was Phyllis Catchpole.

I could see her stout figure pushing a cycle up the slope towards the Hall and knew that she would have been called in to assist with this evening's formalities. Phyllis, however, was a well-known shoplifter; she'd been arrested countless times in places like York, Harrogate, Scarborough, Middlesbrough and Ashfordly where she raided department stores. She stole small items of women's wear, under-clothing in the main, which she tried to sell to unsuspecting clients around the villages. We also had good reason to suspect that she was involved in the drugs scene, possibly as a dealer, but could never catch her in possession of them. Although she'd often been employed at the Hall on special occasions, I always wondered what was in her handbag or shopping bag every time she arrived or departed. I noticed that her cycle now had a basket on the front and decided that tonight I should remind the butler, Johnson, of her criminal proclivities.

I halted my van at her side and climbed out for a chat.

"Work is it, Phyllis?" I asked.

"You know it is, Mr Rhea. Why else would I be heading for the Hall?"

"Just be careful, Phyllis," I held up a finger as a warning. "Mind those light fingers of yours aren't tempted by His Lordship's silver, we don't want any of it finding its way to your mantelpiece, do we? I'll be there later, keeping an eye on things and I'll ask Johnson to search your bike and coat pockets before you leave!"

"You coppers never give up, do you?" she muttered, pushing her bike away from me.

I watched her puffing up the slope, marvelling that in the fairly recent past, this gross and untidy woman had been an hotel proprietor with a gift for organising the big occasion. That's why the Earl employed her; her duties would be centred upon the dining room and servery where she would ensure that everything was done as smoothly and as efficiently as possible, a sort of master, or mistress, of ceremonies. She'd be there to complement the butler's supervision of the staff, allowing him to concentrate upon his other duties. That she had skill was not in doubt but her shoplifting antics had brought about her professional downfall. Abandoned by her fed-up husband, she had lost her business and now relied on casual work for her income — plus, I knew, some ill-gotten gains from shoplifting expeditions. She was clever enough to avoid prosecution but all the Ashfordly market stall-holders were aware of her skills, one of which was the swift and secretive removal of cauliflowers from the vegetable stall. Phyllis could do with cauliflowers what conjurers could do with snooker balls.

As I approached the village, I met Claude Jeremiah Greengrass. With his lurcher dog, Alfred at his side he was trudging down the lane from Elsinby Hall and seemed to be having difficulty walking. When I caught up with him, I could see he was hobbling; so I stopped my minivan and asked if he wanted a lift into the village.

"Lift? Me?" he smirked. "If folks see me in that van, they'll think I'm under arrest and that'll not be good for my image. I'm very particular who I travel with, you know; I'm a man of quality, constable, and I want no false rumours circulating about my honesty and integrity!"

"There's not much danger of that!" I retorted.

"Aye, well, being seen in a police van with a uniformed constable isn't the sort of image I want to cultivate. Besides, I'm not sure Alfred would like travelling in a police van. He's not a show dog, you know — although he could be, with his breeding."

"I stopped to do you a favour, Claude, you're limping. Are your boots too small? Maybe a nail's come through? You're not walking with your usual style and panache!"

"Are you extracting the Michael, constable? I'm not limping! I'm breaking my new boots in, they're just a bit stiff, that's all, they need moulding to my feet."

"Well, they look too small if I'm a judge. I think you've been conned, Claude! Those boots do look as if they're causing pain. You haven't bought them because they were a bargain, have you? From a second-hand stall perhaps? If you have, I reckon you've been done!"

"Second-hand? I don't buy my boots second-hand, Constable Rhea! I believe in quality, I mean, I've had this top coat since the war, my demob coat it was and it's as good as new. Now these boots are good leather, real tough leather; so I'm breaking 'em in. You can't beat a five-mile hike for breaking new boots in."

From the driver's seat, I looked at his footwear. They were a pair of sturdy brown boots in soft, oiled leather, the kind that hikers then favoured and they seemed very expensive. As he stamped his foot on the road surface to emphasise the quality of his footwear, I heard the distinctive sound of metal studs, segs as they are known in this part of Yorkshire.

"Studded like nowt else!" he grinned, showing me the sole. It had rows and rows of small triple-headed segs which had been hammered into the thick leather sole and heel, the pattern on both heel and sole being something like a series of horseshoes, each smaller than the other with the smallest in the centre. Many mountain climbers and ramblers of the 1960s used this kind of sole to facilitate a grip on rocks and rough terrain. But I couldn't imagine Claude going hiking or fell walking.

"They're expensive ones by the look of them," I said. "Did you pay a lot for them Claude?"

"What I pay for my wardrobe is nowt to do with you, constable!" he grinned at me. "It's a sod when a fashionable chap can't walk down a country lane without being interrogated by the law!"

"It's just that they look very high quality, Claude, I could do with a pair myself, for gardening or rambling even. I was wondering where you got them!"

"I'm not saying where I got 'em!" he was teasing me now. "But they're good boots, constable, ideal for tramping around His Lordship's grounds looking for rabbits. Mind you, there's a poacher after his rabbits, Mr Rhea, I've come across one or two lying shot lately, not picked up, just shot and left. Now it's not me doing that, constable, so you ought to be out there catching yon poacher instead of quizzing me about my boots. Catching real criminals, that's what."

"Well, if Viscount Victor or his staff complain to me about the poacher, I'll do something about it. And I trust you're not thinking of gate-crashing Lord Thackerston's party tonight!" I had to issue some kind of warning to the rogue.

"Gate-crashing? Me? I wouldn't be seen dead with that snooty lot!" laughed Claude. "But I'll bet you're there, greasing around 'em, making sure those rich sods get all they want while workers like me have to fight for survival and live on a pittance."

"I shall be on duty, Claude, keeping out gate-crashers and other unwelcome visitors. I thought you ought to know that."

"Well, for all you know, I might be an honoured guest. I mean, me and His Lordship, the old lord, I mean, not Viscount Victor, well, we're mates, you see. We go back a long time, do me and Earl Randy, fighting in the war, having fun, struggling to earn a crust afterwards, rearing pheasants . . . you name it, me and Lordy have been mates . . . just you ask him."

"Well, so long as you present me with your official invitation on the gate tonight, I'll admit you," I smiled at the old rogue. "See you around, Claude."

"Mebbe you will and mebbe you won't," chuckled Claude with a mischievous glint in his eye as I drove away to leave him limping down the lane.

CHAPTER II

"Any man may be in good temper when he's well dressed."
CHARLES DICKENS, 1812–70

At home, I studied the guest list. I needed to identify likely trouble-makers in advance. Local guests included all the long-term tenants of the Elsinby Estate along with some former members of staff and certain prominent people. Among them, were Lieutenant Colonel and Mrs Jordon, she being a magistrate, Captain Fielder, RN and Mrs Fielder, and the Hattertons who owned a chain of sports shops. Both the Fielders and Hattertons lived in Elsinby. Rudolph Burley, the auctioneer, was a guest too, along with his wife and I knew his relationship with the estate was one of long-standing — Rudolph conducted sales of estate livestock in his distinctive booming voice. There were others of similar standing and fortunately, Alison Colburn had included car registration numbers where relevant. That would assist while I was performing my somewhat mundane gate duties; it also meant I could inspect the vehicles which had assembled earlier to determine whether anyone had tricked their way past the earlier gatekeepers. It was quite surprising how people did attempt to gate-crash such parties but without the necessary piece of paper, none would pass me. It promised to be a rather boring and unsatisfying evening's work which should not present any difficulties.

Confident I could cope, I settled down to enjoy the meal that Mary had prepared. Afterwards, I kissed her farewell, climbed into my minivan and left for Elsinby Hall, telling Mary to expect me home just after eleven o'clock.

I enjoyed my visits to Elsinby village, whether on duty or not. It is a pretty community of mellow stone houses with red pantile roofs, and, in accordance with the oft-imagined world of rustic life, many cottages do have honeysuckle and roses around their doorways. There is a castle on the hill above the village and a charming stream which flows beside the main street and in front of the Hopbind Inn. The stream is rich with grayling, a sign of unpolluted water. Close to the inn, the stream disappears underground to re-surface on the outskirts after which it wends its way along the dale to enter Elsinby Beck before joining the River Rye. Many of the cottages and houses are owned by the Estate and this has prevented the intrusion of modern housing developments, thus enabling this beautiful village to retain its character, charm and appeal. Part of that appeal extends to Elsinby Hall itself.

The Hall stands on an elevated ridge of countryside to the north-west of the village with a substantial range of mixed coniferous and deciduous trees serving as a picturesque back-cloth. Thanks to these trees, selected years ago for their beautiful white blossom and nurtured inside the Hall grounds, the house is sheltered from the north. In spite of its elevated position, it avoids the worst of the cold and icy winds of winter. With open views to the front, Elsinby Hall boasts panoramic views of the south and west. To the east is Home Farm which is part of the Elsinby Estate and its buildings partially obscure the views in that direction, although the farm, surrounded by oaks and ash trees, could never be described as unsightly. Spread across the valley is the Estate's extensive parkland comprising undulating meadows replete with sycamores, with further farms in the dale.

These lush fields roll gently towards Elsinby Beck which has alders and willows along its banks. Wild daffodils and bluebells grow in profusion during the spring, while the renowned Elsinby Herd of British White cattle occupies those grasslands. These animals are unlike the equally famous Chillingham herd of wild white cattle in Northumberland — the Elsinby herd are domestic beasts bred for beef and dairy products while those at Chillingham are wild, the descendants of a medieval herd. Elsinby Estate is noted as a breeder of British Whites, while prize-winning Whitefaced Woodland sheep are another of the Elsinby family's farming interests.

The long tarmacadam drive to the Hall runs between the fields and crosses a minor road before climbing the final two hundred yards to the house where the twin rabbit-topped gateposts act as sentinels. Constructed in mellow local stone with a blue slate roof, Elsinby Hall is not one of the county's major country houses. It ranks well below gems like Castle Howard, Harewood House and Burton Agnes Hall, but nonetheless it is a house of substance and style. Comprising two storeys with attics above, it boasts a canted middle bay window (the lounge) with, as one faces it, two bays to the left (the library) and a further two to the right (the morning room). The impressive main entrance boasts a *porte-cochere* with two pairs of Tuscan columns. Renowned for its gardens, former vineyard, white shrubbery and surrounding range of white blossoms, the house occupies the site of an earlier building which was destroyed by fire in 1892. The present mansion was re-built in 1894 and the site has been the seat of the Whitlock family, Earls of Thackerston, since 1667.

The family crest, which incorporates white blossoms, is carved from a slab of granite which is built into the south-facing wall. When I arrived at the main gate at six o'clock, Bill Blades was already there. His staff had been ticking off the names of guests and hired staff who had arrived earlier and he presented me with the updated sheet of paper, saying,

"There's still a few to come, Nick, but most of the house guests have arrived. When you've checked their invitations, send the cars through the arch to park in the yard if you're satisfied they're *bona fide*, and tell them all, particularly any first-time visitors, to head for the front door of the house. There's no footmen these days, so Johnson will welcome them and ensure there's a member of staff to guide house guests to their rooms. Members of the family will know their way around, of course."

And so the evening started rather quietly.

Among the first arrivals during my stint on the gate were people from the locality — The Jordons arrived in their Bentley quickly followed by the Alleyne Floyds in a smart new Ford. Gordon McFarlane arrived too, much to my surprise because he'd once hit the headlines after going berserk with a shotgun over his wife's affairs. He was now alone; his wife had left him and had never been seen again in the village.

Among the tenant farmers I crossed off my list were the Lampkins, the Lees, the Oldhams and the Olivers, all well-known to me because of my regular visits to their farms. If the rumours were true, they would be concerned for their future, so perhaps they would learn something tonight? I wondered what the Earl had in mind — perhaps the sale of part of the Estate?

Few could afford to purchase their farms or cottages, and in these cases, there was always a worry that a predatory estate or property speculator might buy these properties, thus putting the tenants in a state of desperate uncertainty. I was pleased to welcome Sarah Crossfield, the family's former cook and their retired nanny Roberta (Robbie) Whitwell. They were followed by the Estate's efficient and knowledgeable gamekeeper, Roy Cleghorn with his wife Violet, along with the underkeeper Robert Beswick, a bachelor in his early thirties. The family chauffeur also arrived to enjoy an evening off duty; he was called Kenneth Craggs and I noticed he brought Viscount Elsinby's secretary, Josephine Honeyfield, whose husband was a major in the army, serving overseas. Among the house guests already at the Hall upon my arrival were the Earl and Countess of Ploatby, Sir Ashley and Lady Penelope Prittleford, Evelyn du Bartas and Dr Austin Plankenburg.

Also among those who arrived while I was on the gate were Mr and Mrs Henry Powler, the Earl of Thackerston in his gleaming white vintage Rolls, an old couple known simply as Aunt Felicity and Uncle Ben who looked like twins, and a very arrogant fellow bearing the strange name of Edwin Drood. He thought I was there to carry his suitcases.

"I say, you, constable there. Fetch my cases in after me, will you? There's a good fellow," he shouted from his sports car as he sailed through the gate.

"That is not my job!" I called after him.

He braked and reversed towards me.

"I beg your pardon?" His dark eyes studied me from the seat of the car.

"I said carrying your luggage is not my job, I'm a police officer, not a servant of the household," I was emphatic.

"Suit yourself, matey!" there was a poncy tone to his voice. "It'll all change when I have a place like this, I can tell you. People will know their place, and the constabulary will obey me, just like the old days, sunshine!"

He drove away with a shake of his head. I smiled as I watched him hurtle towards the front door, roaring to a halt in a shower of gravel. Johnson emerged unsmiling, and I heard him say to Drood, "I will send someone for your luggage, sir."

Then other cars were heading my way. Of the house guests still to come were the Honourable and Mrs James Whitlock, Ned Powler and his friend Vinnia Phinlay plus some of the late duty staff and members of the three-piece orchestra. Their musical contribution to the evening was due to start after the splendid dinner, probably around 9.45pm. As I busied myself at the checkpoint with my list of personnel, I was surprised at the number of non-guests' vehicles entering and leaving the Hall. It was amazing how much activity such an event could generate, even on a Saturday night. Caterers' vans, guests rushing off to the village for some last-minute object such as a missing ear-ring or a tie-pin from a friend, extra staff arriving, a laundry van, a late delivery from a wine merchant, Saturday evening newspapers for the overnight guests, a last-minute addition to the display of flowers. I checked them all and, as a good policeman should, recorded in my official notebook, all their comings and goings, along with timings and registration numbers. That kept me occupied as the evening wore on.

The Hon. James Whitlock with a beautiful auburn-haired woman at his side, arrived in a splendid blue Daimler about quarter past seven; as I checked their invitations, the Hon. James explained he'd been late leaving home added to which there'd been an accident on the A1 which had further delayed him. The auburn lady was his wife, Lady Sarah, and she insisted everyone called her Sally. I guided them to the front door where someone would assist with their luggage and park the car. Then a battered old three-wheeler car in a dirty yellow coat of paint chugged along the drive and halted before me. I thought it was some itinerant scrap merchants attempting to gain entry, but, somewhat to my surprise, it contained two youthful house guests both dressed as men in trousers and sweaters. Their invitation tickets identified the long-haired man as Ned Powler and his colourfully-dressed companion as Vinnia Phinlay. Dark skinned, her black hair was done in plaits which dangled down her back like curtain pulls. Even though both looked scruffy enough to be scrap merchants, I guided them to the front door.

Their battered old vehicle provided a humorous contrast to the stylish Daimler which was currently being divested of heavy suitcases. I had no idea of the relationship between the scruffy couple and their hosts, although I did notice that other guests bore the name of Powler. Late as they were, they still had time to wash and change before the reception. Johnson welcomed them with the assurance of one who had been some thirty years in his profession and arranged for a man to take their meagre luggage.

The orchestra materialised in the shape of three young men with long hair who rattled towards the gates in a large, untidy and rusting navy-blue van decorated with musical notes in white paint and the words "Stately Tones". Their documents proved their identity and a quick check in the rear of their vehicle did not reveal any stowaways or gate-crashers, merely a collection of drums, amplifiers, electronic keyboards, saxophone cases and other musical paraphernalia. I showed them to the front door where Johnson would summon a member of staff to guide them to the room they'd be using — and I knew there would be supper for these lads, albeit not in the formal atmosphere of the dining room. They'd probably eat in the TV room but in the meantime would have to set up their gear and test it for sound. I wondered what the knowledgeable musicians here present would think about this group — Rudolph Burley, for example, was conductor of the Aidensfield String Orchestra and I knew he preferred Beethoven to the Beatles. With a sense of some relief, I recorded that, before the time specified for the start of the festivities, every guest had arrived and there had been no attempts to gate-crash the event.

The cessation of activity threatened to make my vigil very lonesome. By contrast, I could see everyone enjoying the champagne reception in the spacious entrance hall, the lights enhancing the exquisite oak panelling and highlighting the portraits. Very soon, guests with drinks in their hands wandered into the library, the morning room and the lounge. Johnson, smart in his tail coat, striped trousers, white shirt and white gloves, was buzzing around, stick in one hand and tray balanced upon the other. He seemed to be everywhere, advising guests about the drinks.

His eyes were never still, always watching, always alert. Breathless on occasions, he spent time cajoling the hired waitresses into speedier responses to the guests' constant request for refills. Under the watchful gaze of Phyllis Catchpole, they were all smart in their black dresses, white aprons and frilly hats and were coping admirably. It seemed to be a busy and happy gathering. Even Phyllis had had a bath for the occasion.

Even from the gate, I could hear the babble of loud chatter but my duties were not yet complete. In accordance with the Earl's instructions, I had to remain until 10pm just in case there were any uninvited arrivals during dinner. I wondered why he was so concerned about gate-crashers but rested in the knowledge that I had an expansive view of the parkland in front of the Hall. Even when it became dark, I could detect new arrivals long before they arrived. Likewise, I could patrol a considerable portion of the grounds while maintaining my observations upon the long approach drive. I was confident that no motor vehicle could arrive at Elsinby Hall without my knowledge, although I did appreciate that a truly determined intruder could gain access on foot from the fields at the rear, via the woodland.

Such an intruder would have to be truly determined because it meant a two mile walk across open fields along the borders between Aidensfield and Elsinby, so would anyone go to such trouble? Besides, all the guests were in evening dress which was hardly the sort of clothing in which to tramp across fields and through woodlands while attempting to be secretive. Anyone not in evening dress would be under immediate suspicion.

While the reception was underway, I wandered among the parked cars, through the gardens, behind and around the handsome house, and on one occasion found Johnson on the edge of the White Shrubbery cutting variegated leaves. They were a delightful shade of green with creamy white edges.

"It's weigela," in his formal clothing and still wearing white gloves, he looked out of place and regarded me with an embarrassed grin as he clipped the foliage with secateurs while leaning on his stick. "A somewhat urgent request. Lady Ploatby loves it in vases at table, sir, and like her mother, she doesn't want it higher than the candelabra or obstructing her view of the person opposite."

The beautiful White Shrubbery was noted among horticulturalists, often being featured in gardening magazines and society journals. It comprised a wide range of plants which produced either white blossom or foliage with white or pale portions throughout the year. It included beauties like *rhododendron leucaspis*, *rhododendron yakushimanum*, *elaeagnus*, *viburnum*, *fatsia japonica variegata*, white lilac, weigela and others. It was complemented by wild trees around the Estate and in the woodland which also bore white blossom or had foliage with white upon them. The white candles of the horse chestnuts were particularly spectacular and even the wild plants in the woodland and grounds bore white blossom.

As I admired Johnson's handful of leaves, Bill Blades approached us. "They'll be going in to eat soon, Nick, then we can relax. But we must get these leaves onto the table before they enter the dining room. Everyone's here, by the way, Nick, there's supper for you in the kitchen. Take it into the TV room."

"Thanks, but what about the gate?" I asked.

"I'll get one of my men to keep an eye on it," grinned Bill. "Well, Jasper, I think you've got enough of this greenery. There's enough to decorate a wedding cake. See you," and he wandered towards the rear of the house as Johnson vanished into the entrance hall. I heard the ferrule of his stick tapping on bare floor boards as he made for the dining room. I returned to the gate, the silent white rabbits now prominent in the intensifying darkness.

As dinner got under way, I was relieved at the gate just after 8.45pm by a member of staff and found my way into the kitchen. After some banter with the staff, I collected the tray of supper and drinks which was awaiting and carried it through the corridors to the resident staffs TV room at the rear of the mansion. En route, I heard the crisp sound of a walking stick and rounded a corner to find Johnson heading my way with a tray of full brandy glasses balanced on his gloved hand. He was en route to Viscount Victor's office to position these drinks in case they were required after dinner and he asked if everything was to my satisfaction. I thanked him, saying everything was fine. On my tray was a bottle of beer and a pot of hot coffee in addition to a large plate of chicken with salad, a trifle and a bread bun. When I entered the TV room, the three musicians were already there.

They had their suppers before them and were tucking in with great gusto. I was introduced; they were called Eric, Alan and Simon, Eric and Alan being brothers with Simon being their cousin. They all had regular jobs and in their spare time performed as a band at select small dances, such as the one that would shortly commence at the Hall.

We chatted about life in country mansions, these men performing at many such places, hence the name of their group. From what they said, it seemed they were well known among the aristocracy of the North Riding of Yorkshire and after half an hour or so, I returned to my post on the gate, allowing Bill's man to return to his normal duties. By this time, I could see that the guests were enjoying their meal in the splendour of the dining room, the men in their smart dinner jackets and the beautiful ladies in gorgeous evening wear. Johnson was standing behind Lord Thackerston, slightly to His Lordship's left, eyes watching everyone and everything, there to dispense the finest of wines as the waitresses, under the guidance of redoubtable Phyllis, went about their careful work. It was a glittering occasion, of that there was no doubt.

Even Ned Powler wore a dinner suit and looked very smart — I caught a clear view of him through the full-length floor-to-ceiling dining room window as the lights within the house made me realise that darkness had descended outside. Vinnia, beautiful in a white dress which enhanced her dark skin, looked stunning — an amazing transformation from their earlier scruffy appearance. The next, mercifully short period, on the gate would be lonely but if unwelcome visitors were going to arrive, they would probably do so under cover of darkness.

I resumed my vigil as the house appeared resplendent among the glittering lights. The glow revealed the opulence of the interior and I could see some of the brilliance reflected in the waters of the gushing fountain to my left. It seemed to be working well this evening; Charlie Hirst must be pleased with it.

The remainder of that evening's duty was uneventful, the only highlight being a visit from Sergeant Blaketon. He arrived at the gates in his official car just after 9.30pm and we had a brief chat about nothing in particular as he satisfied himself that I was performing my duties in a manner expected of a member of the North Riding Constabulary. He drove away five minutes later saying he was going to visit PC Alf Ventress who was on duty in Ashfordly and then I heard lively dance music coming from the Hall. I was scheduled to leave at 10pm when Bill Blades came to lock the gates and because I was due off duty at 11pm, it would allow me an hour to check the pubs on my beat. I knew the meal was over because the music sounded and someone began to close all the curtains and lock the outer doors. Very soon the glitter had disappeared, leaving only a dull glow of diffused light to spread across the lawns, the sundial, the fountain, the White Shrubbery and footpaths. The fountain was like a miniature beacon in the darkness, its water reflecting both the softer lights of the hall and the greater brilliance of its own illumination. Just before 10pm, I did a quick tour of the grounds, noting that the conservatory had no curtains and that a few people were standing inside sipping from glasses and chatting amiably.

Because the conservatory door was standing open, I could hear the chatter of guests above the noise of music. On a breath of evening air, I heard the baying tones of Edwin Drood; he was airing his views on the future of country houses. Rather than listen to his opinionated pomposities, I wondered if the conservatory door should be closed, but decided it was not my concern — with all those people in the house, the temperature would rise and some form of ventilation would be necessary — and if the guests frequented the conservatory, no one was likely to surreptitiously enter via that route.

It was a fine, dry night so surely the gathering would spill outside, moving onto the lawns between the shrubbery and the fountain. Some might even use the stone bench near the sundial. At the other side of the house, as I crossed the yard among the parked cars, I saw that the kitchen curtains were not drawn either. I could see the staff clearing up after the festivities, washing dishes, clearing away untouched food and generally making a lot of noise before settling down to their own party. They would not enjoy their own share of the wine and food until they had completed all their chores.

With several unlocked entrances such as the kitchen door and the servants' quarters, the Hall might be considered vulnerable to determined gate-crashers after my departure, but I knew that Bill Blades and his staff would have matters of internal security fully under control. Satisfied that I had done my part of the task to the best of my ability. I wandered back to the main gate where Bill Blades was waiting with the white stone rabbits like beacons.

"Thanks, Nick," he shook my hand. "I know it's a bore for you, doing this sort of thing. It does allow us to relax, I assure you; in the past, people have seen our lights on their way home from the pub or wherever, and have tried to join us."

"I hope the rest of the evening is trouble-free," I said as I prepared to leave.

"I'm sure it will be. Well, some of the early staff have gone so off you go; I'll lock the gate after you. And thanks."

I returned to my minivan, switched on the lights and left Elsinby Hall, shouting my thanks to Bill as I drove away. He closed the huge wood and iron gate behind me and in my mirror, I could see him working in the glow from the mansion, padlocking the gate until morning. Anyone wanting to leave earlier by motor vehicle would have to find Bill to let them out. I checked three pubs on my beat before ending my shift and as I garaged my van I noticed a bottle of whisky lying on the passenger seat. Beside it was a note saying "thanks". I could not return the bottle as an unwanted gift or attempted bribe because there was nothing to say who had placed it there. I would enjoy it in the privacy of my home. When I entered the house at 11 o'clock, Mary was tired and ready for bed.

She was missing the children but asked for a brief account of His Lordship's party, after which we went upstairs and tumbled into bed. In spite of my easy-going duty, I felt tired and was asleep within minutes.

* * *

It was a few minutes before 4am when my bedside telephone rang. At first, I thought it was the continuation of a dream. I'd been dreaming of bells ringing but now there was a shrilling close to my ears and it all came to a swift and painful end when Mary launched a missile attack upon my ribs. Actually it was her elbow, but it was highly effective because it jerked me into fairly speedy wakefulness as she hissed,

"Nick, telephone! Answer it, it might be important . . ."

It required an inordinate amount of effort and self-discipline to respond, but I did manage to lift the bedside receiver to my ear.

"Aidensfield Police," I must have sounded half-asleep at that point. "PC Rhea speaking."

"It's Elsinby," said the well-spoken voice at the end of the line. "Viscount Victor Elsinby. Mr Rhea, you must come to the Hall, urgently."

"Might I ask why, sir?" I had to know the reason for this call.

"Someone's been shot, Mr Rhea. It's Edwin, he was shown as Mr Drood on your lists this evening, he's lying near the White Shrubbery. I haven't moved him."

"Is he dead?" It might have sounded a daft sort of question, but it had to be asked; the state of the victim had to be determined as soon as possible.

"Yes, I fear so, otherwise I should have called an ambulance. He's dead all right, I've seen enough dead pheasants and grouse to know a corpse when I see one."

"Self-inflicted, was it, sir?"

"I think not, constable, there is no sign of a gun." My heart sank at this news. I might have a murder on my patch after all. Even if Edwin Drood had been as arrogant to the others as he had been towards me, it was not an excuse to shoot him. There were less criminal ways of shutting up a pompous nuisance.

"Don't touch anything, sir," I said. "And don't let anyone leave the premises! And please don't let people walk all over the place, especially near the corpse. That's vital. I'll get dressed and should be there within twenty minutes."

I whispered to Mary that there seemed to be some kind of problem at Elsinby Hall and told her I was going to visit the scene; I had to establish the basic facts before raising the alarm at Force Headquarters.

In the dark coolness of the early spring morning, I left the cosiness of my bed to deal with what appeared to be a major incident at Elsinby Hall. As I dressed in my uniform, I did wonder whether or not I should contact my supervisory officers or ask Force Headquarters to alert the CID but, over the years, I had experienced other reports of supposed corpses when the victims had turned out to be drunks or people suffering from fits or other conditions which were not death.

If there had been high jinks at the party, this could be some kind of joke, the sort that students and high-spirited young men might produce, perhaps with a view to causing some embarrassment or alarm at the expense of the local constable. That was always a possibility — a bottle of tomato ketchup can work wonders on a supposed corpse. I decided to visit the scene to check Viscount Victor's story before contacting Force Headquarters, although I did decide to ring Divisional Headquarters, rather than the slumbering Sergeant Blaketon at Ashfordly, to report my actions. Before leaving the house, I called the duty sergeant.

"It's PC Rhea at Aidensfield, Sergeant," I began. "I've had a report from Viscount Elsinby at Elsinby Hall, he's reporting the death of one of his guests, apparently by shooting. I'm about to visit the scene."

"Suicide, is it?" was Sergeant Williams' initial reaction.

"I'm not sure, Sergeant," I had to admit. "The Viscount thinks it's murder. He says there's no gun near the body."

"Oh, bloody hell! Well, get yourself out there and give me a sitrep as soon as you can. How long will that take, do you reckon?"

"I should be there within quarter of an hour, Sergeant."

"Right, well, before I take any further action, I'll wait until I hear from you but for God's sake remember your training and if the death is suspicious, preserve the scene and radio me immediately."

I arrived to find Elsinby Hall aglow with lights and the gate unlocked, albeit with a man on guard. In my police van I drove into the grounds and this time parked outside the main entrance where I saw Johnson waiting just inside. Taking my powerful torch from the van, I went to the front door. The porch light was burning and just inside I could see the pale whiteness of Johnson's features as he stood erect and solemn-faced, leaning slightly upon his faithful stick. He was alone, I was pleased to note, and in the subdued lighting he had the appearance of a plump rook. Black suited with black hair, a reddish face with heavy jowls and dark eyebrows shielding those ever-alert eyes, he was still immaculate, his white shirt sleeves peeping from his jacket to exactly the required length. He adjusted them slightly as he came to meet me. As I entered the house, I realised that the music had stopped and all the guests had been assembled in the lounge — judging by the rumble of voices from that part of the house, they were not wallowing in silence.

"A sad affair, Mr Rhea," Johnson's voice was suitably sonorous for the occasion; he sounded more like a vicar reading the lesson at a funeral than a butler greeting a constable. "I'll inform His Lordship of your arrival."

"Thank you." I waited as he picked his way through the corridors, the sound of his stick marking his progress as he vanished around the far corner.

Moments later, he called me into the presence of Viscount Victor who looked miserable, distraught and harassed.

"Good morning, sir," as he came towards me, I noted it was 4.23am on Sunday.

"We'll use the path around the outside." He ignored the niceties of introduction as he made for the outer door, striding into the darkness beyond. "Even though I'm sure none of my firearms was used, I have locked my gun room, by the way. You remember the gun room, Mr Rhea?"

"Yes, I do, and thanks for closing it." I knew the gun room well; I had to come here periodically to check the firearms which were listed on a certificate and all were kept in that small room. The Viscount, I felt, was acting with immense common sense and calmness. In his early thirties, he was sturdily built and with dark hair long enough to be fashionable. His evening suit looked immaculate even if his youthful face bore signs of anxiety. Against his smart black jacket, the crisp white of his shirt was outstanding in the low lights and with no more ado, I followed him outside. Normally so confident and assured, he was now trembling with the trauma of the occasion and his voice was weak. He was speaking softly as we walked towards the shrubbery.

"Look, constable, this is really awful, a murder at our house, especially one of our house guests. I find this most embarrassing. Our family has always sought to avoid scandal so I really must ask for the utmost discretion and confidentiality."

"Murder, sir? Are you absolutely sure it's not suicide?"

"I think not, Mr Rhea. I did look for a gun, I assure you there is not one near the body, this is murder. That is why I am demanding the utmost confidentiality."

"You can rely on that, sir," I offered. "The police will guarantee confidentiality, but you appreciate we cannot be responsible for the conduct of your guests and staff?"

"I am aware of that, Mr Rhea," he sounded nervous as he led me around the front of the house towards the fountain. It was still flowing and illuminated. "He's over there, near the White Shrubbery," and Viscount Victor halted to point towards the place.

At first I could see nothing, the conservatory lights producing dense shadows beneath the shrubbery and highlighting the white flowers and leaves, some variegated and some backed with white. There was a mottled effect of black and white, making it difficult to identify anything other than the dark shadows and white highlights. I could see a silhouette of the sundial in the lights of the fountain; those lights also served to limit my night vision but as I approached the tall shrubs, I began to play the beam of my torch upon the area, revealing the glister of dew on the lawn. I could identify individual plants in the light, some gleaming white and others producing a creamy image as I walked along the gravel footpath, passing the French windows of the lounge with the bubbling fountain now on my left.

The Viscount was behind me and I heard him whisper. "To your left, Mr Rhea, lying on the grass, behind the fountain as we look at it, beneath the overhanging shrubs."

And there, in the beam of my torch, I saw the body of a man.

CHAPTER III

"He'd make a lovely corpse."
                              CHARLES DICKENS, 1812–70

Recalling my basic training, I told myself that a meticulous examination of the scene of the crime, and an equally meticulous preliminary examination of any corpse found in suspicious circumstances, are both actions of paramount importance. I had not to make a hash of this, the first murder investigation of my career. As I approached the inert and almost invisible form which lay before me, with the worried Viscount Elsinby at my heels, I knew that the approved tactic was to leave everything alone — the CID would deal with the matter when they arrived. But that rule was impossible to obey. There was that awful need to examine a supposed corpse to see if it really was dead. This meant the body had to be touched.

It was an action surely guaranteed to destroy vital evidence but in most cases, it had to be done by the first officer at the scene — and always before calling in the experts. Recognising the risks involved, I asked Viscount Elsinby to remain on the footpath while I ventured across the dew-soaked grass because one can't leave dead bodies lying around the place without doing something about them. It is not surprising that I experienced a sense of foreboding as I approached the object of this exercise; even before I reached the body, my instinct told me that here was death, violent death and that Elsinby Hall was about to become the focus of a murder enquiry.

The beam of my torch played upon the inactive form, highlighting the polished shoes, the dark trousers, the dinner jacket and the white shirt collar of Drood's dress shirt. His dark clothing and white skin, white shirt cuffs and collar matched the shrubbery above him; even at close quarters, he was almost invisible. I noticed a mass of fairly long dark hair curling over his collar. It was a good head of hair with no sign of balding.

I was approaching from behind him and from that angle, he appeared to be lying in slumber or even a drunken stupor. At this stage, I hadn't ruled out either of those possibilities. I recalled being roused at 3am to examine another body — on that occasion, a motorist had discovered a man's body lying on the verge of a road, only a short distance from my police house at Aidensfield. The fellow was lying with his legs protruding into the highway and had all the appearances of the victim of a hit-and-run accident. Upon investigation, that "corpse" had turned out to be a tramp; he was very much alive and was sleeping on the roadside. Many other reported corpses had turned out to be alive and well, and I knew that the man near Viscount Elsinby's shrubbery might not be as dead as we feared.

"You can identify him as Edwin Drood?" I called to the Viscount with as much reverence as I could muster.

"Yes, it's Drood," was the dry response from somewhere behind me. "Edwin Drood. That's his professional name. His real name is Dickens. Edwin Dickens."

"The mystery of Edwin Drood," I stood back to absorb the picture.

"Pardon?" The Viscount hadn't clearly heard my *sotto voce* remark.

"Dickens," I explained, standing motionless as I talked. "Charles Dickens' last book was called *The Mystery of Edwin Drood*, but he never finished it and so we don't know if anyone actually killed Drood, or if he did die, who did it and why. So I find it odd that a modern man using that name, even for professional reasons, has died in mysterious circumstances. Now, I must examine him briefly — you said he was shot? How can you tell?"

"You can see from his other side," Viscount Victor responded and now I could see footprints in the dew. I decided to step alongside them, using those prints as guidance. There were two sets in the dampness.

"Yours?" I asked the Viscount.

"Yes, I expect so, one of the tracks that is. I went that way towards him. And the others will be Lady Violet's. She found him."

As I moved forward with immense care, I noticed that our movements were not being observed from the ground floor of the house, although I did get a fleeting glimpse of someone watching from the large bedroom over the lounge. But as I glanced aloft, the face instantly vanished. There were lights burning upstairs, but not in that room. No one else was watching and I was relieved that all the downstairs curtains remained closed; furthermore, there was no one in the conservatory. Viscount Victor had probably told everyone to keep out of sight.

I was pleased he'd done so because we don't want audiences on these occasions. Now, of course, there was no sound of merrymaking although I was aware of subdued conversation inside the lounge.

Everyone seemed to be gathered there, or at least I hoped they were, because everyone would have to be interviewed.

When I reached the other side of Edwin Drood, a difficult task due to the proximity of the shrubs, I could see, in the light of my torch, the congealed blood on his right temple. He was lying on his left side, almost in the half prone position with his right leg bent at the knee, and the knee resting on the grass. He was facing into the shrubbery and lying practically parallel to it, virtually on the edge of the lawn. Inches in front of his nose was the weed-free soil beneath the shrubs. This position had prevented the body from rolling right onto its stomach; the right hand was dangling behind the back, not quite reaching the ground because the upper arm and elbow were resting upon the torso. The left arm was curled up beneath the body with the hand close to the neck and his elbow bearing the weight of chest. I could see that his mouth was open and almost touching the ground; the eyes were closed and the skin had that awful putty whiteness of death. His legs were pointing towards the house and his head towards the perimeter fence; he was lying almost north-to-south. As I concentrated my light upon his head, I was in no doubt that there was a huge bullet hole in his right temple. The edges were clearly marked with congealed dark red blood and it seemed to be a very large wound.

"I'll have to touch him," I called to the Viscount. "To see if he's still alive."

"I have examined him, constable," came the soft response. "I assure you he's dead."

I touched Drood's brow; it was as cold as ice, and then I lifted the right hand carefully, feeling for the pulse. There was none. The flesh felt like that of someone who'd been dead for several hours.

Carefully, I returned the hand to its original position. That he was dead was not in doubt but how long had he lain here? From my perambulation of the Hall just before 10pm, I felt sure that the body had not been in this position at that time, or had it? Could I have actually walked past without noticing it? The body was very difficult to see, lying in the shadows with the white foliage and flowers providing ideal camouflage for the dark clothing and its white accoutrements. So had he been shot elsewhere and placed here? Had he been shot earlier, even when I was on duty at the gate? It was an awesome thought, but those factors were for the CID to determine.

My next task was to make a brief search for a firearm near the body. If this man had shot himself, the weapon would be somewhere nearby, perhaps under the bushes or even beneath the corpse. It could have been jettisoned a considerable distance. With the aid of my torch and without moving my feet, I quartered the ground within a large circle around Drood, shining my light under the shrubs, across the lawn, into the water of the fountain and along the footpath and then looking beneath the body as best I could without moving him any more. But there was no sign of a firearm. I was now confident that this was not a suicide. I had a murder on my patch. I made a rapid but rough sketch of the scene in my notebook, using a match stick figure for the body and marking those area where I had walked. I included Viscount Victor's and Lady Violet's footprints too.

I estimated the body was fifteen yards from the conservatory door, and confirmed that the dewy grass bore no more footprints and no indication that the body had been dragged or carried to this position. I also noted that the gravel of the footpath had not been disturbed by having anything dragged along it, nor had it been raked smooth afterwards — there were no fresh marks. I asked the Viscount to restate where he had placed his feet and which parts of Drood's body he had touched, and he was able to tell me. Then, before I moved away, I asked if I could use his telephone. I explained that I was now going to call the CID; they would contact the Force doctor, one who was experienced in dealing with suspicious death and he would certify that the man was dead. I explained that a post mortem examination was necessary to determine the cause of death — after all, the shot could have been inflicted after the man had died and all police officers know that external indications are not always a true indication of the real cause of death. Having done what I could, I started to leave the scene, being extra-careful where I placed my feet.

"Aren't you going to move him or cover him up with something?" asked Viscount Victor as I returned to him.

"No," I tried to sound emphatic. "That's the worst thing I could do. I'm sorry to leave him like this, but the body must remain as it was found with the least possible interference."

"It's indecent!" he snapped.

"So is murder," I said, hoping I didn't sound rude. "Now, sir, can you take me to a telephone?"

I could have used the radio on my minivan to make this call but was aware that police radio transmissions are monitored by amateur radio fans who earn a few pounds from tipping off the media about interesting snippets they overhear. A telephone is more secure and he said I should use the one in his office. He was about to lead me through the conservatory door and into his private office which adjoined it, but I decided that this route might contain some useful evidence which should not be destroyed. It was so close to the place in which the body lay — the fellow could have been shot from the conservatory doorway. I asked the Viscount if we could approach his office via the front door of the Hall, and thus leave the conservatory route untouched. He agreed and I followed him through the house to his office. Before making my call, however, there were some other matters to clarify. Standing in front of his polished mahogany desk, I asked, "Lady Violet found Mr Drood, you said, sir?"

"Yes, my sister. Lady Violet Powler, Henry's wife. She went out for some fresh air and went towards the fountain, along the edge of the shrubbery. She almost stumbled over Edwin. She ran into the house and told me; I went to check, thinking he might have fallen or be drunk or something, and realised the worst. Then I rang you."

"So how long did it take between Lady Violet finding the body and you calling the police?"

"Not long, constable. Ten minutes at the most."

"So we can say the body was discovered around 3.45am," I estimated. "And where is Lady Violet now?"

"With her husband, I expect. She was very shocked by it all, she might be in her room."

"And did she or you or anyone else remove anything from the scene?"

"Good God no! I know better than that, constable, I've read a lot of crime novels, you know. And my father's a magistrate."

"Thank you, sir. Now, if I may, I will set things in motion," and I picked up his telephone to break the news to my colleagues. I had to inform Sergeant Blaketon but equally important, I had to notify my Divisional Headquarters who were aware of my presence at the Hall. I therefore rang Sergeant Williams.

"Well, Nick?" he asked as he took my call.

"It's definitely murder, Sergeant," I said. "Shot in the head, no sign of the weapon near the body. A handgun or a rifle was used by the look of it, it's not a shotgun wound, not a twelve-bore or anything like that, although the wound is a massive one. Bigger than a .22, I'd say."

"Fair enough, I'll arrange a full call-out, leave that to me. I'll call CID, SOCO, a doctor, pathologist — the cavalry in other words. So where are you now?"

"At Elsinby Hall, with Viscount Elsinby. None of the guests has left the Hall since the body was discovered nor has anything been removed from the scene. He's also locked the gun room. The body is in the grounds, by the way. Not indoors."

"Nice work so far. You stay with the body, Nick, and preserve the scene. I'll call Control Room, you wait there and don't allow anyone to leave the Hall. No one. And can you remain in contact?"

"I'll stay with the body, Sergeant, and I'm sure Viscount Elsinby will arrange for someone to be near the telephone. It'll be more secure than my van radio." I looked across the desk at Viscount Victor and he nodded, saying,

"We shall be most accommodating, constable, I can assure you. But surely, if the killer is out there somewhere, shouldn't you be organising a search of the surrounding countryside? With dogs and armed officers?"

"I don't think so, sir, with all due respect. If the murder was committed some time before 3.45am, any fleeing killer will be miles away by now, especially if a car was used. So, sir, a massive hunt would be pointless and a waste of manpower. Besides, it could ruin vital evidence at or near the scene. Our officers will be far more useful here, asking questions, interviewing your guests. Now, sir, did you or any of your guests see an intruder fleeing from the scene?"

"No, I did ask. All right, you're the expert, I'd have thought a search was vital but I suppose you know your business."

I was still holding the telephone at this stage and still talking to Sergeant Williams who had overheard His Lordship's conversation.

"I heard it all, Nick. You're right of course, don't let any enthusiastic amateurs start searching the vicinity, it could lead to other deaths if chummy's hiding with a gun. Leave things to me, you return to your corpse guarding duties."

"Thanks, Sergeant."

"And now, I'll start the panic at Headquarters — you can't beat a good murder enquiry at the crack of dawn on a Sunday for causing a flap among the hierarchy. And one in a stately home involving stately people will cause even more of a flap. Now, have we a name for the deceased? It's not a titled person, is it?"

"No, he's called Edwin Drood but his real name is Dickens, Edwin Dickens, and he's a guest at a house party at Elsinby Hall."

"Right. Now you ring your section sergeant, Nick, I'll be busy with Headquarters."

At first, Sergeant Blaketon couldn't believe what I was telling him. By the time I rang, it was almost 5am and in his interrupted slumbers, he had difficulty absorbing the dreadful news I was imparting. But when it did filter through his sleep ridden brain, he almost had a fit.

"You're not telling me that one of His Lordship's guests has been shot, Rhea?" he asked when I had completed my version of events.

"But you were despatched there to prevent trouble, Rhea! To safeguard His Lordship's house and guests! You were specially requested to be on duty to guarantee safety! And now this!"

"The murder happened after I left," I said.

"Did it? How do you know that?"

"Well, I did a tour of the ground just before I finished my duty," I explained. "I walked along the footpath close to where the body was found and I'm sure he wasn't there then. That was just before ten o'clock. The party was under way when I left and it seems to have been going strong at 3.45am when the body was found."

"I don't know what the chief constable will make of this, Rhea, a murder at the home of one of the county's most important people. Right, well, I'll come immediately. As officer in charge of Ashfordly Section, this is my responsibility!"

* * *

Instead of delegating the task to a member of his staff, Viscount Victor Elsinby offered to wait by the telephone in case there were any messages for me. While I was guarding the corpse, he would ask Johnson to notify his household that the police had been called and that a murder investigation was about to be launched. He would repeat my order that no one must leave the Hall.

I left his office and, on my way out, made a detour via the gun room to check that it had, in fact, been locked. Satisfied that it was, I returned to the garden and stood on a slightly elevated portion of the footpath from where I could view both the drive up to the house and the darkly clad corpse in the fading shadows.

It was now light. Dawn had arrived and as I awaited my colleagues in the brightening chilliness of that early spring morning, I contemplated my impressions of Viscount Victor.

Some thirty-two years old, he was a sturdy man, about five feet eight inches tall with a rounded and somewhat florid face, almost like that of a farm labourer who is accustomed to an open-air life. His nose was somewhat prominent in that it was rounded and almost bulbous. This was a family characteristic, I realised, having met other male members of the Elsinby clan. I'd also noticed this feature on the family portraits which adorned the walls of the Hall.

Well-known as a cattle breeder specialising in British Whites, Viscount Elsinby was, like his father the Earl of Thackerston, a countryman with a vast knowledge of wild life and as such was often called upon to speak on radio and television about rural matters. A keen supporter of fox hunting but a vehement opponent of badger baiting and any form of animal cruelty, he was a member of several local wild life groups and he supported many animal charities. He spent a lot of time on committees, some critics suggesting his voluntary work was done at the expense of the Estate. For a young man, he was extraordinarily busy; perhaps this was a substitute for his lack of children?

In the village, he was liked and respected, particularly by the farming community and would always lend his expertise and advice to anyone who sought it. As I pondered my previous associations with Viscount Victor, as most called him, I saw a car speeding along the road towards the Hall.

It turned into the drive and I knew that a bout of feverish activity was about to commence. Moments later, the car entered the grounds, came to a halt in the large turning area outside the front door and discharged Sergeant Blaketon.

He hurried towards the main entrance. I shouted and waved to attract his attention whereupon and he changed direction and headed towards me. Even at this time of morning, having been called from his bed, he had made time to shave and dress smartly and I noticed the gleam of his polished boots.

"Good morning, Sergeant," I greeted him.

"There's nothing good about it, Rhea," he muttered. "So it's true, then? The chap has been murdered?"

"It looks very much like it," I told him. "He's over there, near the White Shrubbery. I'm keeping away from the scene. CID has been informed, they're on their way."

"I can't see any corpse Rhea!" Blaketon peered in the direction I had indicated. "Maybe he's got up and walked away?"

"No such luck, Sergeant. He's lying in the shadows of the bushes, they're pretty dense in the morning light. He's very hard to see from here."

"Got him!" snapped Blaketon after a few moments. "So, who found the body?"

I updated my sergeant with the facts I had ascertained. He listened carefully, adding that I appeared to have done everything correctly, then asked the whereabouts of Viscount Elsinby. I explained that His Lordship was waiting in his office, acting as a volunteer telephonist on our behalf, while the guests had all been assembled in the lounge to await the arrival of the CID. I confirmed that no one had left since my arrival and that the gun room had been secured.

"So," he asked when I had briefed him as far as I could. "Was the victim shot by one of the guests, or was the killer someone lurking outside? Has a motive become apparent? Gossip you know, talk among the gentrified classes?"

"I've seen the body, Sergeant, and don't think it has been moved to that position. There were no marks in the dew or on the footpath. I think he was shot where he fell. And Viscount Elsinby has not suggested any motive."

"The corpse is cold, is it?" he asked.

"The surface skin is cold," I said. "But rigor mortis hasn't set in yet, or it hadn't when I examined him."

"It's a cool morning, Rhea, but even so rigor mortis takes some five or seven hours to begin. So I wonder if the pathologist will be able to indicate a time of death? I just hope he wasn't bumped off while we were responsible for the security of the Hall."

I knew how Blaketon felt, but did notice that he made no attempt to examine the body; he accepted my opinion and had the sense, coupled with long experience, to keep away from the corpse, thus preserving the scene for the attention of the incoming detectives.

He did ask, however, how to find Viscount Elsinby's office.

I told him of the route I had used and directed him through the main door.

"I'll go and acquaint His Lordship with my presence," said Blaketon, and I knew he was doing so as an act of courtesy.

After all, Viscount Elsinby's home and family were about to be subjected to the most searching of enquiries, and I knew Sergeant Blaketon would explain this to him in considerable detail. I remained on the lawn close to the sundial to await the CID and within a further ten minutes, the first car turned into the drive. Moments later, another car was heading towards the Hall. Quite suddenly, there was a steady procession of official vehicles and as I glanced at my watch, I saw it was 5.30am.

The sky was bright with the new dawn for the darkness of night had given way to the rising sun.

A new day was beginning at Elsinby Hall.

CHAPTER IV

"I believe, sir, that you desire to look at these apartments?"
CHARLES DICKENS, 1812–70

The yard behind Elsinby Hall, currently used as a car park by the guests, was large enough to accommodate the incoming police vehicles. A member of staff had appeared, probably at the suggestion of Sergeant Blaketon, and he was guiding the arrivals towards it. In the manner of follow-my-leader, all the swiftly-moving vehicles disappeared around the side of the Hall while I remained near the body of Edwin Drood. Soon, the imposing figure of The Horse appeared from the direction of the parked cars. Gregory Galvin, GG to his friends and "The Horse" to his colleagues, had been a detective sergeant at Strensford when I had served there as a young constable, and so he knew me fairly well. Since that time, he had won promotion, served with the Regional Crime Squad, and was now the detective superintendent in charge of CID in the North Riding of Yorkshire. At that time, the rank of Detective Chief Superintendent had not been instituted in this country and so The Horse was the CID boss.

A highly competent detective, he was likeable, affable and open, and he treated everyone with the same easy charm.

Whereas most senior officers referred to subordinates by their surnames, The Horse preferred to use Christian names. Even as a detective sergeant and detective inspector, he had referred to his own superiors by their Christian names. Rather curiously, no one had objected. I knew of no other officer who had this kind of relaxed relationship with his colleagues.

No one took advantage of his genial nature; he was highly respected by all. Most of the officers of my rank, including myself, called him "sir", although many within the CID resorted to the less formal "boss". In appearance, he was a very large man, some six feet five inches tall, with a correspondingly massive frame. He was not fat, however, just very large with shoulders like a Clydesdale and correspondingly large feet, albeit without the feathering of the breed. His shoes, being size fourteen, were like miniature barges while his smart, well-fitting light grey suits were specially tailored. He always wore light grey suits for work. His shirts were especially crafted too with sleeves longer than normal to cope with his enormous arms. He was always smart "like a Shire horse kitted out for t'Great Yorkshire show".

In his mid-forties, The Horse had a head of superb thick black hair, somewhat like a Clydesdale's mane, for it was always longer than one might have expected upon a senior police officer; it was parted in the middle and beautifully groomed, and this, plus his long, handsome equine features provided a professional splendour that made secretaries and women police officers go weak at the knees. Friendly, warm and very efficient, he came striding around the corner of Elsinby Hall to where I was still guarding the corpse. His commanding but welcome presence brought a sense of relief-it meant my time as a bodyguard was over. Hard on The Horse's heels was Detective Sergeant Bernard Wood, Timber to his friends. Whenever there was a murder investigation in our Force area, Wood and The Horse operated as a team. It is not surprising that they were jointly known as Wood and Horse, inevitably corrupted into Wooden Horse.

Bernard was a smaller man who would never progress beyond the rank of sergeant simply because he had never taken his promotion exams; clever, keen and smart in his tweed jacket, cavalry twills and brogue shoes, he looked like an equestrian orientated country gentleman but was nonetheless a very good and hard-working detective. With his fair hair cropped short and his narrow hawk-like face looking rather like an artist's impression of Sherlock Holmes, Bernard was in his late thirties with a substantial amount of police service yet to complete. Although his boss had constantly pressed him to study for his examinations, with strong hints of an inspector's post as the prize, Bernard had steadfastly declined. The truth was that he hated studying and detested exams. Now the Wooden Horse was heading my way.

"Now then, Nick," was The Horse's greeting. "He hasn't got up and walked away, has he?"

"Not this one," was my response. "He's beyond that stage."

"Well, Bernard," The Horse smiled at Wood. "We'd better take a look, hadn't we?"

As the birds of that spring morning were filling the air with the sound of their joyful music, I remained on my grassy knoll as the experienced pair began their work. They stood back from the corpse to examine it, the strengthening light of dawn providing sufficient illumination for this preliminary scrutiny. Then they executed a wide circle around the remains of Edwin Drood before The Horse asked,

"Who is this chap, Nick? Any idea?"

"He's an artist, sir, calling himself Edwin Drood. His real name is Edwin Dickens, he's a weekend guest at Elsinby Hall."

"They never did find out what happened to the other Edwin Drood, did they?" grinned The Horse. "Let's hope we have more luck. So, Nick, you examined the body?" It was more of a statement than a question. "Which route did you take?"

I began to explain, but he bade me come closer to show him with more precision. Then The Horse made his approach the same way, taking care to tread in my marks which were still visible in the dew. The tracks of Viscount Elsinby's first expedition could also be distinguished and I pointed them out, along with those of Lady Violet. I stressed that no other footprints had been visible upon my arrival, not even those of the dead man. When he reached the corpse after stopping several times en route, The Horse reached down to touch Edwin Drood, confirmed he was dead and said,

"All right, Bernard. Full steam ahead. Get the teams organised and a murder room established. There might be a suitable room we could use here. Where's His Lordship, Nick?"

"In his office, sir, with Sergeant Blaketon."

"I don't want old Oscar messing up my investigation. Wait here, Bernard, take charge of the body for a moment or two. Nick, you show me to His Lordship's office; you know your way around the house?"

"Yes, I've been here several times." Then I added, "You know there was a party here last night, sir? It was a large gathering, family and friends, it went on until the early hours. I've made sure no one has left the premises since my arrival, they're all in the house."

"A house full of suspects, eh? Well done, Nick. I must admit I wondered what all the cars were doing in the yard. Do we know who the party-goers are?"

"I've a list, sir, in my van. The party was for Lord Thackerston who is somewhere in the Hall, he used it to celebrate his 60th birthday which is today. He lives in Chelsea now. His son, Viscount Elsinby — Victor to his friends — lives at the Hall and runs the Estate. I was on duty here last night, from six o'clock until ten, checking for gate-crashers and so on."

"Who asked you to do that?"

"The estate manager, well, His Lordship really, the old man, that is. Lord Thackerston. It seems he wanted a police presence to deter gate-crashers."

"Are you suggesting he anticipated trouble, Nick?"

"He was very insistent, sir, I had to be here from 6pm until 10pm, that's the time most of the guests were arriving, and tickets had been issued to all his guests. No one could get in without one. I checked those who came through the gates during my presence."

"And you'll have a list of all those people?"

"Yes, and their car numbers, plus those of other vehicles which came and went before the party — a florist, for example, evening newspaper delivery van and so on."

"Good, well, we'll have to interview everybody, they're all suspects at the moment so it seems as if we're in for a busy time. Now to His Lordship's office!"

As I led The Horse towards the front door, Detective Inspector Clifford Hailstone, The Horse's deputy from Headquarters, came around the corner of the Hall. A pipe-smoking detective who always wore brown trilby hats and long belted raincoats, he was in line for The Horse's job if and when the big man retired. The Horse stopped to talk to him.

"Cliff, glad you got here. Timber's round the corner with the corpse. It is murder, there's no doubt about that. Can you get things set up? Doctor first, then Scenes of Crime . . . I'm off to ask His Lordship if we can take over one of his rooms as the Murder Room. Nick tells me there was a party last night, lots of guests and family members, plus some concern about gate-crashers."

"They're all in the lounge, sir, the guests that is," I told Hailstone. "Waiting to be interviewed."

"It sounds like something from Agatha Christie," he muttered.

"So long as we don't have Hercule Poirot, Miss Marple or some other amateur sleuth arriving to cock-up the investigation, I don't mind," grinned The Horse. "So, Cliff, off you go, full turn-out."

As DI Hailstone went about his duties, I escorted The Horse into the Hall. We passed the rows of family portraits and the collection of walking sticks, then as we approached the lounge door, which was standing open, we realised the room contained dozens of people in dinner jackets and smart gowns.

Many were still on their feet with drinks in their hands. Others lounged in chairs arranged around the walls but they were now talking in subdued tones. There was no music now. The Horse stopped.

"Guests?" he whispered to me.

"Yes, sir," I nodded.

"They're all suspects now, but I must tell them what's happening," and he entered the room. His sheer presence compelled them into silence and, pulling a chair towards him, he climbed on it to address them, now towering above the crowd like Pantagruel.

"Ladies and gentlemen," he addressed them in a strong bass voice. "I must apologise for this inconvenience, but my name is Detective Superintendent Galvin and I am here to investigate the unfortunate death of one of your number. I fear it is murder. I have just arrived and therefore I am not yet fully informed, but you may know that the body of a man has been found in the grounds. He is believed to be Mr Edwin Drood, otherwise known as Dickens, but I shall need a positive and formal identification. The current situation is that some of my officers have arrived and others will be coming soon, then we can begin the task of talking to each of you. I'm afraid that I must ask you all to remain here until released. I'm sure Viscount Elsinby will provide refreshments and I know that some of you are house guests. I shall speak to Viscount Elsinby before I do anything else, and all I ask is that you are patient a little longer and that you co-operate with my officers when requested. The more helpful and co-operative you are, the sooner we can all go home."

"I trust you will not detain us any longer than is absolutely necessary, Superintendent," said a plummy voice from within the crowd. "I was rather hoping to get to bed before sun-up but it looks as if I shall not see my pillow for some time yet. And I am rather weary."

"Parties are very important, sir, and they are hard work," smiled The Horse with all the charm he could muster, then he added coldly, "But murder enquiries are even more important and, for us, even harder work. You may go to your bed and make acquaintance with your pillow or whatever else is there, when I am satisfied that you are not the killer."

The Horse's smile disappeared and I knew his message had reached the others. The implication that Drood's killer could be among them had a dramatic effect and there was a murmur of assent from the gathering. In those few moments, The Horse had established his authority and as he stepped off the chair, the assembled guests began to mutter among themselves. This was welcome — gossip could provide clues, and he'd ensured they would all gossip. I led him towards Viscount Elsinby's office past the gleaming white piano and into the passage where the door stood open. Sergeant Blaketon was standing before Elsinby's desk; he saw the approaching bulk of The Horse and snapped to attention.

"Good morning, sir," he greeted the detective superintendent. "I was acquainting His Lordship with our procedures and priorities in a case of this kind."

"Very good, Oscar," grinned The Horse. "Good morning, Viscount Elsinby. I am Detective Superintendent Galvin. I'm sorry to arrive in such circumstances."

Elsinby extended his hand; The Horse shook it vigorously with a grip of iron.

Viscount Elsinby said, "I would like to say I am pleased to meet you, Superintendent, but that is not a particularly apt statement just now. Perhaps we can meet socially when this is all over? I wish to provide every possible assistance to you and will put the house, my staff and my facilities at your disposal. I am sure that you and your officers will exercise the utmost discretion in return. Now, if there is anything you need, just ask."

"Thank you," The Horse was very grateful. "I'm afraid we are going to be very disruptive, at least for today. I would hope to conclude my enquiries today, and thank you for detaining everyone, that is of enormous help. What I do need is a large room; it would help me immensely if there was somewhere in which to base my officers and equipment, and a smaller office which I could use. We shall need to install our own telephones, desks and office machinery, all that will be here shortly, and we need the room to be made secure for the safety of our records and equipment if we have to leave them overnight — although there would be a guard, of course."

After more discussion, Viscount Victor suggested a tour of the ground floor with Blaketon and myself in attendance, and having seen the premises, The Horse decided that the morning room would be ideal as the Murder Room. It contained sufficient furniture for the investigation to begin and with a bit of luck, the murderer would be identified before nightfall. "Murder Room" was the name given to the centre of operations at that time (today — 1995 — that room is called the Incident Room).

The morning room was on the south-east corner of the Hall with windows overlooking the long drive to the east and providing wide views of the grounds to the south. It was adjacent to the lounge in which the witnesses could remain pending their interviews, and the thick wooden double doors between the two would ensure adequate privacy. Not wishing to deprive the Viscount of his own office, The Horse decided that he would use that of Viscount Elsinby's secretary. She was not working today, being a Sunday. The Horse explained that while the morning room was being transformed into the Murder Room, the Scenes of Crime team, the doctor and the forensic scientists would begin their examination of the scene and the body. Interviews of the guests would commence in the morning room and he asked the Viscount if he would ensure that everyone had refreshments. The Horse made it clear that the Force would pay for any food or drinks provided, and for any telephone calls made from private telephones. The Horse now required, from His Lordship, a full list of everyone who had attended the party, identifying the house guests. His Lordship said the file was on his desk. Back in his office, Viscount Elsinby pressed a bell button on the wall and I heard it ring in the depths of the house, and this was followed by the tap-tap of Johnson's walking stick. In a few moments, the butler appeared.

"You rang, m'lord?"

"Yes, Johnson. Ensure the guests have refreshments for as long as they need them, will you? Have words with Phyllis Catchpole, get some maids organised. Breakfast, coffee, lunch or whatever. Warn cook that we shall have a large attendance for breakfast and for lunch, a buffet lunch perhaps? And include all the police officers, there will be about forty of them when they all arrive."

"Very good, m'lord," Johnson bowed slightly, turned on his heels and tap-tapped his way along the canvas-floored corridor to the kitchen.

"A very efficient man, Superintendent," smiled Elsinby.

"He runs the household, sir?" asked The Horse.

"With ruthless efficiency, Superintendent. I really could not do without him, he's been with us for some five years now."

"We shall have to interview him about the events of this morning," smiled The Horse. "But we will attend to the guests first, to release them as soon as we can. We can see your staff later. Now, I must find Inspector Oakland who will set up the Murder Room, and then, Oscar?"

"Sir?" responded Blaketon.

"I will need some uniformed officers to supervise the entrance, to check all vehicles coming and going and to maintain security throughout the investigation. I shall also need at least two more constables in uniform to patrol the grounds until our enquiry is complete. I believe this is your patch? That will be your responsibility?"

"The Hall is on PC Rhea's beat, sir," smiled Blaketon. "He can supervise the gate."

"No," said The Horse. "Bring some of your own constables from Ashfordly. I need Nick to work with the CID teams, his local knowledge will be invaluable. Nick, go home now, get washed and shaved, have some breakfast then get changed into civvies. When you've done that, come back here and bring as much information as you can about the local people who came to the party."

"Yes, sir," I replied with enthusiasm.

"And then," continued The Horse. "You will be working in the Murder Room with my officers."

And so, for the first time in my career, I found myself working upon a murder investigation.

* * *

It was astonishing how time had flown during those first hectic hours at Elsinby Hall. By the time I had washed, shaved and changed out of my uniform into a sports jacket and slacks, then had my breakfast and collected my Beat Report, a loose-leaf volume which was almost a compendium of confidential information about people who lived and worked upon my beat, it was almost eight o'clock. It seemed as if the working day was over, but in reality it was just beginning.

I updated Mary on the dramatic events and left the house as the church bells were ringing to herald morning Mass; I would have to give Mass a miss this Sunday. By the time I returned to Elsinby Hall, things had moved forward at a rapid pace. PC Alf Ventress of Ashfordly was on the gate and I could see that the body of Edwin Drood had now been covered by a small green structure resembling a tent.

Officers were conducting a fingertip search upon the ground around it; they'd be seeking the casing of the bullet which had caused the fatal wound, along with any other evidence which might have been discarded. The Scenes of Crime vehicle was parked around the corner and I knew that Doctor Ferguson would have come and gone after certifying death.

I parked my van in the yard among the other police vehicles, lifted out my Beat Report and went to the front door; already, there was a blackboard on its easel in the entrance hall. Looking out of place in these grand surroundings, it bore a large arrow in yellow chalk which pointed towards the morning room door. The accompanying legend said, "Murder Room. Authorised Personnel only."

I knocked and went in. The Horse was in this room and upon noticing my presence, he beckoned me to approach a desk behind which was Inspector Martin Oakland. Oakland was in charge of the Murder Room as opposed to Hailstone who was in charge of the teams of detectives. Thus Oakland's duties were administrative rather than operational because his normal duties were as officer in charge of Force Admin, at Headquarters. His skills in office management were utilised here and he had brought with him two secretaries, Angela Benson and Ruth Morgan, because all murder investigations require a first-rate and very experienced team in the office. The Horse introduced me to them all, saying my role would be that of liaison officer, providing the CID with detailed information about the local community, and about Elsinby Hall and its occupants.

Everyone seemed mightily busy. After my introduction, I looked around the room but no one paid any attention to me. I would have to find my own corner in which to work and I now saw a blackboard on an easel which bore today's date and the name Edwin Drood followed by these particulars:

"EDWIN DROOD alias EDWIN DICKENS, 36 years of age, born 8.3.1931 in West Norwood, South London, profession: artist. Home Address: Aconly Cottage, Little Blandford, Oxfordshire. Height: 5'9", dark brown hair, curly and worn long, brown eyes, pale complexion, average to heavy build, no scars or tattoos. Wearing: black dinner jacket and trousers, white shirt, black dickey-bow tie, black socks, black leather-soled shoes. Apparent cause of death: a bullet wound in the brain, entry via right temple, calibre of weapon not yet known. (Cause of death and location of wound not to be given to the press at this stage — if asked, GG will confirm death is by shotgun wound without giving further details). A

PM has been arranged for 2pm today when the cause of death will be confirmed and the bullet recovered."

Even at this early stage of the enquiry, black and white photographs of the deceased were pinned to the blackboard.

They showed Drood lying in the position I'd found him, with close-ups of the wound and his facial features. There were several views of the deceased from different angles and distances. These had been taken after sunrise and speedily developed in Ashfordly by a willing photographer.

"I'm going to start with Lord Thackerston," The Horse announced. "Angela, you come with me and take everything down in shorthand."

As he and Angela Benson left the Murder Room, Oakland said to me, "Nick, you've brought some gen from your beat, I believe?"

"My Beat Report and what I carry in my head!"

"Right, well, we've got a master list of guests from Viscount Elsinby so if you'd like to find a seat somewhere and go through his list, to see who you know and what you know about them, then that will be a good start. Jot down any details and take your time, care rather than speed is needed here."

Picking up a list of the guests, I went to a spare desk in a corner near the door and began my research. As I settled down, I noticed the arrival of Dr Adrian Butler, the pathologist; he was going to examine the corpse at the scene before it was removed for a post mortem. As he began his work, I started to examine the list of guests and fortunately their addresses were given. It was a simple matter to examine it and abstract the names of people who lived in the vicinity. The first to attract my attention were Anthony and Nadine Ormiston. They lived in a fine detached house on the outskirts of Aidensfield and he was something to do with bloodstock rearing, being heavily involved with horse racing and the flying of private aircraft. A man of means, I had little to do with him except that, once every three years I had to visit him to renew his firearms certificate. He had a collection of fine weapons, both rifles and hand guns, for he was a member of Ashfordly Rifle and Pistol Club. I turned up his name in my Beat Report; it listed all the weapons he held, together with the certificate's dates of validity but there was a star against his name and a note, written by my predecessor, which said, "See Complaints."

I turned to the complaints section of my report and the name was repeated, the time being the subject of regular complaints. A neighbour of the Ormistons had complained about Anthony some five or six years ago, before I came to the area; it seemed Ormiston had a habit of shooting at targets upon his land, but some of his shots went astray and one of them smashed a window of the neighbour's house. When confronted by the neighbour, whose name was Slater, Ormiston had threatened to shoot him. I thought this was worthy of inclusion in the file. The knowledge would be useful during any interview of the Ormistons and accordingly I made a note.

Then I moved on to the next name on the list.

CHAPTER V

"It was a maxim with Foxey — our revered father, gentlemen — always suspect everybody."
CHARLES DICKENS, 1812–70

Lord Thackerston had invited a bizarre selection of villagers. Whether they would have been invited had he known their cloaked backgrounds I could not say, but in my humble opinion, some were hardly the sort of person one would invite to any social gathering. But they were his guests, not mine, and I had no right to criticise his choice. In addition to Anthony Ormiston, an example of my concern was Beatrice May Fielder, the wife of Captain Fielder RN. Beatrice was a woman with an extremely jealous streak; she had been prosecuted six times for sending offensive letters to women in the area and she was also known to sneak into her handbag a trophy from every house she visited. She regarded them as souvenirs; we considered it theft. With both she and Phyllis Catchpole in action at the party, Viscount Victor's silver and antique trinkets were as vulnerable as iced lollies in a heatwave. Beatrice, like Phyllis, stole tiny things like salt cellars or serviette rings, but was seldom prosecuted because her victims were invariably her friends and they always declined to prosecute her. Some simply retrieved their trophies by stealth when next visiting her house.

Alleyn Floyd, the former headmaster of a public school at Ashfordly, could become violent and had convictions for reckless driving and drunken driving and he was also known to beat his wife. She was a well-bred woman who declined to prosecute him.

Just as Anthony Ormiston was careless with his shotguns, so another guest, Gordon McFarlane, had once gone berserk with a shotgun. It had occurred in a fit of anger which had burst upon him after a highly publicised sex scandal involving his wife and five other men. McFarlane was now divorced but continued to run a very successful shop-fitting business from Ashfordly.

The Hattertons, on the other hand, were not known by me to have any criminal convictions or character quirks. Benjamin and Philomena, both in their late forties, were married and were joint owners of a sports shop in Ashfordly, with others in neighbouring market towns. Their shops were known throughout the district as simply as Hattertons, they sold firearms of every kind, including antiques, and these ranged from shotguns to air weapons, as well as up-to-date requirements such as angling gear, hunting clothes, golfing equipment, general sports-wear such as football, tennis and cricket clothing, skis, canoeing or surfing accoutrements — in fact, they could supply virtually anything associated with sport. A handsome couple, both Nordic in appearance and blessed with athleticism, they were highly successful and a credit to Elsinby village.

As I read these highly confidential accounts, much of the information having been gathered by my predecessors, I realised that several of the guests did have access to firearms, and were quite capable of using them. Apart from those who had waved guns around in dangerous situations, my list included the tenant farmers who had been invited as well as the gamekeeper and the underkeeper.

Even gamekeepers could become angry and violent and I then recalled the gun room at the Hall. It contained enough guns to equip half the village and was never kept locked. Anyone could have helped themselves to one of a range of weapons. Also, I contemplated the tenant farmers who had been invited — if there had been a threat to any of them or their workers due to contraction of the Estate, then one of them might have felt compelled to wreak revenge by bumping off the next in line to the throne of Elsinby Estate. Had that been intended? After all, Drood did look rather like Viscount Victor, especially in the darkness. So could mistaken identity be a worthy line of enquiry?

The realisation that there were several possible motives and a number of likely assailants was compounded by the fact that most of Lord Thackerston's guests could handle a firearm with confidence. They were country people and estate workers, people to whom a gun was like a third arm — and that included a large number of women. It suggested that the hole in Edwin Drood's head had been put there by an expert — someone very capable of hitting the correct target. I began to wonder whether the butler, the cook, the chauffeur, the secretary and the former nanny also had access to guns — and thought again of that unlocked gun room. In many ways, it was an open invitation to murder. Had one of the guests or staff, in a sudden desire to kill, helped themselves to a gun last night? Had Drood's obnoxious behaviour stirred someone to kill him?

One of the first tasks by the detectives had been to take the key from Viscount Victor and ensure the gun room was officially sealed.

I wondered if the gun had been returned after the crime? If so, it would undoubtedly be found and identified.

I knew the gun room quite well. When I'd examined the Viscount's firearms certificate in the past, I had inspected the gun room to compare the Estate's complement of weapons against those listed in the certificate. That was done every three years. Now, of course, due to the murder investigation, every likely weapon would be examined by ballistics experts to determine which, if any, had fired the fatal shot. Shotguns, of course, were not then listed on firearms certificates, neither were air guns, air rifles or air pistols and so it was difficult to maintain an accurate check upon those types of gun and their use. At that time, the mid-1960s, shotguns and air weapons could be held without a certificate of any kind, although the use of them outside the grounds of one's home did require a gun licence. These were available at a cost of ten shillings (50p) from the post office as a form of excise licence, just like dog licences (7s. 6d — 37.5p in today's currency). A firearms certificate, on the other hand, could be secured only upon application through a chief constable. Rigorous checks were made upon applicants who had to provide a genuine reason for wishing to acquire such a weapon. For this reason, it was very rare for certificate holders to possess a pistol or a revolver — there were very few acceptable reasons for doing so, self-defence NOT being a valid reason. A very large percentage of firearms certificate holders kept .22 rifles or perhaps something with a larger calibre for competition shooting but few had pistols or revolvers. I wondered if any of the persons here present had ever applied to possess a pistol or a revolver?

From what I'd seen of the wound in Edwin Drood's head, it had not been caused by a shotgun. The hole looked as if it had been made by a bullet fired from a rifle, a pistol or a revolver of very large calibre, but some indication of the type of weapon might be determined at this afternoon's post mortem. There was also the possibility, of course, that one of the guests had smuggled a weapon into the Hall — that would not have been difficult. I knew that the detectives would examine police records to determine whether any of the persons at this party held a certification to possess a revolver, a pistol or a rifle of some kind.

Because I was distracted by these thoughts, it took a while for me to compile my notes based on the list of guests, but after some concentrated efforts, I handed them to Inspector Oakland. He would ensure they were entered in the Murder Room's efficient filing system. He thanked me and then informed me that The Horse had suggested that, in the absence of further specific tasks, I should be used as a statement reader, partly due to my knowledge of the locality and people, and partly because my knowledge of the layout of Elsinby Hall and its inhabitants was better than anyone else's.

He thought I might notice incriminating inconsistencies in some of the written statements. I was happy to do this because it meant I would be in the centre of the enquiry rather than being shuffled to the fringes. The statement reader's job (there were three such readers) was to study every written statement with meticulous care, and then to enter into the card index system any relevant details which were mentioned in the statement.

For example, if the witness referred to the sound of a shot, then there would be a card for "Shots", and upon that card would be entered the date, time and place of every shot that had been heard, and by whom. Any other relevant details would be added. Thus checks and comparisons could be made of every shot or similar noise. Likewise, if someone referred to a sight of the butler in his pantry, or a mysterious black car in the drive or a beautiful woman in a negligee flitting along the corridor at night, then such references would be entered into the system with details of dates, times and places. In this way, every fact could be checked and re-checked and, it was hoped, any discrepancies revealed. Many liars and indeed many guilty people have been identified by this simple but effective pre-computer age method.

Similarly, every reference to a name was checked and entered into the system. If, for example, Mr Powler claimed to have seen Evelyn du Bartas having a quiet smoke outside the conservatory at 1am, then Evelyn would be asked if she had done so at that time. The ground would be examined for ash of the type which would have dropped from her cigarette. And if she said she had smoked a Player and that she had spoken to Viscount Victor at the time, then the Viscount would be interviewed to check the truth of Evelyn's statement.

Every person who was named was interviewed — it was a case of record and check, then double check and check again.

And so the tentacles of the crime enquiry would spread wider and wider, bringing within the realms of a murder investigation all manner of subjects and all manner of people who might never be aware of the role they would then have to play.

Few could anticipate the testing inquisition they would have to endure. I knew how the system worked and I warmed to my task. With some forty detectives likely to be drafted into the enquiry, the flow of statements would be substantial — some people would be asked to make second, third or even further statements if discrepancies were revealed — and I would be kept very busy. It was a far cry from working as a rural constable in the peace of Aidensfield.

The information gleaned from the initial examination of the scene and from the corpse was now written on the blackboard. It said the body had been positively identified by the Earl of Thackerston who, it was noted, was a patron of Edwin who earned his living as an artist. His statement of identification, as opposed to the witness statement currently being obtained by The Horse, was already on file; it said, "I have been shown the body of an adult male person which was found in the grounds of Elsinby Hall this date and identify it as Edwin Drood, properly known as Edwin Dickens. He was thirty-six years old. He was an artist by profession, using the name Drood for his work and I am his patron. My support for Edwin amounted to £400 per annum, paid monthly, along with any other specific requests he might make, say for funding an exhibition or travelling to distant locations to work. Rather effeminate, he could be difficult, temperamental and moody at times but has never hinted at taking his own life and I do not know of any reason why Edwin should have died in this way. I did notice, however, that a gold pocket watch, signed by Frères Sinderby and dating from the eighteenth century, is missing from the body. Edwin always carried the watch, I gave it to him upon his coming-of-age."

The Earl had added that Drood had no known relations. His body had been taken to the mortuary in readiness for this afternoon's post mortem examination and detectives were now undertaking a second search of the ground in the vicinity of the shrubbery, the sundial, the fountain and the conservatory. This fingertip search was done by officers crawling about the ground on their hands and knees; they even parted blades of grass in the hope of recovering the tiniest of clues or the missing watch. The most interesting thing they'd discovered was a piece of chewing gum wrapping paper but the absence of the watch did suggest that robbery might be a motive.

The importance of locating evidence at or near the place the body was found was highlighted in red chalk on the blackboard in the Murder Room. Every officer was reminded that the murder weapon had not been found, nor had the watch, nor had the cast shell of the bullet believed to have caused this death. Everyone was ordered to bear this in mind when moving around the Hall and its curtilage even though every corner, waste bin, drain and hiding place would be diligently searched. A team of two officers, Detective Sergeant Eric Parsons and Detective Constable Paul Craven had been ear-marked to carry out an investigation into Edwin's recent movements and his personal background — at the moment, they were carrying out a meticulous search of the bedroom he had occupied at Elsinby Hall, then his car would be examined. Pinned to a notice board which had been suspended from the picture rail of the morning room was a plan of the Hall, showing both the ground floor and the bedrooms.

Drood's room was in the east wing, next to the butler's quarters. Beyond the butler's room was the shower room and from there a door led out to a fire escape which reached the ground. In the bedroom on the other side of Drood, the side nearest the main part of the house, were the Prittlefords. That room contained twin beds. I knew they would be interviewed to see if they'd heard any altercations or noises which might be associated with Edwin's sudden demise. Uncle Ben Langforte was next to the Prittlefords, Aunt Felicity, his twin sister, next to him and then Ned Powler and his girlfriend,

Vinnia, who shared a double room. All those rooms opened upon a single corridor which led from the main building towards the fire escape.

As I was wondering whether Edwin had been shot in his room and his body carried outside, a most difficult task due to the distance and narrowness of the staircases involved, a Scenes of Crime officer came into the Murder Room. He was carrying a plaster cast of a footprint and took it to Inspector Oakland.

"Sir," he said. "This is a cast of a boot print we found in the shrubbery. It's a solitary print of a right foot, as if someone put just one foot into the earth by stepping off the lawn accidentally. We've had it inked and have photographed the print marks too, so now we need to examine the boots and shoes of everyone at the Hall. The print's a sharp one, so it was made recently. There was rain on Friday night, dying out around 5am on Saturday, so we reckon the print's been made since then. It could be linked to this crime."

I piped up. "I saw Johnson, the butler, in the shrubbery yesterday evening," I told Inspector Oakland. "Just before eight o'clock, he was cutting some foliage for table decorations, a last-minute job. It might be his print."

"He wasn't carrying a gun, was he?" laughed Oakland.

"If he was, he'd hidden it well!" I returned. "So far as I could see, he was just cutting twigs, he was using secateurs."

"All right, Nick, we'll have him interviewed and we'll check his footwear. Joe!" Oakland spoke to a detective sergeant. "That's an action for you. Johnson needs to be eliminated."

On another notice board hanging from the picture rail was a chart showing the tasks currently being undertaken by the detectives, and Oakland entered the one relating to Johnson's footwear. I wondered if there had been a walking stick imprint in the shrubbery too? From the chart, I saw that teams of detectives were already interviewing the guests, one team of two officers per guest, their immediate concern being to discover the precise movements of Edwin Drood prior to his death. Any references to his movements would be checked and entered into the records. To firmly establish his whereabouts at every moment since his arrival at Elsinby Hall would not be easy but it would not be impossible either. On top of that, a motive had to be ascertained — the missing watch offered the possibility of robbery, and a description would be circulated to all antique dealers and others who might be offered it. A note on the blackboard suggested the motive might not be robbery because Drood's wallet did not appear to have been tampered with; it still contained £50 in £5, £1 and 10-shilling notes while his pockets had produced a further £7. 13s. 7d in cash.

Even though some functions of the Murder Room were still being established, the real work of the investigation was moving smoothly into a well-tried routine. Every detective knew his job; two were in the yard where the cars were parked and they were recording every registration number. These would be checked against the list of guests, and then, before the guests would be allowed to leave, every car would be searched meticulously, hoping this would produce some evidence of the guilty person — a letter perhaps, some crudely written note, a hidden threat, some link with the dead man, bullets of the same calibre as the murder weapon or even the weapon itself. A list of names was being telephoned to the national Criminal Record Office at Scotland Yard and to local CROs for checks to be made on the criminal records of anyone at the party. The uniformed constable at the gate effectively turned Elsinby Hall into a prison because no one could leave and no one could enter; of much more importance, it meant that everyone was under arrest which meant, in theory and in reality that everyone was under suspicion — as indeed they were. I had never known a murder enquiry with so many primary suspects, all of whom were technically under arrest. In police jargon, they were all helping the police with enquiries.

"Here's the next statement, Nick," said a woman's voice and I found Ruth Morgan at my elbow. In her early thirties, she had a freckled face and an infectious smile, coupled with a rather plump appearance beneath loose fitting clothes.

A highly efficient secretary, she was drafted into most of the murder investigations in the county where she contributed to the smooth running of the Murder Room. She was issuing copies of the statements which she had duplicated on a hastily installed machine, and I accepted mine. Lord Thackerston's statement of identification aside, this was the first of the witness statements to be completed, and it was made by Lady Violet Powler, the finder of the body. I settled down to read it and enter the salient points into the card index system.

After declining to give her age, Lady Violet did include her address, Barleigh Manor, Chumleigh Barleigh, Devon, after which she said, "I am the daughter of the Earl of Thackerston and sister of Viscount Elsinby, being married to Lady Elsinby's brother, the Hon. Henry Powler. Henry's sister, Lady Lavinia, married my brother, the Viscount, which means a brother and a sister married a brother and a sister. My husband runs the Chumleigh Barleigh estate, which he inherited. We have been happily married for eight years and have two children, Vernon aged six and Violetta aged three. Leaving the children at home with their nanny, Henry and I arrived at Elsinby Hall around 4pm yesterday, Saturday, and the first thing we did was to go to our room to unpack, then have baths and relax before the party. Our room is in the main part of the house, looking east, and it is situated at the end of the corridor which leads to the east wing. We are next to the Earl and Countess of Ploatby, and our room has its own integral shower, bath and toilet."

I looked at the plan of the house and saw that someone had written the names Hon Henry and Lady Violet Powler in the space occupied by that bedroom.

She went on. "My husband and I came downstairs to join the party about 7.30pm. I cannot remember my precise movements although I did chat to friends and relations after taking a glass of dry sherry from a tray in the hall. I began to mingle with the guests. I know I talked to Evelyn du Bartas before going in for dinner because we discussed her new designs. At dinner, I was seated next to Sir Ashley Prittleford who was on my right, while on my left was my husband. Opposite me was Austin Plankenburgh. After dinner, I went into the lounge where there was music for dancing and I danced an Eva Three Step with my brother before finding my father, Lord Thackerston to thank him for inviting us and to wish him a happy birthday. I had lots of dances with lots of men, including my husband, but couldn't put a time to any of the dances although I think most would be before half past twelve. I heard someone playing the piano in the stairwell too, and singing, but I have no idea who it was — except it was a male voice. I was unaware of the time until the grandfather clock in the stair well struck one — I happened to be walking past as it struck, on my way to the foot of the stairs. I was heading for my room, to, well, powder my nose. I remained in my room for about half an hour, lying on the bed for a few minutes because my feet ached. Then I returned to the lounge where dancing was still going ahead and had a dance with my husband. Like everyone else, I was in the lounge when I heard Lord Thackerston give his birthday speech. I never heard any shots nor did I see any intruders on the premises or in the grounds. I knew Edwin, he has been coming to the house since we were children, and I know my father has sponsored him in his work as an artist.

"I had a few words with him — Edwin that is — during the evening and did not sense that he was in any kind of anguish or trouble, certainly there was no hint of suicide, but I can't say whether he was at father's speech. The room was packed, I just assumed everyone was there, and I was not aware of Edwin again until about quarter to four when I saw a man lying in the shadows near the White Shrubbery. I had left the Hall via the conservatory door because it was stifling inside, so hot and airless, and I needed some fresh air. I went outside, onto the lawns and didn't see the man until I was almost on top of him — I thought he was drunk at first and touched him, thinking he might need help but then I realised he was very still and I saw the blood on his head. It was possible to see that in the light reflected from the conservatory. At first, I didn't realise it was Edwin, then I recognised him. I ran back indoors and found Victor who went outside to look and then he said he was going to call the police because Edwin was dead. Victor asked us all to remain in the house and not to go tramping all over the grounds because that would ruin any evidence, he said it looked as if Edwin had been shot. Between coming back to the party and being told of Edwin's death, I spent the time either in the lounge, just talking, or in the library where there were easy chairs and more drinks. The dancing stopped at the news. We all just sat there, stunned. Before finding Edwin, I had ventured into the conservatory from time to time, chiefly to feel the fresh air which was blowing in through the open door and on several occasions, I noticed people standing outside, on the footpath, enjoying the night air.

"I would say most of us went out for some fresh air at some stage. I never noticed any strangers among us, nor gate-crashers. I never saw anyone go into the shrubbery and did not see anyone carrying a firearm, or walking around with mud on their shoes. I was never aware of any unpleasantness among the guests and most certainly never witnessed anything that might be construed as a fight or dispute of any kind. I was not drunk and had some sandwiches to eat around three o'clock, they were brought in by Johnson, Mrs Catchpole and the maids. I had no cause to harm Edwin and did not see anyone behaving suspiciously during the evening. I cannot suggest either a motive or a killer."

The statement ended with the usual clause which said she had read it through and did not wish to alter or change it in any way. I then began to enter the salient details in the card index system, wondering whether the seating plan at dinner was of any consequence or whether Lady Violet's recollection of the striking clock was important. Most certainly, she would have to be interviewed again because this was merely a scene setting statement and she was the person who had found the body. That made her an immediate suspect too. I felt that, with a little prompting, she would know to whom she had been speaking at various times during the evening, and she must have known with whom she was dancing.

Her statement was rather vague, I felt, and lacking in detail.

It was while I was working on the card index that a Scenes of Crime officer entered with the plaster cast of the footprint found in the shrubbery.

"It doesn't belong to Jasper Johnson," he told Inspector Oakland. "When he went to the shrubbery yesterday evening, he was wearing shoes with smooth soles and his feet are size eight. These marks are size nine and they were made by heavy boots with studs in the soles. Farmer's boots, countryman's boots, gamekeeper's boots, that sort of thing. Not the kind of footwear people would be wearing at a country house party."

The Scenes of Crime officers had produced photographs of the marks of that print and these were for distribution among the detectives. I took one and examined it . . . and I knew where I had seen those studs before. The design on the sole was exactly the same as the one I'd seen upon the boots worn by Claude Jeremiah Greengrass yesterday afternoon.

CHAPTER VI

"The dodgerest of dodgers."
CHARLES DICKENS, 1812–70

If I was right and if the footprint in the shrubbery had been made by Claude Jeremiah Greengrass then he had some urgent explaining to do. This evidence put him right at the scene of the murder. Even so, I could not believe Claude was a killer. I was sure he was not — but, as I reminded myself, I knew he kept a .22 rifle as well as two twelve-bore shotguns, one an over-and-under and the other a side-by-side. It wouldn't surprise me if he had a poacher's gun too, the sort that could be secreted down a trousers leg. Faced with difficult possibilities of this kind, possibilities confirmed by positive evidence, a police officer cannot afford to be too trusting. There are times when an unpalatable truth has to be faced and this might be such an occasion. But Claude Jeremiah as a murderer? I must admit I found it hard to believe. And yet, if that mark in the shrubbery had been left by Aidensfield's favourite rogue, then he would have to be interviewed as a prime suspect.

In spite of my in-bred police caution, the possibility did put me in a dilemma. I found myself not wanting to believe Claude was guilty or even under suspicion. I told myself that merely by looking at the plaster cast neither I nor any other officer would be able to identify sufficient detail to determine whether or not it had been made by Claude. A close scientific comparison would have to be made. That could be done only by matching the sole of his boot with the plaster cast itself, or perhaps with the inked imprint it had made on paper.

A large supply of the printed boot marks had been produced by Ruth Morgan and so I took one, folded it and placed it in my pocket. Wondering whether I was doing the right thing by not telling the investigating team at this stage, I nonetheless decided I would speak to Claude before revealing my suspicions to the CID. With a spot of luck, I would be able to do this at lunchtime. Claude always went into the pub for a pint or two before his Sunday lunch of roast beef and Yorkshire pudding in the bar, one of George's most popular meals. Rightly or wrongly, therefore, I decided to keep this piece of information to myself, if only for the time being. In the meantime, further statements had been taken and were finding their way into the Murder Room's system. Before my lunch break, I next read one made by Vinnia Phinlay.

She said, "I am twenty-eight years old and the girlfriend of Ned Powler. He is the youngest brother of Lady Lavinia, Viscount Elsinby's wife, and the younger brother of Henry Powler, the brother-in-law of Viscount Elsinby. Ned and I are lovers. We live together in South London, at Ned's town house which is near Crystal Palace. Because of this family connection, Ned was invited to Lord Thackerston's birthday party with a partner, and so I came along. I'm not accustomed to these country house parties and the lifestyle of those who live in such places but I decided to go because Ned wanted me to support him. He seemed very keen to go to Elsinby Hall for the weekend. I have never met Edwin Drood until this party and did talk to him briefly; it was during the reception before the meal and he told me about his work and exhibitions.

"I considered him somewhat pompous with delusions of grandeur. He seemed to be quite at home in those surroundings, talking to lots of people and saying what he would do if Elsinby Hall belonged to him. I never saw him leave. I never noticed any heated arguments between him and anyone else, nor did I hear any threats against him although I must say that his opinionated behaviour didn't exactly endear him to any of us. He wasn't the sort of chap I'd like to be friendly with. He looked like a homosexual too, very effeminate and affected. I did go outside once or twice, to get some fresh air and to have a smoke, and each time I used the open door of the conservatory, standing outside on the footpath to enjoy my cigarette. Most times, there were other people around, doing the same thing or just talking and drinking. I think Mr Drood came out once or twice too, to get some fresh air. I did see him smoking when he was outside, a cigarette, not a cigar. Viscount Victor Elsinby came out too, with Lady Ploatby with drinks in their hands, but neither were smoking. I think that would be about midnight, but can't really be sure of the time. I never saw the Earl of Thackerston come out for any fresh air, nor Lady Elsinby, the Viscount's wife. I never saw anyone with a gun nor did I hear any shooting. In fact, I heard nothing which made me think Mr Drood or anyone else was in danger. I never went to my room during the evening and so I cannot say who, if anyone, left the gathering to go to their rooms for any reason. I was at Lord Thackerston's speech, but couldn't really say if anyone was missing, I just don't know all the people who were there. I never noticed anyone hanging around the door of the gun room either. I just knew the man as Edwin Drood, not as Edwin Dickens."

As I read this statement, it struck me that it contained a lot of negatives, those things which Vinnia had never seen or known, but such statements were as important as those which produced positive evidence.

As a statement, it was probably typical of most we would receive, especially from comparative strangers to the Hall; most of the guests would be so busy enjoying the party that they would never notice the minutia of the occasion. Further statements of this kind then followed, the detectives clearly sorting through those people with little or nothing to tell; once they had been interviewed and their stories, or lack of them, could be checked, then they would be free to leave the premises — after their cars and rooms had been examined, of course. Uncle Ben and Aunt Felicity proffered similar statements, albeit with Aunt Felicity saying she had gone to her room at lam to get some dyspepsia tablets because the pork had given her indigestion. She'd found it difficult to climb the stairs because of her age, and had remained in her room, taking the tablets, drinking a glass of water and swilling some of the perspiration of the evening from her face before returning to the lounge. Due to her age — eighty-one next birthday — that excursion had taken about fifteen minutes whereas a younger person might have completed the journey in a far shorter time but she had not noticed anyone else in the bedroom areas or on the landings. And she had returned to the lounge in time for the birthday speech. The whole of the landing area, she added, was brightly illuminated and cooler than the downstairs rooms because the landing window was wide open.

In spite of her age, she did enjoy very sharp hearing but had heard nothing when she was in her room, and had not heard anyone passing along the corridor outside. As the floor of that corridor was covered with linoleum and not carpeted, then she felt she would have heard footsteps had anyone passed by. During the early evening, before the party officially began and while the guests were arriving, she had heard people walking backwards and forwards along that corridor, and she'd also heard voices outside her door, although she had not listened to the conversations and could not say what the discussions were about. She had not heard any shots, however, but did remember having a scrambled egg sandwich in the lounge around 3am, she had added as an afterthought.

As I read this statement, I looked at the plan of the house, examining the corridor to which Aunt Felicity referred. As one entered the first-floor corridor from the main concourse of the Hall, Henry and Lady Violet occupied the room which was in the main part of the house, but which adjoined the extension in which a further six rooms were constructed. Ned Powler and Vinnia Phinlay had the first room, then Aunt Felicity, then Uncle Ben, then the Prittlefords in a twin-bedded room, then Drood and finally the butler. Beyond the butler's bedroom was the shower block and then the outside wall, down which ran the fire escape. A narrow corridor extended the length of these bedrooms, terminating at the shower block, although there was an additional flight of stairs which led down to the rooms on the ground floor. I checked that plan next.

Directly below the shower block and butler's bedroom was the gun room, next to which was the TV room for staff, then the butler's private lounge and finally the secretary's office. A corridor ran alongside these ground-floor rooms, leading from the foot of the staircase which led up to the showers and bedrooms, and entering the main Hall via a "Z" shaped passage leading between the servery and the kitchen. It emerged through a doorway at the foot of the main staircase not far from the white piano. Opposite that doorway, across the main hall, was another short passage leading to the Viscount Victor's personal office and the conservatory. Thus it was quite possible for someone to sneak along that top corridor towards the showers, descend the stairs to the gun room, sneak into the gun room to select a firearm, and then hurry along the corridor towards the conservatory. If everyone else was in the lounge, library and morning room, that journey could be undertaken in secret. One snag with that theory was that the conservatory seemed to contain people for most of the evening after dinner, chiefly to get some fresh air just outside the door or perhaps to have a smoke. The gun room had never been locked until after the murder, and if the killer had heard anyone moving along that route while going about his awful business, it would be simple enough to pop into any of the adjacent empty rooms and hide until danger had passed. Another snag with that theory was that

Edwin would have had to be lured into the open when no one else was around so that the fatal shot could be fired without anyone hearing it, and for the killer to make good his or her escape. Unless, of course, Edwin Drood had been killed elsewhere and his body brought here?

That theory could not be dismissed, although the footprints in the dew suggested that Edwin had been killed where he was found. We'd have to establish at what time the dew appeared. But with a party in full flow and with people constantly wandering out of the conservatory door for a smoke or some fresh air, then the placing of the corpse in the situation in which it was found would have been fraught with danger.

I favoured my own view that he had been shot where he'd been found, the missile being discharged from within the conservatory or from just outside the door. Even though the ground-floor curtains of the Hall had been closed before my departure at 10pm, thus shielding the exterior and any external activities from those inside the house, I could not visualise the killer carrying or hauling the corpse into its discovery position while the party was in progress. There'd been no marks of dragging on the ground; they would have shown up very clearly on the grass, the gravel or in the dew, and I had not noticed evidence of any such activity upon my arrival. There was always the possibility, of course, that Drood had been shot from beyond the grounds of the Hall, perhaps by someone hiding in the shrubbery and even in the darkness beyond; a rifle could have killed him after being fired from the parkland which surrounded the hilltop site. One of the tasks of the Scenes of Crime officers, and the forensic scientists, would be to determine from where the shot had been fired, a task made easier by the position of the body and of the wound.

"Lunchtime, Nick," it was Inspector Oakland organising breaks so that the room was continuously staffed. "We've brought sandwiches, we're used to this kind of thing! You can share some of ours."

"No thanks, sir. Mary will have my lunch ready at home," I told him. "I can be there and back within my allocated three quarters of an hour."

"Right, off you go, and we're not like the Sergeant Blaketons of this world, I'm not tying you down to a mere forty-five minutes for lunch!"

All policemen were allowed three quarters of an hour for refreshments during a tour of duty, but I would take longer today because my first job after leaving the Hall was to examine the pattern of the studs in the soles of Claude Jeremiah's boots. With that in mind, I drove into the car park of the village pub. I knew Claude would be there, indeed his old truck was parked outside. Inside, I ordered a pint from George, the landlord and asked whether Claude had got himself a drink.

"He'll never say no to a free pint, Nick!" grinned George, as he pulled an additional glass for my quarry. "He's over there, near the fire, with his cronies. His roast beef and Yorkshire pudding will be there in ten minutes, tell him."

I was moderately surprised that George did not mention the murder investigation at Elsinby and I guessed that news of the crime had not yet filtered into the village. Due to the isolated nature of Elsinby Hall and the fact the police had arrived so early in the morning plus the fact that everyone had been detained on the premises, secrecy had been maintained. Not even village gossip had been generated, nor had any newspaper reporters arrived. But they would come!

The secret could not be maintained for much longer. I walked across to Claude's table carrying the pair of pint glasses and sat down facing him. He didn't notice me for a few moments, then he saw the pint standing before him.

"Cheers, Claude," I raised my glass as he noticed my presence.

"Are you trying to bribe me or summat?" were his first words.

"No," I smiled at him. "Just a drink for an old friend, that's all."

"You're scheming," he looked at me with some suspicion. "You're after summat, setting me up . . ."

"You're not a copper's nark, are you, Claude?" asked one of his pals.

"I am not!" he snapped, and I could see he was embarrassed by my presence, so I decided to put him to the test. I pulled the print of the footmark from my pocket, unfolded it and placed it on the table. He stared at it, along with his cronies.

"That's just like the sole of your boot," I smiled. "As soon as I saw this picture, I said to myself, that's a picture of the sole of Claude's new boots."

"Are they special boots?" grinned one of his pals. "Where'd you get 'em, Claude? Are they nicked?"

"That's never from my boots!" Claude began to blink as he avoided my direct gaze. "I've never put my foot in stuff that'll make marks like that . . . is it soot or summat?"

"Ink, Claude. Fingerprint ink in fact, taken from a plaster cast of a boot print. Anyway, I'm sure you won't mind if I check the sole of your boots, Claude, the right one, isn't it? So, off with it and I can compare the stud marks with this print."

"Take my boots off in a public place, constable? You must be joking . . . I'm a man of pride and principle, no man in my position takes his boots off in public."

"Not with your sweaty socks, eh, Claude?" chuckled his pals. "By gum, Mr Rhea, you're a brave man, risking what'll happen if Claude takes his boots off. I've seen flowers wilt at the stink and pigs turn tail and run . . ."

"All right, Claude, up with your leg. Let's have your right foot, put it on my knee . . ."

And so he had to oblige.

I made him position the sole with the face outermost so that I could place the print beside it and check the position and design of the studs. I knew that those studs were the work of one of our local cobblers, they had not come from the factory already fitted to the new boots and so the design would be unique. And the design matched. I told him to lower his boot to the floor at which he took a long sip from his pint and looked at me, puzzled, but saying nothing.

"There we are, Claude, a perfect match! So what were you doing in the grounds of Elsinby Hall yesterday?" I asked him. "Me? Yesterday? No, Mr Rhea, you've got it wrong."

"This footprint was found in the shrubbery, Claude, the famous White Shrubbery no less. It's your footprint. It appeared last night, after the rain of the previous day, and this is a copy of a cast we made. It matches perfectly. It means you were there yesterday, Claude; I bet you were snooping in the dark, probably while the party was in progress. You can't deny it, Claude, this is our evidence."

He blinked furiously, his eyes avoiding mine as he took a long draught from his glass.

"I wasn't doing anything, Mr Rhea, not poaching or pimping or anything. I just went for a look, you know how it is, to see how the nobs enjoy themselves . . . I never did owt wrong, I just waited in the shrubbery, watching 'em . . ."

"I know you do that sort of thing, Claude, wander around folks' houses at all hours of the night looking in, although God knows why. You could be arrested as a pimper if you're not careful but I suppose if you happened to see a pheasant on the way home, you might just have been tempted to give it a lift back to your place, eh?"

"No, I never took any pheasants, it's the close season anyroad. They're nesting. You don't take pheasants when they're busy producing lots more pheasants for us to take. Look, I stayed there for, oh mebbe twenty minutes, watching the stupid buggers drinking themselves silly and trying to out-talk each other."

"So at exactly what time were you there?" I put to him.

Again he blinked in his agony and said, "Well, I dunno, not exactly."

"Approximately, then?" I offered. "Roughly what time? Ten o'clock? Midnight? Dawn this morning?"

"After closing time last night," he was screwing up his face as he tried to recollect the events of yesterday evening. "Latish, getting on for one o'clock mebbe."

"One o'clock, eh? So what did you see from the shrubbery?" I persisted with my questioning, still not revealing the true reason for my interest in his boots.

"You're asking a lot of questions for a feller that's done nowt," he grumbled.

"I'm trying to establish whether or not you really did do nothing," I said seriously. "So who did you see or what did you see from the shrubbery?"

"Well, I saw a chap come out for a smoke. He stood outside the conservatory and lit up. I couldn't see who it was, he could have been Lord Thackerston's lad but he was like a silhouette, you see, constable, even to one whose eyes are trained for night vision, like mine. The Hall was lit up, upstairs and down so he looked indistinct. Smart he was, though, in his dinner jacket. He looked a bit like the Viscount but, well, I couldn't be sure."

"Anybody else?"

"No, not then. He was alone, until a woman came out and talked to him."

"What woman was that?"

"Search me, I don't know who she was. Youngish, blonde, hair in a bun . . ."

"Did they talk for long?"

"No, they chatted for a bit, I couldn't hear what they were saying, then she went back inside. I sneaked away, I came home. Without any pheasants, mark you . . . now, wasn't that an exciting evening for a feller, constable?"

"Claude, I have no idea why you want to pry into people's lives like you do, but on this occasion, it's landed you in bother. You'd better come outside," I said quietly, placing my drink on the table.

"Bother? Outside? But I haven't had my dinner yet, my Yorkshire puddings will get cold . . ."

"Your puddings haven't been served yet, Claude, so come outside. Now, just you and me. For a chat. Right?" and I made my move.

Under protest, Claude followed me into the rear yard of the pub with Alfred, his dog, on his heels. I kept going until we were out of earshot, then I said,

"Claude, there was a murder at Elsinby Hall last night. That footprint was found in the shrubbery . . ."

"Murder?" He swallowed hard now, and genuine fear began to show in his eyes. "Hey, you don't think I did it . . ."

"No, I don't, that's why I want to find out just what you saw and why you were there. That footprint is a real giveaway, Claude, the CID will want to ask you more questions, you might have been the last man to see the victim alive. He was a man called Drood, Edwin Drood."

"Never heard of him. Was that him I saw?" he asked.

"It's possible but I can't be sure," I told him. "Clearly, there's a lot more enquiries to be made, we need to determine Drood's movements during the evening, but I want you to come with me, to the Murder Room, to tell the detectives why you were there and what you saw."

"They won't arrest me, will they? God, I mean, a murder suspect . . . Mr Rhea, I mean, you and me are pals, good pals. We've had our ups and downs, but you know me, I'd never kill a chap . . ."

"I know Claude. But you must come with me voluntarily, that'll be a good indication of your innocence and your willingness to help us. Now, not a word to anybody in the pub about the murder, no one knows about it yet. I'll pick you up after you've had your roast beef and Yorkshire pudding, eh? In say, half an hour?"

"You'll look after me, Mr Rhea, won't you?" he almost pleaded and I promised him I would.

And so, after lunch, I returned to the Murder Room with Claude in my van and took him to meet Inspector Oakland. I explained about the boot print and Claude stood there, his old army greatcoat around his shoulders and those new brown boots on his feet as the inspector listened to my tale. Oakland then called a detective sergeant across, explained the matching patterns on Claude's boots, and took Claude away for an in-depth interview and, I knew, a searching interrogation.

"I didn't do it, Mr Rhea, you know that," he was almost weeping now but I waved and promised he would be in no difficulties if he told the truth. Telling lies, however small, during a murder investigation was the worst thing anyone could do, but for Claude, his reason for being in the shrubbery in the early hours would not convince the CID. I knew his propensity for wandering at night, they didn't; they'd think he was an accessory to murder. As poor old Claude was led away for his interrogation, I settled down to my pile of statements; it had grown considerably during my absence. I found one made by Robert Beswick, the estate under-gamekeeper, who said he'd seen Edwin outside the conservatory door at ten minutes to one, smoking a cigarette and talking to Brenda Armitage.

Brenda was the blonde with her hair done in a bun. Beswick had gone out through the same door for a walk in the fresh air and had executed a tour of the Hall before regaining entry via the back door of the kitchen, a route familiar to him in his work. Johnson, the butler, had seen Beswick enter the kitchen around one o'clock, but Beswick, a keen-eared countryman, said he had not heard any shots, nor had Johnson noticed Edwin again. Johnson's mission to the kitchen had been to see if there was a pot of tea on the go because he'd felt thirsty. But these accounts did tend to back up Claude's story and his statement about the time of his presence in the shrubbery. I must admit I worried about poor old Claude — he would not be able to satisfactorily explain his presence in the shrubbery and he could get himself high on the list of suspects if he wasn't careful.

I spent the next hour or so wading through the growing pile of incoming statements, happy that the detectives were endorsing most of them as "witness only", a means of informing us that, in the view of the detective who had interviewed the witness, that the statement-maker was not under suspicion. As the afternoon wore on, many of the local people — the tenant farmers and their families, were allowed to leave Elsinby Hall. None of them had heard a shot, something to which their ears would be attuned, especially in the early hours of the morning. The Horse clearly felt that many of the guests could now be eliminated from the enquiry.

I saw that the Lampkins, the Lees, the Oldhams and the Olivers had all been interviewed and allowed home, as had the former nanny, Robbie Whitwell and the former cook, Sarah Crossfield.

It seemed that other local people were still being interrogated — I noted that they included Lieutenant Colonel Jordon and his wife, Mr and Mrs Floyd, Gordon McFarlane, the Hattertons, the Ormistons and the Fielders. And so the process of elimination was proceeding quite speedily, the police knowing, of course, that if they wanted to interview the local people again, they would be able to do so without much trouble. It was then that I received the statement made by Roy Cleghorn, the gamekeeper for Elsinby Estate. This statement was marked for special attention because one of Cleghorn's responsibilities was the gun room. Aged 46, he was married to Violet and they lived in the Keeper's Cottage behind the Hall; they had no children and Violet sometimes helped out in the Hall where she was particularly skilled at flower arranging.

I studied his words with care, itemising his references to named people whom he had noticed during the festivities — he'd seen Lord Thackerston walking out of the lounge some time before half past twelve and he'd noticed His Lordship in earnest conversation with Edwin Drood earlier that evening, around eleven o'clock, when the pair had been chatting in a corner of the library. He'd also seen Uncle Ben laughing uproariously at something said by Lady Ploatby and had seen Lady Violet heading for the door of the lounge, but couldn't be sure of the time. It was not too long before the birthday speech. That could confirm her story about going up to her room to rest her feet, but Uncle Ben had also seen Ned Powler creeping away from the lounge at quarter to one that morning.

His statement said, "It was the way he crept out of the room that drew my attention to him. It was as if he was hoping no one would see him. He sidled along with his back to the wall, avoiding people, and when he got to the doorway, he paused to smile at someone who was coming in — I think it was Lady Penelope who was entering and she just smiled at him — then Powler vanished around the edge of the doorway. I was most curious so I hurried towards the doorway which gave a wide view of the hall and heard someone walking upstairs, walking in a rush, almost running in fact. I could not see who it was but heard someone on the landing and as I did not see Powler anywhere, I assumed it was him. I have no real idea if it was Powler or not but I never saw him again until we were assembled in the lounge after the discovery of Mr Drood's body."

An endorsement on this statement said, "Powler now a suspect."

CHAPTER VII

"I am ruminating on the strange mutability
of human affairs."
CHARLES DICKENS, 1812–70

Ned Powler's distractive exit was, for him, a necessity because he had split his trousers. He'd done so while dancing a particularly vigorous Dashing White Sergeant with Evelyn du Bartas. Upon being interviewed about his perplexing behaviour by Detective Sergeant Crisp and Detective Constable Arkle, he had collapsed in a fit of laughter, albeit after some tense initial moments of worry and concern. Ned explained that a gaping hole had appeared in the seat of his pants when the seam had been rent asunder as a direct consequence of his contortions. His spotted red underpants, not the most glorious of sights, had then been placed on public display. He had fled upstairs to repair the damage. This event had been witnessed by Evelyn who confirmed Ned's story. Highly embarrassed at the display of secret things, he had manoeuvred himself along the wall of the lounge, always with his rear in concealment and his front towards any potential sightseers. Once free of the crowds, he had bolted upstairs to his bedroom while clutching his gaping trousers with a free hand. He wasn't sure of the time of this memorable incident, but agreed it might have been around a quarter to one.

His statement went on, "The lounge was stifling because the French windows were closed and curtained. Although I was perspiring somewhat heavily due to the heat, and was keen to get some fresh air outside the conservatory.

"I was also anxious to return to the party as soon as possible. The incident with my trousers meant I did not get outside and I wanted to return as soon as I could because Lord Thackerston was expected to make his birthday speech around 1am. I didn't want to miss it. I had to work fast to get my trousers fixed in time. There had been a rumour among the family that the Earl might be thinking of making some announcement about the future of the Estate. I knew that Viscount Elsinby, the heir apparent, hadn't been able to produce his own heir and was not likely to produce one. On top of that, we knew the Estate wasn't generating enough income. The Hall itself is a financial drain on very strained resources and there were suggestions, unofficial ones among the family I might add, that it ought to be used to provide an income — even if it meant opening it to the public. For all those reasons, the family was expecting some dramatic decision which, as it turned out, never transpired. During his speech, the Earl didn't refer to any such changes, nor did he mention anything about his future plans for Elsinby Hall or the Estate. He merely thanked everyone for coming to his party, thanked them for their good wishes and presents, and said he was going to have a large brandy in the library before going to bed. After repairing my trousers, I had returned to hear that speech, I'd fixed the seam with some cotton that Vinnia always carries, plus a couple of strategically placed safety pins. It wasn't very professional but it did survive the night. When I was upstairs, I did not see anyone on the landings nor did I hear any one in their rooms — sometimes, you can hear toilets being flushed or people moving about, closing wardrobe doors and so forth, but the landings were deserted by this time.

"I found the landing very comfortable, much cooler than the downstairs rooms because someone had drawn back the curtains and opened the large window at the top of the stairs to allow a circulation of fresh air, at least on the first floor. I did not hear any shots either, when I was upstairs. Viscount Victor hadn't wanted us to open the ground-floor windows because of his father's worries about intruders, although he'd agreed to one door being left open — the conservatory that was. There was someone in the conservatory for most of the evening, on and off, except during dinner, so I don't think a stranger would have tried to gate-crash via that route. They wouldn't have been able to get past us and Johnson had locked the door while we were dining. Anyway, I was glad of a bit of cool air and stood by the open window on the landing for a couple of minutes, taking several long and deep breaths, and then I returned to the lounge. I must admit the heat in there was stifling; the place was very crowded and I thought everyone was present during the speech, but to be honest, I didn't attempt a count of heads. There was no cause, after all; I guessed that, with the anticipated announcement, everyone concerned would be there, especially members of the family, and they'd all be listening with bated breath."

The detective who had taken down this statement, DC Neville Troughton, had completed a short statement of his own which was attached to Powler's. It was short and simple, Troughton saying he had inspected the dinner suit worn by Powler and the trousers had been repaired, somewhat clumsily, with some black cotton and safety pins. It seemed that Powler was telling the truth.

By this stage of Sunday afternoon, the tempo of the investigation was increasing. On the Murder Room wall, there now hung from a picture rail yet another noticeboard, this time a white board with black felt tip writing — this bore the names of all the guests and family members. As each one was interviewed, so a tick appeared against his or her name; likewise, ticks appeared against names which had been compared with CRO lists, although the results were publicised here. They would be kept confidential for the time being.

Now that some of the suspects had been allowed home, gossip about the murder would surely be circulating Aidensfield, Elsinby and district. The freed guests would find such gossip irresistible as the detectives whittled away at the backlog of waiting guests. Already, some had been interviewed several times and their statements cross-indexed — the aim was for everyone's name to be crossed off that list.

It was at this point, that the Wooden Horse returned to the Murder Room. Both men looked shattered . . .

"Anybody got a cup of tea?" The Horse sounded hoarse. "God! Talk about a marathon interview!"

The Wooden Horse had been interviewing Lord Thackerston. During the investigation he had kept out of the way, preferring to sit in his bedroom which was directly above the lounge. His aristocratic breeding kept him away from the sordid work now underway, but he had not escaped The Horse. The interview had been a long and exhausting process, His Lordship believing that such interrogation was beneath him.

In spite of his efforts, The Horse felt Lord Thackerston had not revealed everything about his family but at least he had abstracted some evidence about the events of the night. When Angela Benson appeared bearing a tray with a tea pot full of newly brewed nectar, The Horse and Wood relaxed in a corner with a mug apiece. No one interrupted them during those few moments of peace — Inspector Oakland signalled that we should not pester the couple until they were ready to impart their knowledge to us. That moment came some twenty minutes later when The Horse, suitably refreshed, rose to his feet and said, "Right, everybody. I think we should arrange a conference of detectives, we should include everyone who is engaged on the enquiry. Can we do that, Martin?" he asked Oakland.

"Give me half an hour," said Oakland. "I'll get Cliff Hailstone to bring his teams in for a tea break at the same time. They've earned a short rest."

"Agreed," said The Horse. "Do that, and I'll address them all. Now, any major developments? Has the murder weapon been found? Any spent bullet casing? Anything else of value?"

Frustrated to some degree by a negative response to those questions, Oakland began to update the boss, referring to Claude Jeremiah's sighting of a man and a woman outside the conservatory shortly before 1am. That same sighting appeared to have been confirmed by the underkeeper, Beswick. He had stated the man he'd seen had been smoking and this appeared to place the living Drood at the place where his body was found.

From the descriptions available, it was fairly certain he'd been talking to Brenda Armitage, another of the house guests. Oakland added a few words about the known movements of the witnesses around the building, joking about Powler's trousers, referring to Lady Violet's visit to her room at one o'clock and to Aunt Felicity's visit to her room around the same time. Nothing of any further consequence had emerged from the completed interviews, other than there had been considerable traffic in and out of the conservatory door throughout the evening with people standing outside only yards from where the body was found, some smoking and drinking and others merely congregating in the cool night air.

The Horse listened intently. "Right, well, me and Timber will interview Brenda Armitage next. If she was the woman seen talking to Drood, she might well have been the last person to see him alive. But if he'd been shot around that time, say 1am, is it feasible that no one saw him lying near the shrubbery until Lady Violet raised the alarm about 3.45am? Could he have lain there for nearly three hours without anyone noticing? A lot of people were using the conservatory doorway to go outside for fresh air and some of them must have been standing very close to the body. What time did the dew descend? And have we got the result of the PM yet?"

"No, sir," said Oakland. "It should be finished around now. DC Staples said he would ring us the moment he had any news."

"OK, Martin," beamed The Horse. "Get the troops in for a conference, and afterwards I'll interview Brenda Armitage."

Some three dozen operational detectives led by Detective Inspector Hailstone crowded into the Murder Room half an hour later and were each given a mug of tea and a choice of buns and biscuits, courtesy of Johnson, Phyllis Catchpole and the domestic staff. There was nowhere for them all to sit and so they crowded around the place, jostling for comfortable positions so they could lean against the walls or the furnishings which had been edged aside to accommodate the paraphernalia of the murder investigation. Then The Horse rose to address them, standing on a chair to elevate himself even further above their heads. Both secretaries, Angela and Ruth, were waiting with shorthand notebooks at the ready, eager to take down all his words.

"Timber Wood and I have just completed our first interview of Lord Thackerston," he told us. "I think we should all hear what he has told me because his knowledge might help us during this investigation. Clearly, this will be a shortened version, we do have a full statement from His Lordship which will be typed up very soon and distributed in the usual way. Now, the Earl and late Countess of Thackerston were the owners, by inheritance, of Elsinby Hall and the surrounding estate which comprises Elsinby Hall, Home Farm, several other farms and some thousands of acres of parkland and pasture. When the Countess died in 1956, aged only fifty — she was older than her husband — Lord Thackerston later decided to move to London to live. He wished to continue his business interests in the City and to hand over the running of the country estate to his eldest son, Viscount Elsinby.

"The Viscount is known locally as Viscount Victor and upon the death of his father, he will become the next Lord Thackerston.

"He was not made the owner of the Estate, in fact, he is not yet the owner, he merely runs the business because his father remains in control. At the time he took over the running of Elsinby Estate, Viscount Victor was only twenty-two years old. Lord Thackerston has three children — Victor who is Viscount Elsinby, now thirty-two, The Honourable James aged twenty-seven who is the second son and Lady Violet who is the youngest in the family at twenty-five. It was assumed by all that when Viscount Victor married, he would produce an heir to the Estate and so provide a natural successor. It has always been the case with Elsinby Estate that it passes from father to eldest son, a long-standing Yorkshire tradition even with small farms. That line of succession was decreed by the first Earl and it has continued ever since. The title, of course, must descend by the bloodline; it cannot be inherited by illegitimate or adopted children but there is no legal reason why the Estate and the title cannot be separated. The present Earl is a stickler for tradition, though, and so the current family have problems. Viscount Victor married Lavinia Powler; they're both over thirty and doctors have said they'll never have children. Lord Thackerston's second son, James, also got married. His wife is Lady Sarah, known to everyone as Sally. She's that gorgeous redhead who seems to have danced with every man in the room. Her maiden name was Hammett and they too could never produce children. They adopted two youngsters, Irwin and Vanessa, a brother and sister whom they found through a highly regarded adoption agency.

"The agency specialises in finding youngsters for adoption by the aristocracy. Their parents died in a fire and the children are not yet of school age. Irwin is four and Vanessa is only two.

"The dilemma facing Lord Thackerston is whether or not to make a will which, for the first time, will change the course of Elsinby family history. He does not wish to deny Victor his inheritance but he *does* want Elsinby Hall and the whole estate to remain within the family in perpetuity if that is possible. If he willed it to James, it would descend to the eldest of James' two adopted children, Irwin, whom the Earl thinks is of unknown character, breeding and reliability. He is not happy about an adopted child inheriting the family estate, especially when there are other members of the family, linked by blood, who might be more suitable. Irwin could not inherit the title, of course; in that case, it might die out.

"That is one of his worries. There may be unseemly disputes or problems in the future unless His Lordship settles things now, in a will. His daughter, Lady Violet, is also married. Her husband is the Honourable Henry Powler, brother of Lady Lavinia who is the Viscount's wife. This means that the Hon. Henry and his wife are related to Viscount Elsinby from two sides — a brother and sister have married a brother and sister, and so the family ties are strengthened. The Powlers have two children both of whom were born naturally to them — Vernon is now six years old and Violetta is three. If my knowledge of inheritance by bloodline is correct, then, providing that neither Viscount Victor nor the Honourable James produce any natural children and there are no other distant relatives who are claimants, young Vernon could, in due course, inherit the title and even the Estate.

"Another problem is that the Earl does not trust his son-in-law, Henry Powler.

"Henry, in spite of his privileged background, is a businessman who is ruthless and untrustworthy, and Lord Thackerston believes that Henry's sole reason for marrying Lady Violet was to manipulate things so that he became part of the family with his own children being possible heirs to the Estate. Henry knows that neither Victor nor James can produce children and there is no doubt that Henry has his beady eyes on the Estate — and he is not concerned about any accompanying title. Lord Thackerston does accept, however, that Henry, with his business acumen, would make a success of running the Estate and his efforts could ensure that it remains in the family — if Henry can be trusted to keep it within the family and pass it to his own children. All sorts can go wrong in families — deaths of children, re-marriage and so on. The Earl wishes to stabilise things but to whom should the future of Elsinby Hall and the Estate be entrusted? That is Lord Thackerston's problem — and one he has not yet resolved. So, how does all this relate to the death of an obscure artist, albeit one sponsored by His Lordship? The death of Edwin Drood would not, on the face of it, have any links with the inheritance of Elsinby Estate. But has it? That is what we must determine. Was Drood deliberately killed or was he mistaken for someone else? I have quizzed His Lordship at length and he says he cannot help any more on this matter. The Earl has sponsored Drood for several years, having taken pity on the plight of this talented youth; his mother could not afford to keep him. I do not wholly believe the Earl; I feel sure he is keeping some important information from me, hence my frustration at this interview. I sense a family scandal, gentlemen, I'll be honest.

"Now, the movements of Lord Thackerston. After dinner, he had a brandy with Victor in Victor's private office, spent a little time in the library and then went to his room to rehearse and consider the content of his birthday speech. That was about half past twelve. He came down at ten past one; meanwhile, Johnson had mustered everyone in the lounge in readiness for the speech, and the Earl began at twenty past one. He talked for twenty minutes. Afterwards, he sat around chatting to guests and family until the sandwiches came at 3am, then he went to bed. He was roused by Victor after the body was discovered; the Earl was up and dressed by the time we arrived — he got downstairs at 4.15am, but while he was in his room, which is directly over the lounge, he heard no shots or other noises outside. He said he would have done, even above the noise of the party because his bedroom window was open. So what we must do, every one of us, is to examine the facts which come to light to see whether this family problem, the question of inheritance of the Estate, which is at present unresolved, has any bearing upon our investigation. Now, Eric and Paul, you are engaged in the Drood actions, so have you anything further to report at this early stage?"

Detective Sergeant Eric Parsons, accompanied by his aide, Detective Constable Paul Craven, raised their hands to indicate their whereabouts and Eric said,

"Sir. We've given Drood's room a thorough search. The first thing we sought was signs of blood from the shooting, or indications that a struggle had taken place, or even bullet holes in the walls. We found nothing; we therefore conclude that he was not shot in his room. Scenes of Crime have dusted it for fingerprints — initial conclusions are that no one else has been in that room since Edwin's arrival yesterday. His prints are on the washbasin, the mirror and his personal belongings. We did find some others, but they were left by the maid — we found identical prints in several other rooms, left behind after dusting and cleaning. Drood didn't bring much with him. There are two sets of casual clothes — jeans, sweaters, shoes, socks, underwear and so forth, and he was, as you know, found dead in his evening suit. There is nothing in his room to provide any hint of a motive for his death — one odd fact is that we found nothing to indicate his profession as an artist. No business cards, no paint or brushes or notices about exhibitions. We also searched his car with similar results. From what we found, no one would believe he was an artist. I would have that any artist would have taken this opportunity to do some work but in fact, there was nothing to indicate any profession. On the other hand perhaps he likes an occasional weekend away from work. One thing we did find in the bedroom were lots of perfumes, hair spray, toiletries and other items which supports the idea that Drood was a homosexual. Another motive perhaps? With regard to the car, it is registered in the name of Edwin Dickens, his real name, with an address at Aconly Cottage, Little Blandford in Oxfordshire. I have asked the local constabulary to find out what they can about him, his antecedents and so forth. It will be interesting to see if they can provide any clues as to why Drood should be murdered, with due emphasis upon the homosexual element."

"And was Drood known to many of the people at this party?" asked The Horse.

"He was known to the family, sir, and to members of the staff, such as the butler and gamekeepers. He came here quite regularly when Lord Thackerston was in residence, he was only a child then, of course, but was a frequent visitor. He hasn't been since Viscount Victor took over ten years ago. Lord and Lady Thackerston, when she was alive, did care a great deal for him, according to the staff, and treated him like a member of the family. He was the son of a former member of the Earl's staff."

"All right," smiled The Horse. "Keep digging, we need to know a lot more about Edwin Drood or Dickens. We'll see if the PM throws up anything about his homosexuality. So, I think we can call this conference to a halt. I'll suggest another meeting late in the day, say five thirty this evening? Now, Cliff, it's time for me to interview Brenda Armitage. Can you locate her please, and ask her to come along to the Viscount's secretary's office. It's in the east wing, on the ground floor. I'm sure she will know where to find it."

And as the assembly was dispersing, the telephone rang. It was the first incoming call on our specially installed line and as I was nearest, I answered it. It was Detective Constable Staples, ringing from the hospital.

"Death was caused by a missile in the brain," Staples told me. "A single shot, probably fired from fairly close range, although there are no burn marks or signs of powder on the skin or clothing. The forensic pathologist has discounted a small handheld weapon such as an automatic, a pistol or revolver. He believes a rifle was used but the bullet is not a conventional one.

"It's a ball, a round lead ball which is five-sixteenth of an inch in diameter. The pathologist thinks it might have come from an antique firearm of some sort. We have recovered it for examination by the Ballistics Lab at Nottingham. The body was otherwise in good condition, well-nourished and with no other signs of bruising or violence. There are indications, however, of Drood's homosexual tendencies — the familiar funnel-shaped rectum in particular. No skin or fibres were found beneath the finger nails, thus discounting a close struggle and it is believed the body fell where it was found. There are no indications that the corpse was moved after death or dragged to the position where it was found. His estimated time of death, based on body temperatures, is between midnight and 3am."

I relayed this to The Horse who cried, "The time fits, but let me have a word about that bloody bullet!"

We all waited as The Horse asked Staples to repeat what he had told me, and then he turned to his officers, with Staples still on the line, and barked, "The pathologist thinks an antique gun was used? How the hell could he be shot with an antique? Was it taken from the gun room? Check it out, have all the unconventional firearms examined. Something has fired a lead pellet into Drood's brain, a small one, like a little marble. What the hell would do that?"

Having instituted that secondary enquiry, The Horse returned his attention to Staples and asked, "So what about the homosexual element, Norman?"

Staples told The Horse that the corpse had a funnel-shaped rectum, a hallmark of some homosexual men.

The Horse thanked him — another motive had been presented to the teams. After replacing the handset, he turned to us all. "Not a word out of this room, any of you, about the exact cause of death. Just say it was gun-shot wounds. We're looking for a gun that fires little lead pellets, one that seems to be accurate and lethal over a considerable distance. Now, the body will now be put into deep freeze in case we need another investigation and Staples will be returning here. The time of death is given as between midnight and 3am — we know Edwin was alive just before one o'clock. That narrows the search somewhat. So all we have to do now is to find that gun and then find who fired it; we must find out what everyone was doing between 12.45am and 3am. And so long as we fail to find that gun, it remains available to the killer!

It might be pointing at any one of us. So find it we must. Right? Wesley and Neville? That's down to you. Tear the walls down if necessary. It must be somewhere on this site. And remember this — because it inflicted the fatal wound, it could have been fired from a considerable distance. It must be quite an antique if it's as accurate as that. It's a sobering thought. So have we a sniper? Was it someone in the village fooling about and shooting at light bulbs in the big house? Someone who was jealous because they'd not been invited to the party? Was it a stray shot? Was it accidental death, in other words, or was the killer someone here with access to such a weapon? And who'd kill an obscure artist? Don't let us forget the possibility of a mistaken identity. Drood does have a look of the Viscount from some angles. So, Martin," and he turned to Oakland again. "We need to search Headquarters firearms certificate records to see how many people living hereabouts have antique weapons. I know they can be kept without certificates if they're a hundred years old or more, but have them all checked. Seize every likely weapon and pack them all off to the Ballistics Lab to have them matched with the pellet. And what about the gun room here? Anything on that? Any strange types of ammunition in store? Any weapons missing?"

Detective Sergeant Wesley Dale acknowledged The Horse's instructions and his colleague, Detective Constable Neville, said, "Sir, I did a check of the gun room with Mr Cleghorn, the gamekeeper who's responsible for it. Unfortunately, the room is never kept locked — this dates to a time when an earlier Lord Thackerston saw a pheasant on his front lawn and decided it was ideal for dinner. He dashed inside for his twelve-bore, but the gun room was locked and his keeper had the key. So he couldn't get a gun out in time, and the pheasant made good its escape. Ever since that time, 1896, the gunroom has never been locked. It's a tradition of the house."

"But surely all the weapons in the room are listed on either a firearms certificate, or an estate inventory?"

"Yes, sir. All the Section 1 weapons are on the Estate's firearms certificate — there are some .22 rifles among them, along with a captive bolt humane killer which is kept in case of problems with the cattle, and there's a Lee Enfield .303 rifle. But all were present when I checked the locked room. The Viscount had locked it before we arrived, we now have the key.

"There's a range of shotguns, as one would expect on an estate of this kind, but it seems that several friends of Viscount Elsinby's, who came here for weekend shooting parties, left their guns behind. They kept sets of weapons here and among them were some .22 rifles, used for pigeon and rook shooting and some small calibre pistols, for use in Ashfordly Pistol Club competitions, according to the certificate. I have no note about any antique weapons being kept here. Until we've contacted all the friends who might have left their guns here, we can't be too sure how many are missing, if any."

"Well, the killer got access to a peculiar gun of some sort, and it might have come from that gun room. So keep the pressure up, keep asking the gamekeeper to dredge his memory. The snag is that the sight of a man carrying a gun in these surroundings isn't unusual."

"We'll keep trying, sir."

The Horse kept us for a further half an hour, checking and re-checking the facts while trying to see if there was some angle we had overlooked, some movements that might prove significant, some snippet of speech which might betray a secret or personal jealousy among the family. Had something become sufficiently volatile to culminate in murder? He, like all the other detectives, felt the secret lay in this Hall and among these people. He was sure the death was not the result of a stray shot from afar, but a deliberate killing, coldly executed for some reason yet to be identified, always with the possibility that the wrong man had been shot.

He did add that a man was currently helping the police with their enquiries — his name was Claude Jeremiah

Greengrass, the man whose footprint had been found in the shrubbery, but he was refusing to say why he had been there around 1am this morning, the likely time of death of Edwin Drood. Questioning of Greengrass was continuing. Satisfied that, at the moment, little more could be deduced from the available evidence, The Horse dismissed his officers to resume their duties. Chattering to each other, they filtered out as Oakland called to one of them, Tan, find Brenda Armitage and take her to Mr Galvin's interview room, it's the secretary's office."

"Sir," acknowledged the detective, rushing out and turning towards the lounge. Those still awaiting interview were there and Johnson had ensured they had all been given lunch, courtesy of the efficient kitchen staff. But as the numbers were reducing, so their tiredness and frustration was beginning to show.

"Who's next for the chop!" I heard someone shout as Ian Cassell opened the lounge door.

"Brenda Armitage," he called.

There was a long silence, and then he called again, "Brenda Armitage? Is she here?"

"She went out some time ago," said one of the women. "She said she was going for a walk in the grounds . . . !"

"A walk! Everyone was supposed to remain here until called. Right, thanks, we'll find her."

The reaction from The Horse was immediate. "Gone? She had no right to go outside. Find her, all of you and bring her here."

But Brenda Armitage had vanished. She was not in the house, not in her room which was in the loft, not in any of the bathrooms, toilets or private suites of the Hall. Detective Inspector Hailstone organised a swift and immediate search of the car park — her car, an MG Midget was still in its parking space — and so he arranged a search of the grounds. At first, loud-hailers were used to call her name among the trees and white-flowered undergrowth of the woodland at the rear of the house and among the beautiful, white-blossomed ornamental trees of the grounds. But there was no reply. She seemed to have disappeared without trace.

And then one of the uniformed constables who'd joined the search shouted across the garden to The Horse.

"Sir," he said, running towards the boss. "I think I've found her. At least, it's a woman, sir, in the ice house. I think she's dead."

CHAPTER VIII

"That 'ere young lady," replied Sam.
"She knows wot's wot, she does."
CHARLES DICKENS, 1812–70

The Horse told us to remain at our posts while he and Timber Wood examined the constable's grim discovery. He did not want us all to go tramping around the woodland and grounds to destroy any lingering remnants of evidence and so we waited as the detectives hurried from the room. None of us worked during those next few minutes; we sat and waited, stunned and horrified that another death could have occurred literally under our noses. If this was a second murder which had been committed in broad daylight, in the midst of an on-going murder investigation attended by more than three dozen police officers, then everyone had a right to be afraid and worried. It meant the killer was ruthless, fearless, skilled and determined.

I knew the ice house. During my visits to the Hall, I had been shown around the gardens and grounds by various members of staff and each had shown this relic to me. Not far from the remnants of the Victorian vineyard, it comprised a large oblong hole in the ground, rather like a giant grave; it was some forty-five feet long by fifteen feet wide and six feet deep. The excavation was lined with stone while a curved stone-built roof covered the entire structure. At one end there was a door with a flight of steps leading down into the pit; that descent into the darkness was rather like stepping into a subterranean cave which lacked light and warmth.

I could imagine Victorian staff being scared out of their wits at having to enter this place by lamplight in order to fetch His Lordship a game bird. Because the ice house was no longer used, the wooden door had been allowed to rot and disappear, so leaving an unrestricted opening but even without a door, the place lacked light and airiness. When I had last looked into the ice house several months ago, the base had been filled with straw on top of which were items of rubbish like old bottles, jam jars, broken chairs, discarded bedsteads, chests of drawers, wardrobes even, discarded furnishings of every type. Other unwanted junk had been thrown here too like old electric irons, kettles and worn-out household goods. Some of the objects would, if repaired and sold in an antique sale or auction, bring a useful sum of money. A good deal of it, though, was worthless.

In days of yore, every self-respecting country mansion boasted an ice house. It was the equivalent of the modern refrigerator. Blocks of ice were manufactured and placed in the base of the ice house and then covered with straw. The ice remained intact and cool even during the heat of summer and the household would use it to store meat and game, the coolness of this dark crypt-like place keeping the food fresh until required. Elsinby Hall's ice house was deep in the wood behind the building, the route to it now being almost overgrown with woodland vegetation such as briars and elderberry bushes. The footpath to the ice house had become almost obscured through disuse; the curved roof was also difficult to see due to the unchecked growth of vegetation which had practically covered it. Ferns, moss and ivy thrived on the roof while briars and nettles protected it from most woodland approaches.

In many ways, the old ice house was like a secret underground chamber — indeed, during the war, it had served as an air-raid shelter and many a secret romance had been conducted upon those bales of dry straw. For some reason, so it seemed, Brenda Armitage had seen fit to pay a visit to that place and had been killed. The reason for her visit, the knowledge by her killer that she was heading that way and the sheer daring of her death in the present circumstances would present a difficult puzzle for The Horse and his men. Had she known the whereabouts of the ice house? Had she been lured there by someone who had every intention of killing her? Or had this been an opportunist killing? A panic killing? A professional killing, even?

It was while awaiting the return of the Wooden Horse that the door of the Murder Room opened after a gentle knock, and the face of Lady Lavinia Elsinby appeared somewhat nervously around the edge of the woodwork.

"Oh, excuse me," she said quietly to anyone who might listen. "We have a press reporter on the telephone, the call's come through to the house. I don't know what to say to them, they've heard about the murder, rumours in the village apparently."

"I'll deal with all press enquiries, Lady Elsinby," Inspector Oakland told her. "Please say nothing at all to the press, we don't want our enquiries jeopardised. What are they asking?"

"They've heard there's been a murder at the Hall." She looked very frightened. "They were just asking for confirmation, and the name of the victim."

"We must not reveal the name of the victim at this stage," Oakland was insistent about that. "There may be relatives who have yet to be told. Tell any callers to ring me, Lady Elsinby, we now have a direct line into the Murder Room, it's 222."

"Thank you," she sighed with some relief, then disappeared. "I thought we couldn't keep it secret for long," sighed Oakland. "God knows what they'll write about the second death if it is a murder. I wonder if it's a suicide? You know the set-up — Brenda Armitage kills Edwin Drood and then puts an end to her own life . . . that sort of scenario. It's happened before and it'll happen again. Murky secrets among the aristocracy. The newspapers would have a wild time publishing all that. Mind, our boss is good with the press; the newspapers, radio and television can help us enormously if we handle them correctly. But there are no evening papers tonight, so time's on our side. Let's hope we can give them some positive news by catching the killer before their deadlines."

While we waited for some positive news from the ice house, I decided to continue with my statement reading. The next one I picked up was made by the Hon James Whitlock, the younger brother of Viscount Elsinby. In the prelude to the statement, he gave his age as twenty-seven and said he was married to Sarah (Sally) nee Hammett, and they had two adopted children, Irwin aged 4 and Vanessa aged 2, the adoptions being due to the fact that they were unable to produce their own children. They lived at Waldentoft Hall, a fine mansion in Wensleydale in the North Riding of Yorkshire where James ran a small estate and reared thoroughbred racehorses.

He was a noted trainer too, having won the Derby, the Oaks and the Ebor Handicap in the same year. From his statement, I noted that the children had been left at home in the care of their nanny and that he and Sally had taken the opportunity to enjoy a relaxed weekend away from their demanding young family. They occupied one of the main bedrooms in the big house; it was above the library, a fine room with southerly views, although a second window provided views to the west. That window overlooked the shrubbery and enjoyed views across the parklands that lay beyond — as far as they could see the Pennines and the Vale of York.

"At the party, there were many people I'd never met before," James' statement went on. "They were father's friends rather than mine such as Evelyn du Bartas who was next to me at table, and so it's difficult for me, not knowing them all by name, to state where any person was at any particular time. I did know Edwin, of course, because he had been to the house on many occasions when we were children but I can think of no reason why he should be murdered. I had heard that father was going to make an announcement about the future of the estate but when I saw that his party guests included tenants and estate workers, I couldn't imagine him airing family matters before them. I mean, that sort of thing is just not done. I did leave the dancing from time to time; I went into the library on occasions where you could have a smoke and a drink in moderate comfort and because the interior was so bloody stifling I popped into the conservatory quite often because there was a blast of fresh air from the door. Like nectar, it was. I didn't see much of my father during that time, but I did see people standing outside the conservatory, chatting, puffing cigarettes, drinking wine or just breathing in the crisp night air. I did not notice any arguments or antagonism among them. I can't be sure that I saw Edwin out there, nor can I remember what time I popped out. I can say that I never noticed a body lying there. I think I would have done, although to be honest, when people stood outside they did make a very effective barrier and it was virtually impossible to see anything behind or beyond them because of the darkness. The only thing I can recall from those outings is the fountain — it was playing throughout the evening and the lights of the house reflected in the waters to give it a most romantic effect. In the darkness of that night, it produced a most remarkable picture. I know my brother went to extraordinary lengths to ensure the fountain worked properly for father's birthday party. During those visits to the conservatory, I never saw anyone holding a firearm of any description nor did I hear any shots. To be honest, there is simply no information I can give which will explain Edwin's death. He was making his name as an artist, I believe, thanks to father's financial support, and I was thinking of asking him to paint my portrait. Drood was his professional name, of course, his real name being Dickens. I knew him as Edwin Dickens when I was a child."

Reading these words, I was unable to isolate any times or people from the prose, other than to confirm that Evelyn du Bartas had been seated next to James at dinner. James had been on the top table, on the extreme left of the Earl of Thackerston, and Evelyn had been on the sprig, the nearest of her table to the top one.

Ned Powler had been next to her and, as I was examining the table plan on the wall, I saw that Drood would have had his back to James Whitlock — but Drood was seated directly opposite Brenda Armitage. Was that significant? But, with an effort of concentration, I returned my attention to the statement before me. It was another classic non-committal statement, on the surface appearing helpful and truthful, but in truth devoid of any relevant hard facts, names, times and places. In my own mind, I felt that James would be re-interviewed by The Horse because he must have experienced some positive moments during the evening. When I read the name of the officer who had taken this statement, I saw that it was that of a young detective; probably, he had been overawed at having to interrogate a man of James' stature and background. The Horse would not be deflected by such considerations, I felt sure.

Having abstracted what little positive information that I was able, I filed James' statement and then The Horse returned. He strode into the room looking grim and said to us, "It's another murder," he sighed heavily. "Same cause of death by the look of things. A shot in the head, right temple. It'll take a PM to determine the calibre of the bullet, but my bet is it's the same calibre and the same bloody gun — and therefore the same person. So, gentlemen, it seems we have a ruthless and dangerous killer in our midst. I have issued instructions for armed officers to patrol the grounds from this point onwards — Headquarters will be sending armed reinforcements. Now, the dead woman is Brenda Armitage, although we haven't a positive identification.

We're starting to trace relatives — Martin, put a team onto Brenda Armitage, trace her background, contacts, place of work, domestic arrangements . . . the lot. So, gentlemen, the question is: why? Who killed her, and why? Did she know who killed Edwin Drood?"

He paused to allow the import of those words to sink in and we all knew that, on the balance of probabilities, Brenda had known the identity of the murderer and had died as a consequence. But if the killer was using the same weapon that had launched Edwin Drood into his heaven-bound journey, where was it hidden between the two killings? How had it avoided the scrutiny of skilled detectives? Every known gun on the premises had been impounded by this time. Experienced police searchers were examining every possible hiding place. Clearly, a thorough search would take a long time, but in spite of the presence of so many officers within the house and grounds, the killer had penetrated that network to carry out a second murder. It was a chilling thought.

For my part. I knew that I must search my growing card index system for references to Brenda Armitage or any other woman who might have been seen with Edwin Drood, or with anyone else who might be the killer. I knew Brenda was blonde haired and so I began to check my cards. To begin with, I listed her neighbours at dinner. She'd been seated at the centre sprig; she had been adjacent to the top table with the Earl of Thackerston to her left, across the top table, Col Jordon on her right at the sprig and Edwin Drood directly opposite. Helen Jordon, the Colonel's wife, had been seated next to Drood.

I had no idea whether there was any significance in this seating arrangement but it did seem odd that the two people at the head of the sprig, those closest to the Earl, had both been murdered. As I worked on the statements, a detective began to chalk Brenda's details on the blackboard. He wrote:

"BRENDA MARY ARMITAGE, home address York, occupation: solicitor. Unmarried. Next of Kin to be traced. Aged 34, 5'4" tall, long blonde hair fashioned into a bun, blue eyes, fresh complexion, average build. Wearing a pale cream blouse with long sleeves, a dark green full-length skirt, black high heeled shoes. Apparent cause of death — a bullet wound in the head, to the right temple. PM being arranged."

I reminded myself that Claude Jeremiah Greengrass had seen a man, surely Drood, talking to Brenda outside the conservatory just before one o'clock this morning. Beswick's testimony confirmed that. With Drood being seated opposite her at table, their acquaintanceship was not surprising. I wondered now whether or not they had known each other prior to this party?

Immediately after this sighting, Claude had gone home and so he had not observed what had befallen the man, or where he had gone after enjoying his smoke in the fresh air. But from the evidence of those two witnesses — poacher and gamekeeper — it was clear that the woman had been Brenda Armitage. No other woman at that party had had blonde hair in the form of a bun. As I pondered Claude's role in this enquiry, I realised I had not processed his written statement. Had his interview been concluded, I wondered?

Was he still helping the police with their enquiries? I flicked through the pile now awaiting my attention and there was nothing from Claude, so I asked Inspector Oakland.

"Sir, about Claude Jeremiah Greengrass. I brought him here at lunchtime, and I can't see a statement from him yet. Has he been interviewed?"

"Twice, Nick. He's in the frame, is your friend. He's the favourite right now too! He refuses to give an acceptable reason for prowling around these grounds in the early hours of the morning. In the absence of any valid reason, and in the absence of any witnesses favourable to him, he's put himself right in the firing line. He might be the last person to have seen Drood alive, Nick — and talking to a woman who has also been murdered. It doesn't look too good for your Mr Greengrass, does it?"

"Claude was here, sir, being interviewed, when Brenda died, surely?" I spoke in defence of my old adversary. "He can't have killed her."

"You know him well, Nick?"

"I know him as well as anyone, sir, and I know he's not a killer. Poacher, trespasser, picker-up of oddments he finds in other folks' grounds, petty thief, but he's not evil, sir, not in the way that he'd steal from the poor or kill people. He'd be prowling these grounds simply because we were here. He'd want to see what was going on, nothing more. Nosying about. Snooping. He does it all the time. If there's a party at any large house in this area, Claude won't be far away on the night. And if a pheasant happened to drop in his lap, or if His Lordship happened to invite him into the kitchen for a supper or a drink, well, that would be a bonus."

"He's known to His Lordship, then?" asked Oakland.

"Yes, over a long period, sir. In fact, Claude claims they served together in the war, but I've never checked that tale with His Lordship — we're talking of the Earl, by the way, not the Viscount. The Earl of Thackerston was CO of a unit during the Second World War and I know Claude was a soldier too. He claims to have been Thackerston's official driver, sir. Private Greengrass as he was then."

"Well, let's see what emerges during these interviews. If Claude's not guilty, he needn't worry but I get the feeling he knows more than he's admitting, Nick."

"In that, he's true to form!" I grinned. "OK, sir, I'll wait until I get his statement in."

It was then that the CID were endeavouring to trace the last known movements of Brenda Armitage. From their enquiries, it emerged that she had waited in the lounge to be interviewed and had eaten a salad lunch on her knee. Lunch had been served late, for which Johnson had apologised on behalf of the Viscount, and she had finished her plate about 2.40pm, that course being followed by a small dish of trifle left over from last night. She'd then waited for a while before a cup of coffee had been brought by a maid; the maid had entered the lounge carrying a tray full of cups of coffee and had served the waiting guests one by one from the tray. Brenda had taken her cup and had waited a while after drinking it, and then she had risen to her feet and said, "I feel so full after all this eating, I'm going to stretch my legs."

From preliminary enquiries made by the detectives, it seemed that two people had heard Brenda make that statement. Lady Penelope Prittleford and Ned Powler. Each said she left the lounge a few minutes after 3pm and both had no idea she was going outside. They thought she was going upstairs to her room or to the toilet or perhaps just for a walk around the ground floor of the house as the others had all done from time to time. Her body had been found at 4.14pm — she had died within that hour and a quarter. Currently, the detectives had no idea which exit she had used to leave the house because not all had been guarded by police officers and in fact, on the ground floor there were seven or eight doors which led outside, not to mention the French windows of the lounge, the conservatory door, both of which were now unlocked, and the first-floor fire-escape route near the shower room. The question now to be answered was: who had been absent from the Hall between 3pm and 4.15pm?

CHAPTER IX

"She's the sort of woman now," said Mould,
"one would almost feel disposed to bury for
nothing; and do it neatly too!"
                        CHARLES DICKENS, 1812–70

The Horse asked, "Is it significant that Brenda left the lounge while the detectives were in the morning room for their conference? Did she take advantage of their absence to slip out? If so, why? Why did she want to sneak out of the house without us knowing? We were all in here, apart from the uniformed constables who were patrolling the grounds. Nick, get me Sergeant Blaketon."

I found Sergeant Blaketon talking to a constable near the ice house. He looked extremely worried when I said The Horse wanted words and followed me to the morning room, asking what was in store for him. I pleaded ignorance and ushered him through the door ahead of me.

"Ah, Oscar, good of you to come," beamed The Horse. "Now, tell me this. When we were attending our conference, where were you and what were you doing?"

"I sent my men in for a refreshment break, sir, one at a time. We never left the grounds unattended. There was always three officers out there, two constables and myself. We maintained our patrols."

"The woman in the ice house, Sergeant, she is called Brenda Armitage. She's thirty-four and blonde with her hair in a bun. Quite distinctive in appearance. Did any of you men see her leaving the main building? It seems she went outside sometime around 3pm. She was found dead just over an hour later.

"What's important to us is whether anyone else was seen in the grounds during that time. So, get out there and quiz your officers, Oscar. Did any of them see Brenda? Did any of them see anyone else? Let me know as soon as possible, negative as well as positive answers. It does look as though a murder was committed right under your nose, Sergeant!"

"Sir." I watched Sergeant Blaketon wither beneath The Horse's gaze and then he turned and marched smartly outside.

"Right," said The Horse when Sergeant Blaketon had gone. "Back to your actions, everyone. Martin, we need to allocate more men to the lounge on statement taking. How many people are still in there, waiting to be interviewed?"

Inspector Oakland did a quick calculation, "There's about thirty, sir, but most have been interviewed about the Drood murder. I think there's eight or nine whom we've not yet seen about that crime, plus members of staff who've not been questioned yet, and now, of course, we've got to start all over again. None's been interviewed yet about Brenda Armitage."

"Good. Get Cliff to organise ten detectives to drop whatever they are doing and start in the lounge, then you come with me. I'll address the waiting people to tell them what's happened, and I'll ask if anyone can tell us about Brenda's movements just before her death, then I want anyone who can help to be interviewed immediately. So let's go. Statement readers, you come too, you need to hear as much as me at this stage."

As before, The Horse entered the room and selected a chair upon which to stand for his address. Everyone lapsed into a strained silence. I noticed that the Earl of Thackerston, Viscount Victor and Lady Lavinia were not among them, neither were members of the household staff. They would have to be told separately. Already, stories of another death had circulated and I could sense fear among these people as the huge man clambered upon the dining room chair and stood on the seat.

"I'm sorry to have to tell you that there has been another death," he spoke softly and his voice carried tremendous feeling and sorrow. "A lady, one of your number, had been shot in the grounds; we have discovered her body in the ice house which is to the rear of these premises. I must insist that no one leaves the Hall for any reason, no one. It seems we have a sniper in the grounds and it is possible that her death is linked to the earlier crime, although there is nothing yet by which we can positively associate them."

"Your men are not giving us much protection, Superintendent," said the plummy voice which had earlier spoken about delays.

"When we issue advice about remaining indoors, sir, we do so for a good reason. With all due respect, the deceased lady ignored our advice. We are, of course, carrying out an immediate investigation coupled with a search of the grounds. The victim is Brenda Armitage, she was a solicitor, she is thirty-four years old and she was easily recognisable by her blonde hair which she wore in the form of a bun. My officers need to know her movements and contacts before she left this room at around 3pm."

"What's he want?" the distinctive voice of Aunt Felicity rose above the murmur of conversation.

"He wants to know if anyone saw Brenda before she went out," said a woman's voice, loud enough for Aunt Felicity to hear.

"I did," and a woman's voice was heard. "I spoke to her shortly before she went out. I saw her leaving and remonstrated with her, I told her we weren't supposed to leave the building but she said she must, if only for a breath of fresh air."

"And your name, madam?" asked The Horse.

"Mrs Alleyn Floyd."

"Did she give any other reason for leaving?" asked The Horse.

"No, Superintendent, she said the heat in the house was overwhelming and she needed to breathe some pure Yorkshire air, and that was it. She left the lounge."

"Alone?" asked The Horse.

"Yes, I watched her leave via the main door. She turned towards the staircase but didn't go up it, she was heading towards the conservatory, I think. She was alone and I thought she was hurrying rather."

"Hurrying? What gave you that impression? Do you think she was meeting someone?"

"It's hard to say. But when people walk away from you, you can sense if they are in a rush, can't you? You know, she walked very quickly without glancing behind and seemed keen to get away from the room, anxious not to be stopped en route. Perhaps she was feeling faint in the heat."

"Thanks, that might be important. Now, did anyone else see her?"

One or two of the gathered guests raised their hands and said they had spoken to Brenda after they had gathered in the lounge but could offer no explanation for her disappearance or subsequent fate. The Horse explained that his officers would now interview everyone and reminded them that no one should go outside the Hall until the killer was traced. He added that a meticulous search of the exterior was being organised by Detective Inspector Hailstone, and that any possible hiding places for a killer would be examined, albeit without any risks to possible evidence and, of course, without incurring undue risks to the searching officers. A disorganised random hunt by amateurs could never be sanctioned, it was far too dangerous. If a killer was lurking outside, then everyone was at risk, police officers included. After thanking the guests for their continuing patience, GG descended from his makeshift platform, wiped his brow with his handkerchief and said,

"My officers are doing all within their power to find the killer, I assure you. I should be pleased if you would all be as helpful and co-operative as possible to my officers. Please remind yourselves of your own movements, and those of Brenda, before she left the room. I am going outside for a look at the grounds. Nick, you know your way around the grounds, so come with me. Martin, you make sure that Lord Thackerston, Viscount Victor and the family know of Brenda's death."

As the giant man strode away, the lounge began to buzz with excited conversation but I could sense the pervading aura of fear; those people were very frightened indeed but, somehow, his sheer presence had produced a calming effect. I knew that might only be temporary. As we swept along the corridors towards the rear entrance, he was saying to me,

"Don't forget it's dangerous outside, Nick, so keep your ears and eyes open for intruders," he cautioned me. "Now, I'm interested in access to the Hall grounds from the rear. I need to know the whereabouts and routes of local footpaths, bridleways, lanes and farm tracks. Can you show me any which might have been used by the killer? I need to know where, when and how they approach the boundaries of the Hall, and where they come from. It is significant, is it not, that both deaths have been out of doors?"

"And both have been committed when the Hall was full of people, sir, — and full of policemen in the latter case."

He grunted in agreement. "But if the killer is from outside, a sniper for example, would he or she know the Hall was full of policemen? Last night's events must have shown that the Hall was full of people — cars parked around the place, lights on, music, dancing, people going out for fresh air or a smoke, that sort of thing. That's when the first death occurred, with all those people around. But now only one car looks like a police vehicle (yours, Nick) — not even Blaketon's has police insignia on it, so that doesn't indicate an unusual police presence. If a sniper is responsible — a sniper taking random shots into the grounds — he might never have seen the policemen, not even those in uniform. There's only two officers patrolling the grounds, and one on the gate at the front. He's out of sight of any approach from the rear and your van is now in the yard, also concealed by the surrounding buildings, so our killer might be out there now, waiting for a chance to let loose another of his lethal lead pellets not realising the place is swarming with police — maybe not even realising he's killed anyone. You know as well as me, we can't search all this woodland, not effectively, not even with forty officers. We could make only a show of searching it but that could be counter-productive."

The idea of random shots being recklessly fired into the grounds could not be dismissed, and I remembered Claude's rabbits now. Had they died from the same cause? Some idiot firing from a long distance? Some idiot not knowing where his shots were terminating? But by this time, we had left the Hall through the rear door, the one opposite the butler's room, and we were striding across the yard which led us past the estate office and domestic staff accommodation and into the woodland. A sheltered route. A mass of newly foliated trees surrounded the Hall at the rear, many bearing lush white blossom. There were acres of them. Did they hide the killer?

"Is Claude Jeremiah Greengrass still here, sir?" I asked as we picked our way across the yard through the mass of parked vehicles.

"He is. My last information was that he's refusing to say why he was prowling around the grounds last night. Why do you ask?"

"It's just that he will know all the footpaths and tracks better than anyone," I suggested. "And he wouldn't have a reason for being here, he's like a moth attracted to light. If there's any event in the villages, he'll be there, sir, skulking in the darkness, watching without any sinister motive and without any good reason."

"You sound like a defence lawyer, Nick!" boomed The Horse. "OK, he's in the TV room, being grilled. He's still a suspect, you realise. Go and fetch him; bring him to meet me at the ice house."

And so I turned back towards the Hall, hurrying through the parked vehicles with the hair rising on the back of my neck as I made my way indoors. As I entered, Johnson was emerging from his room with a tray in one hand, balanced precariously as he manoeuvred himself, the tray and his heavy walking stick through the doorway.

"Just had my five minutes sit down," he smiled briefly at me. "It's been a long night, we've had no sleep, Mr Rhea, the staff that is. But what a shocking business. The household is very very upset . . . I'm keeping them busy through it all, of course, supplying drinks and refreshments to the guests in the lounge. Everyone needs to be kept busy. So can I get you something?"

"I'd love a break, Mr Johnson, but later. You see to the guests and your staff."

And as he made his way along the corridor, I marvelled at the way he balanced the tray while using the stick almost like a crutch on the linoleum, and I waited until he had negotiated the Z bend before turning towards the TV room. The Elsinbys had a dedicated butler, I realised; he'd been on the go right through the night and all through the day so far, ministering to the guests, caring for the staff, making sure the police were looked after and never forgetting the needs of his master and the family. The door of the TV room was closed and so I knocked; a detective opened it.

"I'm here to collect Mr Greengrass," I told him. "Detective Superintendent Galvin wishes to speak to him, at the ice house. I'm to take him there."

"I thought you'd come to rescue me, Mr Rhea!" came the plaintive cry from within. "These Gestapo officers think I killed that chap, and I didn't . . ."

"They're only doing their job, Claude. If you refuse to explain why you were near the shrubbery last night, you can only blame yourself if they're suspicious. But come along, Mr Galvin is keen to talk to you."

The detectives allowed Claude to emerge and said, "We've finished with him, Nick. He's admitted snooping and we're satisfied he's not the murderer of Edwin Drood. But he has admitted stealing those boots, Nick, the ones he's wearing now."

"Claude!" I was ashamed of him. "Stealing boots? Where from?"

"I wasn't stealing, they'd been chucked out, they were rubbish. They were in the ice house. A few nights back, it was, before all this carry-on . . ."

"You were in the ice house?"

He blinked at me, lowering his head as he said, "Well, yes, just looking around, you understand. You know how it is. I help myself to rabbits from time to time. And I allus look in the old ice house because that's where stuff gets thrown out. Stuff that's got some value left in it, old chairs, settees, beds . . . I once got a good settee from here . . . and last week I found them boots. They'd been chucked out, Mr Rhea, and you can't do me for pinching stuff that's been abandoned, see. I know my law, eh? Besides, His Lordship said I can help myself to stuff in the ice house, Lord Thackerston that is, or was. The new regime doesn't mind either. I get rid of their junk for them and earn myself a bob or two at the same time."

"So if you took those boots from the ice house, where are your old ones?"

"I left 'em there, changed on the spot. No point in keeping old boots on when you've got new 'uns, is there?"

I groaned. "Claude, they'll still be there, in the ice house? Your old boots!"

"Aye," he grinned. "It'll prove I'm not lying, eh? My old size tens, black leather, with a hole in the right one, near the little toe . . ."

"Claude, you'd better be telling the truth . . ."

The presence of those boots would now need to be explained. They placed Claude at the scene of yet another murder! Leaving the two detectives to speak to Johnson about some refreshment, I led Claude through the yard, past the estate office and along the track which took us to the ice house.

"Does he want to apologise for all the hassle, eh?" Claude asked me.

"He wants your expert advice, Claude," I said. "We need to know all about the footpaths behind the Hall, where they go, where they come from, that sort of thing, and whether the killer could have used them to get into the grounds."

"Aye, well, I know this estate like the back of my hand, me and Lordy being mates, you understand. He knows I come here, constable, he never objects and says I can help myself to a sniggled rabbit or two if I want . . . mind you somebody else has been potting rabbits recently, so that's one reason I've been coming here, to catch poachers. I don't want poachers on my patch, constable. Fancy that, eh? Me catching poachers!"

"It takes one to catch one," I said as we approached the ice house and I could see the puzzlement on Claude's whiskery features as he saw the police activity,

The Scenes of Crime department, police photographer, a forensic scientist, several detectives and two uniformed constables were assembled near the ice house.

"It looks as though they've found my old boots," he whispered to me. "They're making a fuss about 'em, eh?" he chuckled.

"Claude," despite police protocol, I decided to break the news to him. "This isn't to investigate the discovery of your old boots. It's another murder victim, a woman, Brenda Armitage."

"Brenda? Lordy's solicitor lass?"

I nodded. "You saw her talking to Edwin before he was shot."

"Her with her hair in a bun?" He sounded surprised.

"Yes, that was Brenda."

"I never recognised her, constable, not with that sort of a hair-do in that darkness. I've never seen her with her hair done up like that. You said she's been shot, an' all?" There was horror on the old rogue's whiskered features.

"Yes, I'm sorry to say. She was shot sometime between 3pm and 4.15pm this afternoon, Claude. It happened while you were helping us with our enquiries, so you're not a suspect. But you might have to explain how your boots came to be at the scene of this murder!"

He made no reply; the shock of his involvement in this second death had reduced him to silence, and as we approached, The Horse came forward.

"Ah, Mr Greengrass, the footpath expert, so Nick tells me."

"Aye, well, about them boots . . ."

"What boots?" asked The Horse.

"Well, them lads of yours who was quizzing me, well, they got me to confess taking these here boots from the ice house," and he lifted up one boot. "Cast-offs, they were, you understand. His Lordship says I can take stuff that's put in the ice house, old chairs, stuff like that, so that's how my old boots got left in there."

"You mean those old black leather ones with worn-down heels and a hole in one side?" smiled The Horse.

"Ay, well, they were my second best, you understand."

"Well, Mr Greengrass, I can put you out of your misery. We know they've been there for a few days because a robin's building her nest inside one of them, so your boots are going to become home to a brood of chicks. That means we know the boots were there before the victim was killed, so you're not a suspect any more. Now, has Nick explained why I need your services?"

"Summat about footpaths?" There was relief on Claude's face now.

The Horse explained his requirements after which Claude, myself and The Horse walked to the entire edge of the plantation to survey the landscape beyond. He highlighted one or two possible routes, one of which led from Aidensfield into the rear of Elsinby Hall's land, but when we examined the lane, there were no recent footprints. He took us to a stile, then a kissing gate thick with cobwebs and then wandered along several obscured pathways, all deserted and little used.

Claude, with his poacher's wisdom and countryman's knowledge, assured us that no one had used any of those main routes or any of the minor paths, since Friday evening's rain.

"So you can swear nobody came in this way last night or today?"

"Swear? In a court of law you mean?" he cried.

"I don't think it will amount to that, Mr Greengrass, but I would like you to make a statement, for our files, to the effect that, in your expert opinion, those routes have not been used since Friday. All I want to be able to say is that no one entered the Hall by those routes either on Saturday or today."

"Aye, well, I can say that. You can tell, you see, when you're an expert like me, a tracker who served his country well in the war, you understand. Folks allus leaves tracks, Mr Detective Superintendent, and there's none here, not recent that is, not along the entire boundary. I'd stake my reputation on that."

"Good, well, Nick can take a statement from you to that effect, and, Nick, refer to those boots, will you? I want them eliminated from the enquiry now, we don't want Scenes of Crime disturbing a robin at her nest, do we? We'll soon be clear of the ice house so she can resume her work, and we'll leave your boots there, Claude. You'll soon be dad to a little brood of chicks."

And so I went back to the house to take a short written statement from Claude. At least the mystery of the boots had been solved and after seeing Claude off the premises, I found Bill Blades, the estate manager in his office. I mentioned Claude's visits to the ice house and he nodded.

"It's true," said Bill. "We do throw rubbish in there which might have some other use, and Claude has permission to take it away. Old crockery, pots and pans, furniture and so on, it's dry in the ice house and it makes a useful dry store. And Claude is allowed to take rabbits, pheasants and so on. He's right about serving with Lord Thackerston during the war. Claude was His Lordship's driver. His Lordship thinks a lot about Claude, he shared a lot of experiences with Lord Thackerston, that's why Claude's permitted these small privileges, Nick."

And so the mystery of Claude's tight-fitting boots had been solved and his relationship with the estate confirmed, but a new and sinister mystery remained.

Brenda's murderer could not have entered by the front of the Hall due to the police presence, so if he or she had not entered the Hall secretly by those back routes, then he or she must be one of the people currently on the premises.

Every policeman knew that. Every policeman knew the killer could strike again. Every policeman knew that no one at Elsinby Hall was safe.

CHAPTER X

"Father is rather vulgar, my dear."
CHARLES DICKENS, 1812–70

When I returned to the Murder Room, no one was speaking. The only sound was of detectives and staff at work among piles of paper. Members of the Murder Room staff were ruffling papers, reading papers, filing papers, checking papers, sorting papers and cross-referencing papers and if these activities could be said to be of a hurried nature, then so it was in Elsinby Hall. Everyone in that room considered that urgency in their work would solve the crime, that their unique clerical abilities would detect and arrest the killer or killers. It was to this subdued but determined atmosphere that I returned. I settled at my desk and felt dismayed at the huge volume of statements which had accumulated during my brief absence. Some were short, less than a page perhaps, while others ran to several sheets.

Outside, things were very different. I knew that the Scenes of Crime department, already on hand and soon to be aided by the returning forensic scientists, were examining Brenda's body *in situ*. Once that examination had been concluded, the bed of ice house straw would be examined in minute detail by Hailstone's officers. In fact, every shred would be removed until the floor was revealed — who knows what lay hidden within those straw-covered depths? Another body perhaps? That straw had been there for decades. I knew that whatever was found would be retained for examination so that it could, where necessary, be eliminated from the enquiry.

I wondered how they'd cope with the nest in Claude's old boots. His discarded footwear would be the first of the eliminated objects, I reckoned, and allowed to remain for the female robin to continue her work — she alone built the nest. From what I had learned after listening to informal chatter among the detectives, it seemed that Brenda had been shot outside the ice house, albeit very close to the doorway, and that her body had been dragged inside for rapid concealment. That meant she had wandered fairly deep into the woodland, probably out of sight from the cinder footpath and certainly beyond the vision of anyone in the house and outbuildings. Her clothing did not appear to have been interfered with, thus suggesting that her attacker had not been driven by any sexual motive and her handbag was intact, thus ruling out robbery. She had been hauled head first across the deep, old bed of straw until her body was lying away from the patch of daylight formed by the ever-open doorway, and she had been left on top of the straw with her clothing in place. Even without being concealed beneath the straw, she could have remained here for a considerable time without discovery, certainly long enough for the killer to return and hide the corpse. But it seemed those plans had gone awry — she'd been found very quickly. The method of disposal of her corpse looked hasty — a determined killer would surely have buried her in this place. The straw was four or five feet deep, ideal for burial — and no one, not even Claude Jeremiah during his irregular visits, would have had reason to search beneath the centuries-old bed of straw. To have selected this place did suggest the killer was familiar with the practices of the household and with the geography of the grounds.

But someone with that knowledge would have realised that the ice house was used regularly to deposit unwanted items of the kind that Claude gathered up and sold in second-hand stores. He or she would have known the body would be discovered — unless it had been buried. And it hadn't been buried. A stranger, on the other hand, might consider this dark, damp place deep in the woodland an ideal hiding place of a more permanent nature. Those thoughts were openly circulating the Murder Room. I was not sure — if the murder had been done in haste with people likely to appear at any time, then the shelter of the ice house would offer an immediate hiding place for something as awkward to dispose of as a corpse. It was out of sight and might have remained so for some time had it not been for us searching for Brenda.

Among the activity around the ice house was the police photographic unit who were recording everything on camera, the Task Force who were searching every inch of the woodland for evidence, particularly any spent cartridge, concealed or abandoned firearm or other clues left by the killer, and two teams of firearms officers who had been recruited from Strensford. Recent arrivals, these four officers, all trained in the use of firearms, were told to search the woodland and patrol the boundaries of the estate. Apart from their protective role, they had to disarm and arrest anyone seen carrying a firearm.

All this external activity was separate and quite distinct from another form of urgent work — that of interviewing all the remaining guests once again — at least once, twice or even three times in some instances.

Even at this stage, there still remained a few guests who had not been interrogated about the death of Edwin Drood and so The Horse now decreed that those people should wait in the library. They had to be separate from the Brenda Armitage interviewees. Once they'd been quizzed about the Drood murder, they would rejoin the others in the lounge to undergo further questioning about the death of Brenda

Armitage. So far, none of the staff had been subjected to a detailed interview about the death of Edwin Drood — those who were resident on the premises, could be seen later. Some had, however, been quizzed to clarify statements made by the guests. The guests took priority, especially as some wanted to leave for home this evening. During all the interviews, particular attention was paid to the movements of Edwin Drood just before one o'clock this morning. The detectives kept asking: Where had he been? To whom had he spoken after leaving Brenda? Had he been to his room?

What was emerging was that no one had seen Edwin Drood after Claude and Beswick had noticed him outside the conservatory. I knew The Horse now required an even more detailed account of all his movements, especially between, say, 12.45 am and 1.40am, the time Lord Thackerston had ended his speech. Every sighting would now have to be analysed in the context of the movements of Brenda Armitage.

The police knew and accepted that, by this stage of Sunday afternoon, many guests and staff would be extremely tired but The Horse felt it was essential to get everyone's first statement before being allowed to leave the premises.

Those who felt it absolutely essential to have a short refreshing sleep were allowed to do so, either in the easy chairs or in their bedrooms, provided the rooms in question had been thoroughly searched by CID officers. Viscount Elsinby did, in fact, supply two camp beds which were positioned in the dining room for anyone to use for catnaps. It was a trying time; people incarcerated in the lounge were not accustomed to being told what to do by anyone, especially not police officers, but the fear of possible slaughter by an unknown armed killer did render them more malleable.

By late afternoon, with the prospect of a long night of interviews ahead, they resigned themselves to the fact that they would have to remain in this lounge and library for an indeterminate number of hours. Fear of sudden death rather than respect for the police ensured their co-operation and, at least, they were well-cared for.

Shortly after 5pm, the body of Brenda Armitage was removed from the ice house and placed in a makeshift coffin called "the shell" for its journey to the mortuary. A post mortem examination would be conducted the moment the corpse arrived; the job would be undertaken by the same pathologist who had operated upon Edwin Drood. I watched the small personnel carrier moving slowly down the drive with the shell in the rear and a detective by the side of the uniformed driver; few people on the road would realise that this innocuous vehicle contained the mortal remains of a murder victim.

We should know the cause of Brenda's death within a few hours and everyone engaged upon that enquiry wondered if the killer had used a round lead ball similar to that which had killed Drood. If he had, where were those missiles coming from? Someone must be manufacturing or selling them. I wondered if the Hattertons would be able to help. I walked across the room to speak to Inspector Oakland to remind him of the Hattertons' skills.

"Thanks, Nick," he said. "We've already got a team with the Hattertons; the minute we're given the all-clear from here, they'll visit the Hattertons' local shop in Ashfordly to check their weapons. We can't show the Hattertons the Drood pellet because it's not returned from the PM. Staples will bring it after Brenda's PM. We might have two pellets by then!"

I returned to my statement reading. As the later statements filled my in-tray, it became clear that the detectives were certain that Drood's murder had been committed between 12.45am and 1.40am, the times of Drood's last sighting, and the time of the end of Lord Thackerston's speech when everyone had been together in the lounge, the time the conservatory had been empty of potential witnesses. The guests had assembled at 1.20am for the birthday speech; Lord Thackerston had come down from his bedroom shortly before 1.20am and he had spoken for twenty minutes or so. So who had been missing in that time? From the contents of each statement, it was evident that the witnesses had been closely questioned about their movements during those critical minutes, and they had also been quizzed about the behaviour of Edwin Drood.

Apart from a widespread agreement about his arrogance, few could help. Most of the statements were of little or no evidential value; the witnesses were unable to offer any real assistance. Few of them outside the family and staff had known Mr Drood in person and even a physical description of the victim failed to elicit any further useful information about his movements around the house at the critical time. There'd been a lot of men who were similar in appearance and all had been dressed alike, making it almost impossible for an outsider to be of any assistance.

One factor that did emerge was that many of the guests had formed themselves into small cliques after the meal, and had remained within those groups for most of the evening. Diligently, I waded through the mass of paperwork, sometimes querying a word or a name with my colleagues, sometimes halting my work for a few moments as the effort of concentration began to create a headache and sometimes checking in my growing card index to settle questions which were created in my mind. I realised that the factions at the party had not mixed very well. The tenant farmers had grouped together in the lounge, not far from the French window and had remained there for most of the evening, accepting drinks proffered by the busy Johnson and his staff while enjoying the occasional dance. As dance partners, they had selected people from within their own group, not wishing to intrude upon the upper-class family members and their friends. On one occasion, six of them had wandered out of the lounge, along the corridors towards the library and then outside via the conservatory door. They'd stood outside in the cool night air for about half an hour, chatting and drinking, with some smoking, before returning to the lounge.

That had occurred around twelve midnight, but none could help with sightings of Edwin Drood or anyone who might have been talking to him. Members of the Stately Tones band had also been interviewed, but could not help; after their meal in the TV room, they had come into the lounge to set up their equipment and had remained there throughout the evening, apart from a twenty-minute break during Lord Thackerston's birthday speech. In that time, they had gone to the gents' and had returned to the TV room for a sit down, a drink and some sandwiches. One of them, Simon, thought he recognised Edwin Drood from the description we provided, but couldn't be sure — he did see a man answering such a description outside the conservatory just before one o'clock. He'd noticed the fellow from the window of the gents' loo, the top portion of which had been opened for ventilation. The man outside had been smoking, according to this witness, but he had not noticed the blonde woman with her hair in a bun.

Of the other statements, Robbie Whitwell said she had seen Edwin wandering about in the entrance hall by himself, head down, and apparently muttering something as he walked up and down between the main entrance and the lounge door. That had occurred about twelve thirty, she believed, before Lord Thackerston's speech; she hadn't taken too much notice nor had she spoken to Edwin because she thought he might be rehearsing some kind of thank-you speech for this evening's occasion, the thank-you being for years of sponsorship and support. He'd also been seen at that time and in that place by Anthony Ormiston, but apart from confirming Robbie's testimony, he could offer no further help.

Edwin had been alone, the statements confirmed. As I read these pieces, I wondered if Edwin Drood had let himself out of the main front door, which had been locked at 10pm. Had he then walked around the front of the house to meet his death at the shrubbery? That was speculation, unless of course someone else had seen him during the interim period. I knew it was possible to let one's self out of that door and lock it behind because it had a Yale lock in addition to the mortice lock; the key to the mortice lock was always left in the solid oak door. Thus you could unlock it from the inside quite easily, but not from the outside.

Then I found another statement which might confirm my own thoughts. It was a note in a second statement from Lord Thackerston, taken by The Horse himself. Lord Thackerston had gone to his room around twelve thirty to finalise the preparation of his birthday speech and, under close questioning by The Horse, he said he had heard the main door crash shut just after half past twelve. As near as possible, the sound had been at 12.40am, he added; his room was directly above the main door and lounge. His bedroom windows had been open giving wide views across the lawns, the fountain and the White Shrubbery and the solid crashing of the huge door had been very clear and distinct. Immediately afterwards, he'd heard footsteps moving along the gravel path from the front door towards the western end of the house, i.e., towards the conservatory. He had peeped out of the window but, because all the ground-floor curtains were closed, the light was poor. He had, however, seen the figure of a man dressed in an evening suit; the man was walking towards the conservatory and he was alone.

But in the darkness and from the awkward angle of the bedroom window, he'd been unable to identify the man, not even being willing to estimate his age or provide the colour of his hair — he was not bald, however. That was one point which could be established. The Earl was unable to say whether he thought the man was moving quickly or slowly, for his progress had been singularly lacking in distinction — he had not been running or trotting, merely walking in what Lord Thackerston believed was an ordinary manner, nor could he say whether the man had been smoking. The Horse had also asked whether the man had been carrying a firearm. Lord Thackerston had said he believed not — he did add, however, that a pistol might well have been concealed in the fellow's clothing but most certainly, he'd not been carrying a rifle or a shotgun. His hands had been empty, of that Lord Thackerston was quite sure.

So had that been the victim or his killer? Once again, the fact that all the men had been wearing almost identical clothing had not helped. I puzzled over those probabilities as no doubt The Horse and his officers would also do, but thought that, if this had been the killer, he might have made some effort to conceal his movements. After all, he could have walked on the grass, thus making no noise, or he could have moved away from the house to move in the far darkness across the grass, and thus been both out of sight and out of hearing. But the fellow had not done that — quite openly and without any hint of concealment, he had strolled along the gravel path, past the morning room window, heavily curtained, past the French windows where the dancing was taking place, past the library window which was also heavily curtained and which was a sort of quiet room next to the lounge, and then towards the conservatory which had no curtains and whose door was standing open with people milling around in it for much of the evening. I concluded that the person had known his way around the house and had been quite confident in opening the door as he had done — and Edwin Drood had known the house very well indeed, having been a frequent visitor in the past. I now wondered whether he had been summoned to a meeting near the conservatory — if the mystery man had been Edwin, his departure from the house did coincide with other reports of a man's presence at or near that place, including Claude's — except that Claude had thought it was one of the Earl's sons.

There was no doubt the detectives on the case would be examining every possibility but these were things I must bear in mind while reading my pile of statements.

I resumed my work in earnest.

CHAPTER XI

"Bless the Squire and his relations."
CHARLES DICKENS, 1812–70

Among the paper mountain which had accumulated in my in-tray, I sought and found Lady Violet's original statement. I wanted to check upon the precise words she'd used to describe her discovery of the body of Edwin Drood. I thought the account she had given of those few minutes was vital to the investigation. When I traced her statement in the thickening file, I studied her words. She said, quite clearly, that she had gone to her room at one o'clock, that she had heard Lord Thackerston's birthday speech at 1.20am and that she had not heard a shot nor seen any intruders in the grounds. Thus her evidence was of little value at that stage — it did not cover the relevant period, the period between 12.45am and 1.40am. Later on, however, it did become vital because it was she who found the body — and the person who finds the body of a murder victim is perforce a prime suspect. I studied her account again.

Prior to finding Edwin Drood, Lady Violet had left the Hall via the conservatory door because it was stifling inside. It was about 3.45am and others had commented on the overwhelming heat and lack of fresh air within the main building; many had ventured outside to get some fresh air. No one doubted that because most, at differing times, had congregated very close to where the body was subsequently found. Lady Violet said she had walked outside, onto the lawns, and did not see Edwin until she was almost on top of him. She'd thought he was drunk and had touched him because she thought she might be able to help in some way, but then she'd realised he was very still. She then saw the blood on his head in the light reflected or emitted from the curtainless windows. Her statement did not clarify whether or not she had known he was dead, but she had run indoors to get her brother, Viscount Victor; he'd taken over, and, in the circumstances, had performed rather well.

Her account had a ring of truth about it, but the detective who had written it down had not thought to refer to the dew; the dampness must surely have affected her shoes. Now in retrospect, Lady Violet's succinct account did raise a lot of unanswered questions. She said she had seen a man lying in the shadows near the White Shrubbery, but where had she been when this had come to her attention? Did it matter where she was? Had she been alone? What had drawn her attention to the body in the shadows of the bushes? She had touched him? If so, where? On the face? Hands? Body? Did it matter where? A lot of people in that situation would have gently kicked his legs with their own foot . . . but she had touched him, so she said. There was no reference to any firearm lying nearby, or any other possible weapon — that question should have been asked by the interviewing officer. She should have been asked to comment whether or not she had noticed anyone or anything suspicious there at the time. And had the dew fallen by that time?

I raised my head and attracted the attention of my neighbouring statement reader, Detective Sergeant Milburn.

"Serge," I asked. "Has Lady Violet Powler made a second statement?"

"Yes, it should be in your in-tray, Nick. Number 105. If you haven't got one, I can fix you up with a copy. Why, is there a problem?"

I explained some of my queries to him and he smiled. "The Horse is ahead of you, Nick, he read her first account and sent the team back to interview her again. Her next statement should answer all your questions. But keep up that standard — the solution to this case could depend on the likes of you and me raising questions — and that's why we are here. And we believe the dew settled around 3am."

As it transpired, her subsequent statement did answer my immediate queries. Lady Violet had been alone when she'd decided to take a walk in the fresh air around 3.45am this morning. She had left the house through the conservatory door which had been standing open, and as she had walked through the conservatory, from within the house via the passage past the library, there had been no one else inside the conservatory. No one had seen her which meant no one could confirm those movements, and there had been no one outside either, no one smoking or chatting or having a drink on the lawns. No one could confirm her statement and so no one could produce evidence of her guilt — or innocence. From what I had understood from previous statements, the conservatory had seemed full of people for most of the night after the dinner, and so it seemed she had chosen the one moment, the one rare moment, when it had been deserted. That's if she had used that route. Suppose she had gone another way? Suppose she had walked around the exterior of the house, perhaps via one of the rear doors, then no one would have seen her.

I wondered if, from the statements we had gathered, it was possible to say that the conservatory had been empty at any particular time. Logically, if it had been deserted, no one could tell us so! And if it had been empty, even for a minute or two, then that period was long enough for someone to stand there and shoot Edwin when he was standing just a

few yards from the open door. If that had happened, then the spent cartridge case might be somewhere in the conservatory, hidden among the flowers and the house plants, wedged between the tiles of the floor or lodged in some other inaccessible place. Thus the emptiness of the conservatory, albeit for just a few moments, could neither confirm nor contradict her claims but it could have provided a place in which the killer could operate unseen. As I read this account, I next wondered if the question of the dew had been determined — and it had. As I read the words, I recalled an old verse which says,
With dew before midnight, the next day will be bright.

But Violet had said that, after returning from Edwin, her light dance shoes had been soaked, and so she had changed them. The statement was endorsed by a detective who said, when searching her room, he had seen the wet shoes.

It all seemed very neat but was Lady Violet telling the truth about finding the body or had she shot him, and then, much later, produced this account of "finding" the corpse? This was a device resorted to by many murderers — some seemed to think that by reporting the body to the police they would be exonerated whereas precisely the opposite was the general case in most murder investigations.

But so far, we had not found anyone who had seen any of the guests or staff carrying a firearm nor had anyone heard a shot. Would Lady Violet be able to secrete a firearm upon her person, in her handbag perhaps? I knew that, in the earlier part of the century, fashionable ladies did carry small and rather ornate revolvers in their handbags for personal protection — some had revolvers with mother-of-pearl handles and in other cases, silver handiwork upon them was not unusual. Had she had her handbag with her when "finding" Edwin Drood, I wondered? If so, had it concealed the murder weapon? Had the CID searched all handbags, I pondered . . . people did carry illicit weapons around with them, in spite of current legal controls?

And then, as I pondered, I recalled Lady Violet's earlier statement about going upstairs at one o'clock, lying on her bed for half an hour and then coming down to hear the birthday speech. That was impossible — the speech had begun at 1.20am, only twenty minutes after she had allegedly gone upstairs. So was she lying, or had she made a genuine mistake? Had she misjudged the time spent in her room?

I began to realise I was treating this lady as a suspect without any sound reason — unless the inheritance issue provided her with a motive? I decided I should examine many more statements before making public my uneasy feelings about her. As I picked up the next statement, I realised it was from another member of the Viscount's family, this time Lady Lavinia herself, the Viscount's wife. It was clipped to several other statements from the Viscount's relations, some secondary statements and others primary.

Before reading Lady Lavinia's statement, I wondered whether the rumoured changes to inheritance of the estate could have provoked a desire to murder? If so, why kill Drood? If Lord Thackerston had plans to bequeath the house, estate and benefits of being master of Elsinby Hall to another person, who might he have had in mind? He had refused to co-operate with The Horse on such matters. Might it be the Honourable James and Lady Sarah? Or Lady Violet Powler and her unattractive, untrustworthy husband? Did Violet have a strong enough motive for killing someone in an attempt to ensure the estate came to her and her children? If so, had she killed Drood by mistake?

We all agreed that Edwin Drood did have a strong resemblance to Viscount Victor — same shape, size and colouring, with even some similarity in his facial characteristics. I could hardly believe Violet would kill an artist, even if it was one her father was sponsoring, so had she mistaken him for her brother? Others had done so in the darkness, so why not she? It was a thought which could not be ignored. And how did the Drood death relate to the death of Brenda Armitage?

With a plethora of thoughts racing through my mind, I now turned to Lady Lavinia's statement. At the moment, there was just one statement, and it said very little. She was a quiet person, it transpired, who could not relax at parties, nor did she enjoy large gatherings of strangers. Shy and retiring, she liked outdoor pursuits and was far happier tramping across the field with a pair of binoculars as she sought birds and wild animals than she was dancing and making polite conversation.

In her statement, Lavinia said she had spent a lot of her time in the library during the celebrations, chatting to her sister-in-law, Sally Whitlock, and to others she knew well. From time to time, she had popped into the kitchen and the staff quarters to make sure Lord Thackerston's orders were being carried out but had spent very little time actually in the party. As hostess, she'd been far too busy to waste time in petty conversation. After the meal, she had been particularly busy for she'd helped to supervise the staff, making sure everyone had a drink or nibbles and generally supervising things. She'd introduced strangers to one another, shown newcomers around the house, requested music from the Stately Tones and generally kept herself occupied with the functional aspects of the party rather than as a participant in the festivities. She had spoken to Edwin on several occasions during the evening, usually to introduce him to one or other of the guests, but she had never noticed any overtly indiscreet behaviour from or towards him in spite of his own unremitting arrogance and baying voice. He'd even gone so far as to say he intended to be master of Elsinby Hall, an ambition he had nursed over many years.

Lavinia's statement did produce a crop of names and times — she could say, for example, that Edwin had been in the library at midnight, talking to Ned Powler; she'd seen him in the hall too, wandering around alone just after half past midnight but on that occasion had not seen where he'd gone next. Upon being pressed for answers, she had been able to state several positive times and places where Edwin had been seen talking to other people between ten thirty and eleven thirty — he'd been in the library most of that time, for example, looking at one of Viscount Victor's art books when

Johnson had approached him to ask if he required a drink. Sir Ashley Prittleford had accosted him shortly afterwards to ask if Edwin would paint his portrait and Lady Ploatby, a cousin of Viscount Victor, had sought his opinion on the works of John Constable — all within a very short space of time.

Another person who had been in the library for most of the evening was Doctor Austin Plankenburg. Of mixed Dutch and English parentage, he was an interior designer and revelled in visits to country houses whose internal decor he tried to emulate in his work. In his early thirties, Plankenburg was extremely tall, at least six feet five inches high, and his companion, lover and partner in his work was Evelyn du Bartas, a one-time actress whose skills in interior design and decor were rapidly gaining favour with people in the public eye — it was rumoured that she'd even been commissioned to decorate a room at Buckingham Palace but her professional ethics forbade her to discuss that high spot in her career. She and Austin Plankenburg were a famous team. He was a serious man, however, not given to frolicking the night away by dancing and drinking and so he had also spent a lot of time in the library, examining books on interior decor down the ages, with particular emphasis on Victorian country house styles of furniture and curtaining.

I had no doubt that, before too long, the next Plankenburg designs to hit the market would be based on something he'd discovered at Elsinby Hall. I could imagine him making good use of the White Shrubbery in his designs.

Both his statement, and that of Evelyn du Bartas, were helpful in the sense that they did confirm what Lady Lavinia had said about Edwin Drood; both of them had been acquainted with Edwin and could confirm that he had spoken to several people in the library around midnight, including Lady Violet. Every one of the persons mentioned had been interviewed by the detectives and, apart from one case, they all agreed with the sightings of either Lady Lavinia, Doctor Plankenburg and Evelyn du Bartas. Lady Violet added that she had spoken to Johnson when he was in the library on one of his rounds — she concurred that it would be around midnight, the time the butler had himself been talking to Edwin Drood while proffering drinks from a silver tray. Someone, it was thought, had seen her speaking to Johnson when in fact Johnson had been close to Drood . . . such a mistake, it was accepted, could happen.

From what the statements revealed, it seemed that yesterday evening after dinner, and well into the early hours of this morning, the library had been the focus of more gentle leisure, a sanctuary from the more noisier elements of the party, a place where people with ample time to spare had assembled to talk among themselves. Viscount Victor had been there for most of the evening after dinner. Drinks had been in constant supply through the attentions of Johnson and the ever-attendant maids. From the statements I read, it became clear that those who had relaxed in the library were mainly members of the family and close friends of the Elsinbys, the sort of people for whom dancing was the amusement of the lower classes.

Most of them knew each other, thus the CID were able to obtain names of those present, a very useful adjunct to their enquiry.

At least it was known that Edwin Drood had been in the library around midnight, and in the entrance hall at half past twelve. He was alive at that time — that was the confirmatory message from those interviews. It seemed that the library had not been neglected by the staff — they had gone round to dispense drinks every half hour at least, probably more, but at the moment we had no detailed statements from the staff.

The next batch of statements came from people who lived in the nearby towns and villages, chiefly Ashfordly, Aidensfield and Elsinby. The tenant farmers and their wives did not know Drood and were unable to help — all they had seen was a lot of men in penguin-style clothing who were accompanied by ladies wearing flashy gowns and jewellery. The Lampkins, Lees, Oldhams and Olivers, plus Robbie

Whitewell and Sarah Crossfield had all been interviewed and allowed home. They had been quizzed about their movements around the house after the meal, but it seemed they remained in the lounge for most of the time, with occasional forays outside via the conservatory door or to the toilets on the ground floor. The farmers among them had been asked if they had heard a shot at any stage of the evening, but none had. Most of them said that if anyone had fired a gun, be it a rifle, pistol or shotgun during the night, one or other of them would have heard it. Likewise, both Roy Cleghorn and Robert Beswick, the gamekeepers, had never heard a shot; they accepted it might have occurred during a particularly loud piece of music in which case they would not have heard it.

Both felt that, if a shot had been discharged near the shrubbery during a lull, then it would have been heard, especially by people in the conservatory and even by those in the library. But, as I ploughed through the statements, I realised that no one had heard a shot — and everyone in the house had been asked. The absence of evidence about anyone hearing a shot suggested either that a silencer had been used or that Edwin had been killed at some distance from the building, and carried here for disposal. The latter sounded somewhat unrealistic for practical reasons and also because there had been no signs of dragging movements near the body; this did tend to support the theory that a silencer had been deployed. I wondered if there was a silencer listed on the Estate's firearm certificate or in the inventory of the gun room?

It was while I was ploughing my way through the mass of words on these foolscap sheets that Detective Sergeant Parsons and Detective Constable Paul Craven returned to the Murder Room. The Horse saw them and beamed a welcome.

"Ah!" his happy loud voice filled the room. "The Drood experts. Well, lads, any news?"

This team had been specifically enquiring into the background of Edwin Drood and Parsons said, "Yes, sir, one matter of major importance." He stood before The Horse and he looked pleased. "We've been talking to the force where Drood lives. Or Dickens as they know him."

"Yes?" There was a quizzical look on The Horse's face.

"Drood's mother, sir, is called Alice Dickens, they've learned that from documents found at Drood's address, but it seems he was illegitimate. A birth certificate has been traced but does not give the name of Drood/Dickens' father. His mother is dead, by the way, she died last year and one document they found related to the wording and an estimate for the costing of an inscription for her headstone at the grave. Drood paid — or Dickens to give him his real name."

"Then I need another word with Lord Thackerston to see what he knows about all this," said The Horse. "He's been keeping a lot from us, I reckon, but keep this to yourselves for the time being. Treat it as highly confidential. So was Drood a genuine artist, Eric?"

"It would seem not, sir, the local force have found no evidence of his work at the flat — no easel, paints, studio, brushes, artists' equipment and so forth. Not a sign, not a thing, except a large amount of art reference books. He seems to have been a student of art rather than a practitioner. I wonder if he was a conman, sir, pretending to be a struggling artist while blackmailing Lord Thackerston for some reason? Just a theory. At this point, we don't know what Drood/Dickens did for a living, although he's never suffered hardship, it would seem. Lord Thackerston did pay him some kind of allowance — unless it was blackmail, sir. Blackmail disguised as an allowance, perhaps?"

"All right, lads, thanks for that. Put it all in writing, enter your findings in the system and thanks. Now, I must have another word with Lord Thackerston."

And The Horse strode out of the room just as Johnson was passing with a tray of sherries balanced on his free hand, it now being after five in the evening.

"Ah, Johnson," beamed The Horse. "Just the fellow. Can you find Lord Thackerston and ask him to see me please? At his convenience, of course. I'll be in the secretary's office, waiting."

"Very good, sir," said Johnson without a smile. He turned about with a remarkable display of agility and, with the tray held high and his heavy stick padding along the floor, went to find the Earl of Thackerston.

"There's something very puzzling about this family," said The Horse as he vanished into the depths of Elsinby Hall.

CHAPTER XII

"I know their tricks and their manners."
CHARLES DICKENS, 1812–70

As The Horse went to see Lord Thackerston, I resumed my reading. I found a small batch of statements which had been clipped together and headed "The Murder of Brenda Armitage". It implied, I felt, that The Horse had not yet decided whether there had been two murders by one suspect or two murders by two suspects. The first real clue would be the cause of death, yet to be determined by the pathologist, with subsequent confirmation, through ballistics examination, that the fatal missiles had each come from the same source.

I decided to read these statements immediately in the hope that I would find some meaningful association between Brenda and Drood, or between his death and hers. There were the obvious links — the style of killing, the fact that both murders had occurred at Elsinby Hall, that both had died on the same day, that both victims had been guests at a society party, that both had been murdered out of doors, that they'd been seen speaking to each other shortly before their deaths . . . but was there another link? Had we overlooked some other clue? What was needed, of course, was a positive sighting of Brenda as she left the Hall for her final breath of fresh air, her fatal journey, plus any sightings of individuals in the grounds around the time of her death. Anyone seen in the grounds must be a suspect — but no one had been seen. So had she been shot from the house? Or from elsewhere? Those possibilities seemed unlikely, bearing in mind the place of her death.

I was acutely aware that the grounds were being patrolled by police officers at the time, so had the killer, with foresight, been able to avoid their watchful eyes? And had Brenda also deliberately avoided their scrutiny?

The first statements came from the policemen on duty in the grounds. Among them was Sergeant Blaketon. Prior to Brenda's death, there had been one constable on the gate, one supervising the distant boundaries beyond the trees and a third patrolling the grounds around the Hall. In charge of them was Sergeant Blaketon; he had been on duty, like the rest of us, since the early hours of this morning and according to his statement, he had been told that all the detectives had been summoned to a conference at 3pm. Knowing it would continue for about an hour and that refreshments would be served, Sergeant Blaketon had used the same opportunity to provide his men with a break and some refreshment. It had been a thoughtful decision by a caring sergeant. While two of the officers in his charge had taken advantage of this break to have a well-earned sandwich and a cup of tea in the kitchen, he had placed the patrolling constable on the gate. Blaketon himself had patrolled the exterior of the Hall, looking out for suspicious people and generally maintaining the sort of security that is required at any premises which are the focus of a murder investigation. During his time on patrol, Blaketon had not seen anyone walking within the grounds, not even a member of the family or staff; he had gained the impression they were all having a tea break, maids and estate staff included. Sergeant Blaketon's expression was "It was as quiet as a vicarage lawn after a church fete."

His account left no doubt that, between 3pm and 4.15pm, he had not seen Brenda Armitage in the grounds of Elsinby Hall. Furthermore, he had not seen anyone else there but we all knew it was easy to conceal oneself in the undergrowth. In Blaketon's opinion, no one had ventured into the grounds from outside the Hall. Alf Ventress, one of the constables who'd been on the gate, echoed his sergeant's words, saying he'd dealt with one or two journalists who had appeared at the main gates but he had not allowed any to pass, nor had he given them any information. Bearing in mind the persistence of some reporters and photographers, the uniformed constables had been instructed by Blaketon to pay extra attention to the boundary fences, but, to date, no difficulties had been caused by unscrupulous or over enthusiastic journalists trying to enter the grounds by unofficial routes. Alf Ventress had left his post at the gate, under the orders of Sergeant Blaketon, and had walked into the Hall via the rear of the building, through the kitchen entrance, where he and PC Alwyn Foxton had been welcomed by the kitchen staff. After ensuring the detectives and the waiting guests had had a cup of tea and some biscuits, the kitchen staff had settled down too, along with the local girls and women who were acting as maids. They'd not been allowed home and were still on duty. They had welcomed the presence of the uniformed constables; it was an opportunity for a bit of good-humoured banter, along with a good deal of gossip about the on-going drama. Johnson, the butler, had told the staff to rest for half an hour or so; he had come into the kitchen too, to compliment Phyllis Catchpole, the cook and their staff upon their hard, sustained work and their calmness in the face of the current problems.

He'd then collected a tray bearing his own teapot and biscuits. He'd taken this into his own ground-floor room along the rear corridor, between the secretary's room and the staff TV room. There he could enjoy his own refreshments in some privacy — this boss never mingled with his subordinates when off duty.

And so, for about half an hour, there had been a lull in the frantic activity at Elsinby Hall. In the traditional English manner, everything had stopped for tea. And that's when Brenda Armitage had slipped out of the house to her death. She, and her killer, had managed to avoid being seen by anyone, even the vigilant Sergeant Blaketon and his patrolling officers. Brenda had managed to get herself shot near the ice house without anybody noticing and her body had been dragged into the darkness of that dank place by her assailant, also without anyone noticing. From my own knowledge of the grounds, I knew there were several routes from the main building towards the ice house — it lay close to the end of a cinder path. In large houses, paths in the grounds were often made from surplus cinders taken from the fireplaces of the household; the cinders kept down the weeds and so the residue from fireplaces was recycled in this useful way. The cinder path which led into the woods curved through the trees as it led past the cats' graveyard, then the dogs' graveyard, each complemented with miniature tombstones bearing the deceased pets' details, Pussy being the most recent cat fatality. The path led towards the far boundary, to terminate at the swing gate where Claude had shown us all those cobwebs. The route to the ice house branched off that cinder path.

Once, it had been a flagged route with twin tracks for horse drawn vehicles but lack of use had caused the track to dwindle into a single neglected footpath, albeit with the old stone flags still in position beneath the leafy deposits of the trees. Now overgrown with briars and undergrowth, the path was difficult to find; the ice house was even more difficult, being obscured by thick shrubs, ivy, trees and undergrowth. The dumping of household rubbish would not be a regular event, nor, I guessed, would sorties by Claude Jeremiah Greengrass. Besides, with his countryman's skills, he would be able to pick his way through undergrowth and briars without much difficulty. It would be highly unlikely that a stranger would have known of its existence among the trees — very few, in any, of the villagers hereabouts would be aware of that old ice house although some older inhabitants of Elsinby had used it as an air-raid shelter during the Second World War. They would know where to find it. So did the presence of Brenda and her killer at that disused, somewhat secret place, suggest a killer's knowledge of the ice house and a good knowledge of the grounds of the house? I felt it did. I was sure she had been lured to her death. I got the impression she had gone there specifically to meet someone just as Edwin Drood may have done. But who and why? The "who" was probably both her killer and his killer — the "why" remained a mystery in both cases. That, in turn, suggested to me the killer was still in the house, still with us and therefore still extremely dangerous. It was a frightening thought. I decided to reveal my worries to Inspector Oakland and sought him during a quiet moment.

He listened intently as I expressed my belief and my concerns and said he would have words with The Horse the moment he had concluded his interview with the Earl of Thackerston. I felt I had made a useful contribution to the investigation. Feeling better, I settled down to re-read several statements taken from guests but quickly began to appreciate that few of them really knew Brenda; as a solicitor to Lord Thackerston, she had had very little connection with other members of the family and few, if any, links with the other guests. A pretty woman, she had attracted some attention because of her blonde hair in its bun style, but even so no one could say when they had missed her presence from the house. In one or two cases, some of the guests were able to confirm they had spoken to the young woman with the blonde hair fashioned into a bun but had not noticed her departure from the building. Lady Penelope Prittleford, for example, had chatted to her in the lounge when they'd discussed the family portraits of the Elsinbys, with Brenda showing a surprisingly deep knowledge of the Elsinby ancestors. But that talk had been around lunchtime, just before one o'clock, according to Lady Penelope. Other statements told me that Brenda had been seen speaking to Viscount Victor on several occasions, generally with the Viscount showing no warmth towards her;

Lady Lavinia Elsinby had also talked to Brenda from time to time, at one period for some twenty minutes in a corner of the lounge during the dancing last night where no one could overhear their chatter due to the music. After his birthday speech, the Earl of Thackerston had been with her in the library, both sitting on a commodious settee while he sipped a brandy and she had a glass of white wine.

They had talked in earnest, so the witness said. That witness was Ned Powler. And so, according to witnesses, Brenda had moved around a good deal, especially during the festivities of last night.

Colonel Jordon had been seated next to Brenda at the dinner, with Helen Jordon, his wife, opposite; next to them, sitting opposite one another, had been Brenda Armitage and Edwin Drood. Brenda, a single woman, had been seated opposite Edwin, a single man, and both were on the central sprig directly opposite Lord Thackerston; at either side of Lord Thackerston had been Lady Violet on his right and Lady Lavinia on his left. Had they been seated there for a reason, opposite one another and so close to the top table? Statements taken from Colonel and Mrs Jordon were testimony of their conversations with Edwin Drood and now did likewise in respect of Brenda. But they were not helpful — the chief angle in the detectives' questioning had been whether or not Brenda and Edwin had exchanged any words which might reveal some antagonism, some motive for their killings or any other clue to these tragedies. But neither of the Jordons could recall any harsh talk from the murder couple. By five thirty, I was exhausted. In spite of regular breaks, my head ached with the concentration of such intense reading over such a prolonged period and I sat back in my chair and sighed. Oakland heard me.

"The Horse might break at six," he said to us all. "It's been a long day. I guess he'll allow more of the witnesses to go home, once he's satisfied they are not the guilty parties — and a police guard on the premises will ensure no one leaves without his authority. It looks as if we'll be back tomorrow."

"I'm going for a walk around the house," I said to Inspector Oakland. "Indoors, I mean, just to get a break."

"Don't venture outside, Nick, not now. We don't want a policeman being the next victim."

I thanked him and left the morning room, strolling through the splendid panelled hall with its antique hat-stand, collection of walking sticks, ornate mirrors and beautiful candelabra highlighting the family portraits. From there, I went into the lounge where a few people were still sitting around, some being interviewed there, others being in one or other of the ground-floor rooms. Johnson, with his silver tray balanced on his hand, was asking Mrs Floyd if she would like a sherry or some other form of aperitif before dinner.

"Ah, constable," Johnson's round, serious face did not break into a smile. I noticed he was leaning very heavily upon his walking stick, his frame looking tired after his recent exertions and he was slightly breathless. "I am on my way to the morning room to speak to your Inspector Oakland. Viscount Elsinby has authorised dinner this evening, for everyone who remains on the premises. The meal is being prepared now; perhaps you can pass the word to your colleagues? An idea of numbers would be helpful. The police officers will be more than welcome to join us in the dining room. Extra tables will be laid. The meal will commence at 8pm. A gong will sound to announce it."

"Oh, thanks, I'll pass the word on." I had expected to finish around six o'clock, then go home for a bath before crashing onto the settee for a lazy evening.

This was a new and unexpected offer, one which I felt The Horse would accept. After all, his men did need feeding and a sumptuous dinner in these surroundings would be better than a fish-and-chip shop.

Following my chat with Johnson, I wandered into the library where more people were relaxing; Some were smoking, others enjoying a drink from a glass, Johnson clearly having been to this room with his tray and his offer of an aperitif. Some of the people smiled at me and said "Hello" but I did not remain; I was just wandering about wanting a little exercise and a change of scenery, however brief. From there, I moved into the corridor which led towards the conservatory and turned in that direction. As before, the conservatory was full of people and no one noticed my arrival. I pushed through them, noticing they all bore glasses of sherry, whisky or some other aperitif and found myself at the door. It was standing open as it had been throughout the tragic events of this weekend and in the evening light, I could see the splendid White Shrubbery. It was not quite opposite the door but slightly across to the right, stretching away from the near edge of the lawn towards the perimeter fence. The beautiful white blossom was a picture but as I stood here, breathing in the delightfully cool air, seeing where Edwin had lain, I felt sure the fatal shot had been fired from this doorway. The point where Edwin had lain was about thirty yards from this doorway, well within the range of most firearms however small or lacking in power. I looked about me — the conservatory, a semi-circular glass walled structure, contained a range of indoor plants, some of which stood in pots on the tiled floor with others hanging from the roof in baskets.

There were cane chairs too, along with straw mats and two bamboo tables but as I stood here, looking out, I realised that if Edwin Drood's killer had operated from here, he could have done so without being seen from the house. Next door, on the left as I peered out, was the library, but the separating wall was solid stone with no windows; if everyone had been inside the house, gathering for the Earl's birthday speech, then this conservatory would have been deserted with no possibility of anyone from either the kitchen, the house or the bedrooms looking into the conservatory. It was easy to look into it from the outside, especially at night with the lights blazing, but it was surprisingly isolated from any other part of the house.

I imagined Drood being called outside, waiting in the shadows of the shrubbery to meet someone, and being shot from this very doorway... the more I stood and gazed across the peaceful garden, the more I thought it feasible. And, equally feasible, was the fact that Brenda had been lured from the house . . . and then I saw the way she could have walked.

If everyone had been called in for a cup of tea this afternoon, the conservatory might have been left empty, if only for a few minutes, but long enough for her to walk into it, leave via the open door, turn right and walk through the gardens towards the ice house without anyone noticing her. It seemed such a logical route. And if she could have used that route without being seen, then so could her murderer.

It was a further indication that the killer was amongst us and I began to shudder but it wasn't caused by a breeze from the open doorway. It was the realisation that tonight we would all be together again.

We had been summoned to another meal, dinner this time. And while we were there, the conservatory would be empty again. If the killer was going to strike for a third time, I guessed it would be during dinner. But who might be the intended victim?

I knew I had to voice my concerns to The Horse the moment he concluded his interview with Lord Thackerston. I turned on my heel, my lungs now filled with fresh air, and returned to the interior of the house. Finding myself passing the beautiful white grand piano at the foot of the stairs, I galloped up the flight to examine the landing window. It was a sash window with the upper portion lowered and the curtains were drawn back. I could feel the flow of incoming fresh air. To gain a better vantage point of the grounds, I climbed on the window sill; it was a low one, almost like a window seat. From there I had a clear view of the White Shrubbery and the lawns around it. I could see the point where Drood had lain — the CID's equipment was still there.

It was quite possible to have shot Edwin from this window. There was a clear, uninterrupted view, even if it was over a considerable distance. This window presented a perfect sniping position, I realised. Upon returning to the Murder Room, I wanted an urgent word with The Horse about my findings, but he was in deep conversation with Inspector Oakland. While waiting for an opportunity to talk, I settled down to my statement reading yet again. I could not concentrate, however, not until I had aired my views about the conservatory entrance or the landing window being used in the way I had come to believe.

After some ten minutes, The Horse addressed us: "We are all invited to stay to dinner tonight," he said. "A nice gesture by Viscount Elsinby and as I did not intend finishing today's work until 9pm, I think we can avail of ourselves of his courtesy. Inspectors Oakland and Hailstone will inform the other officers who are busy conducting interviews around the house; dinner is at eight, gentlemen. The gong will announce it, and separate tables will be erected for our use — and for those who see this as a bribe or attempted bribe or unauthorised gift, I can assure you that the Force shall be paying for all the meals consumed. It means we can finish work earlier, we shall knock off at eight and return tomorrow. Arrangements will be made to accommodate any guests we have not talked to but I anticipate we shall have finished with most of our witnesses by that time, except for the resident staff. A night duty officer will remain in the Murder Room overnight.

"I have told Johnson of our acceptance and he will inform His Lordship and the kitchen staff, so that the necessary meals can be served. Now, back to murder. Inspectors Oakland and Hailstone and I have studied most of the statements and have decided which of the witnesses can be released before dinner. A list will be placed on the notice board when Angela has typed it — they include most of the local guests, the lads in the band, some of the locally recruited staff and one or two of the resident guests. It means that those people are not on our main list of suspects anymore and that I am confident that I am not releasing the murderer but, as you all know, we all make mistakes. I'm sure you all realise that I cannot hold everyone here indefinitely, and so, tomorrow, we shall begin interrogating members of the resident staff. Regarding your

Mrs Catchpole, Nick — we found six knives and forks in the saddle of her bike, nicked from here! Lordy doesn't want to prosecute — she's escaped with another warning! She's gone home, by the way. The guests who will be remaining will be having an early night, as will the staff but our restrictions upon access and egress will continue overnight. We resume tomorrow morning at 9am. So tonight, it's dinner! Johnson has been told and he will make the necessary arrangements for tomorrow, and, of course, there will be uniformed police presence in the house and grounds during the night, as well as our own night duty CID officer in the Murder Room. Now, gentlemen, I have just interviewed Lord Thackerston about Edwin Dickens alias Edwin Drood. Lord Thackerston does assure me that the fellow was a genuine artist, specialising in landscapes which feature in classic English novels.

"He worked from a studio and kept his private life quite distinct from his work, hence the lack of artistic materials with him during the weekend and at his home address. Lord Thackerston showed me an oil of a scene in Wessex taken from Thomas Hardy's *The Woodlanders* as an example of his work — it was signed Edwin Drood. I am not sufficient of an art expert to know whether the work was genuine or not. I am assured that he is also a very competent portrait painter and that he is well known in art circles by the name of Drood. I questioned His Lordship about the payments he has been making to Drood and the Earl assures me they are not blackmail monies, gentlemen, he is a sponsor and has a list of the exhibitions at which Drood, under that name, has exhibited his works.

"I see nothing sinister in this use of a pen-name, gentlemen, it happens with authors, people in the acting profession and others. I did ask His Lordship about the background of Drood but other than acknowledging that Dickens/Drood was illegitimate, Lord Thackerston cannot help any further. He is only interested in his work and his future . . . well, he *was* interested in Drood's future, but that has now come to an abrupt end.

"His Lordship will not be drawn on the future of the Estate simply because he has not made any decision — he did, however, admit there were long-term problems because of Viscount Victor's lack of an heir and from financial pressures, but he could not offer any explanation as to whether or not that was in any way linked with the death of Edwin Drood. His Lordship, by the way, is extremely distressed about these two deaths, both victims meaning a lot to him.

"Miss Armitage was his private solicitor; although her practice is in York, she does manage His Lordship's personal matters, the practice for whom she worked having enjoyed a long association with the family and their estates. When Miss Armitage joined Brooke, Brooke and Rhodes, her legal skills brought her to the attention of the Estate, and eventually Lord Thackerston who had by then, of course, moved away." Inspector Oakland asked, "Sir, so the two victims were both closely associated with His Lordship in a private and rather confidential capacity?"

"Yes, I suppose you could say that. Do you regard that as significant, Martin?"

"I just wondered whether His Lordship had some secrets which these people might have had access to, secrets denied to even his family? I know you have considered blackmail as a means of income for Drood, or Dickens or whatever we are going to call him, and those payments might even be blackmail disguised as sponsorship, then there is Brenda, the solicitor, well, she must be privy to much of his private affairs. I am asking whether the Earl has a guilty secret? Something not even his closest family know about?"

A frown crossed the big man's forehead. "Are you suggesting that Lord Thackerston is the killer?"

"He's certainly in the frame, sir," said Oakland with confidence. "If these two did have something on him, he might have bumped them off. We can't overlook the possibility. He wasn't in much evidence at the party between the end of dinner and his speech. He claims he was in his room, checking his speech and if so, he was in a position to have killed Drood by shooting from an upstairs window — his own bedroom window for example. Inspector Hailstone has viewed the grounds from that window, with His Lordship's permission and knowledge, and there is a good view of the White Shrubbery from there."

"But no weapon has been found in his room?" remarked The Horse. "Although, I do accept that he could have paid someone else to do his dirty work. So Martin, get Inspector Hailstone to put a team onto the private life of Lord Thackerston and run a check, a very close one, upon all his movements during the celebrations. Get his London address and start to dig deep, ask at Scotland Yard if they have any confidential notes on him — we do know he has a very active social life, and apparently always has had, and we also know he's involved in many other businesses apart from this estate. But I must say that when I asked him if he was being blackmailed by either Drood or Armitage, he categorically denied it. And I believed him. But we need to find out for sure."

When The Horse had concluded his briefing, I went up to him to express my theory about the conservatory doorway and the landing window.

"You'd better show me, Nick," he said.

I decided I would also express my concern about the way the two deaths had occurred while the entire household, guests and staff alike, had been assembled in one place. Just as we would be at dinner tonight.

CHAPTER XIII

"It is a melancholy truth that even great men
have poor relations."
CHARLES DICKENS, 1812–70

Keen to explain my theory about the conservatory's position in relation to the rest of the house, and how the corridor leading to it from within the building could have been used by the killer to facilitate both murders, I led The Horse from the morning room and along the central passage. This extended directly from the front door right through the heart of Elsinby Hall until it reached what might be termed a crossroads at the western end of the house. At this coming-together of corridors there was, on the right as one faced west, the ornate and stylish staircase which curved from the ground floor in a peerless sweep to form a graceful flight to the first-floor rooms. The landing window was in the west facing wall, directly at the top of the flight. A grandfather clock, ticking away majestically, stood at the foot of the stairs with its back to the wall and the gleaming white grand piano with its lid propped open, stood on the polished wooden floor in the stair well; behind the wall, I knew, was the servery, but there was no direct entrance to it from here. A second corridor used by the waiters, cooks and kitchen staff ran behind the wall which supported the curving staircase and led into the kitchen, this being a fairly recent extension to the main building. Thick carpet runners in deep maroon pile formed a cross at this point. One of them went to the right, past the grand piano and into the Z shaped corridor, doors from which entered the kitchen to the west and the servery to the east.

The Z shaped passage then straightened out and led into the rear extension which housed the secretary's office, the butler's room, the staff TV room and the gun room. A door led from that corridor into the yard at the rear, the yard being overlooked by the kitchen windows which faced north; through that yard, one could approach the estate offices, gardener's cottage and the wooded grounds at the back of the house. The ice house could also be reached via this route.

Straight ahead at the carpeted crossroads was a short passage, only some fifteen feet or so in length, and on the left of that was a door which led into Viscount Victor's office. The kitchen wall, minus windows but decorated with coaching prints, formed the north wall of that passage. Some distance to the east of the crossroads was the main door of the house at the end of a long through-corridor which led from off the main hall. To the south lay the route to the conservatory. The short passage had once been a side entrance, windowless, it ran for some ten or twelve feet between Viscount Victor's office and the western wall of the library, neither of which contained windows. The door, with its glass panels, had once led directly into the gardens, doubtless being a convenient route outside for whoever was working in the small office adjoining, but it now led into the conservatory, a comparatively recent addition to the Hall, circa 1921. Almost circular in shape, the former exterior wall of the library, without windows, and the former outer wall of Viscount Elsinby's office with a window, formed two walls of the conservatory, i.e., two solid sides of a square.

With these walls forming the rear to the north, and a side on the east, the almost-circular conservatory with its pointed roof of glass panels had been constructed to form a welcome extension to the main house. With a low stone wall, it comprised large panes of glass built into white wood and it protruded a considerable distance from the building-line of the original house, matching perhaps the outer lines of the lounge and its huge bay, central to which were the French windows. By standing in the bay of the lounge or in the bay of the bedroom above the lounge, and looking to the west, it was possible to see the conservatory's protruding section, but I had not lost sight of the fact that, at the time of the first murder, the lounge curtains had been closed. They were open at the time of Brenda's death, however.

It was a large conservatory, probably equal to the morning room in floor area, and its door was on the south-west corner, overlooking the White Shrubbery. With that door standing open, the killer could have positioned himself or herself in the north-west corner of the conservatory, completely out of sight of anyone in the Hall. From there, it would have been fairly simple to shoot at the victim only yards outside the door. During the dancing, that door had remained open to permit entry of fresh air, and so had the connecting door near the library/office passage. It was with these factors in mind that I led The Horse through the corridors to expound my theory. Even as we walked, the Hall appeared deserted; had it not been for the noise of subdued chatter in the lounge and library, and CID activity in the morning room, I could have imagined the place deserted even though it was full of people.

If they were fully engaged upon some group activity, it would be easy for a killer to prowl the building without anyone noticing him or her and that heavy carpet which formed the runners of the hall and corridors was thick enough to silence any footsteps. Even the domestic staff were silent — they would be busy with dinner preparations, their range of movement extending little beyond the kitchen, the servery and the dining room. I led the big man to the foot of the stairs. I indicated the landing window so we climbed to examine it; The Horse climbed onto the low window sill as I had done and muttered,

"Right, Nick, thanks. I agree — it is a possible firing point. So I wonder if Drood was shot from here? But not Brenda, I feel, we can't see the ice house or anywhere near it."

Satisfied I had expounded my own concerns, we returned to the foot of the stairs, Johnson passing en route to the lounge with yet more drinks borne aloft on his silver tray. I showed The Horse the carpeted sections of the polished wooden floor to explain the various routes from here. He nodded in understanding. I showed him the short passage which led to the door of Viscount Victor's office; tapping on the door and receiving no reply, he opened it and peered inside, noting one window which overlooked the gardens to the west and another that looked into the conservatory. He noted the absence of windows in these walls of the library and the kitchen, and then I led him into the conservatory. I left the house door open, it folded back against the wall of Viscount Victor's office where it was held open upon a small spring-loaded catch.

He halted and looked back into the house — from this position, there was a clear view of the crossroads in the hall, with the grand piano and rising stairs partially in view. The foot of the stairs and the grandfather clock were not within view from this point, but there was a clear sight of the corridor which ran due north, before it entered the Z shaped link between the kitchen and the servery. I heard the grandfather clock strike five thirty; the sound filled this part of the house.

"If somebody stood here, Nick," said The Horse. "They might be seen by anyone passing along those corridors, that crossroads is a busy place, as you know. Waitresses looking after the guests, Johnson serving drinks, people coming and going, climbing the stairs, stopping for a chat, going to the toilets."

"But if someone steps into the conservatory, sir, and takes two steps to the right, they're out of sight from the crossroads. They'd be sheltered by the wall of Victor's office because his window is further to the right; anyone in his office would not see a person standing against that wall. And there are plants around too, to add to the cover."

"I can't imagine many people being in his office late at night," said The Horse. "I doubt if any of the guests would enter it; his wife and secretary might, of course, and members of the staff, plus Viscount Victor himself, but no one else."

"No one with a legitimate purpose, you mean, sir!" I smiled, and then I moved into the position I had described as he watched me.

"From here," I said, "I have a clear view of lawns outside, right through the open door of the conservatory; I can see the place where Edwin Drood was found dead. When I arrived in the early hours of this morning it was still dark, but the subdued lights of the house enabled me to see the White Shrubbery. Light from the fountain helped but it was difficult to see the fallen man. I'm sure, sir, in the light from the house and the fountain, the killer would have been able to see his victim standing out there in the garden, especially in his white shirt."

He came to my side and nodded. "Right, that's one scenario. The same theory applies to a view from the landing window, doesn't it? Now walk towards the door, stand in the doorway, Nick."

I obeyed. The Horse walked back towards the Hall, into the corridor which led to the crossroads, and said, "Now I can't see you . . . the conservatory door's offset, isn't it? It is not directly opposite this rear entrance, so chummy could have stood anywhere in the conservatory to the right of the rear entrance, and not be seen from the house. And, as you said earlier, Nick, everyone was busy anyway — listening to Lord Thackerston's birthday speech. Well, everyone except the killer. So who missed his speech, Nick? We don't know, do we? I'm convinced he was killed during that speech or just before it. The fall of the dew, the pathologist's opinion and the timing in relation to the birthday speech all conspire towards that theory."

"It's virtually impossible to say, sir, from the statements alone, just who was absent. We need more evidence to identify the person who was not there. But there's more, sir," I added.

"Go on," he invited.

"If you leave the house via this route, through the conservatory door, and walk west into the gardens, you are also out of sight of the people in the house," I told him. "The kitchen has no south-facing windows and none facing west, whereas any other exit is overlooked in some way. Even if you leave the house via the fire escape above the gun room, you could be seen, perhaps from the dining room or even from the kitchen if you walked towards the woodland."

"What are you suggesting now, Nick?"

"That the murderer of Brenda Armitage left the house through the conservatory having possibly arranged to meet her at the ice house; he or she could do this without anyone noticing. And remember everyone was in the house, having a cup of tea, sir; except for two policemen who were in the grounds — and one of those was on the gate. It would have been a simple job for a determined person to dodge one patrolling constable. And what concerns me is that everyone had been drawn together to hear the birthday speech — like you, sir, I think that's when the first murder occurred. And tonight, we're all invited to dinner!"

"You reckon a third murder will be committed, Nick?"

"I don't really know, but it would not surprise me, after all, sir, the conditions would be just right."

"So who would the victim be?"

I smiled. "That's the problem. Of the people expected at dinner, we'd have to see who was missing."

"It's all very feasible, young Nick, but it's all conjecture, is it not? We need something more, don't we? We've searched the grounds and the conservatory for evidence of the probabilities you are highlighting, but we've found nothing. No spent cartridges, no forensic evidence to suggest the killer's presence, nothing in fact. There is absolutely no firm evidence to suggest the killer stood in the conservatory to fire the lethal shot at Edwin Drood. Our men searched it and found nothing, no spent cartridge, nothing. The fatal shot could have come from beyond the perimeter fence, and so could the one which killed Brenda Armitage. Some shots are lethal over a huge distance."

"I realise that, sir, but I repeat my concern. I think Drood was shot where he was found — the lack of a suspect's footprints in the dew tends to support that. But what bothers me now is that we've all been invited to dinner tonight, everyone who is here. It means that yet again everyone will be assembled in one place and I wondered if the killer would take that opportunity to kill again . . ."

"Then we'll set a trap," was all he said. "We've plenty of officers to do that. Now, if your theory is correct — and I do think it has merit — we need to examine all those statements again, don't we, for evidence of people who were not present at either the cup of tea ritual, or Lord Thackerston's speech. More reading, then?"

"Yes, sir," I said as I turned back into the Hall.

* * *

It was clear that The Horse wanted to be alone for a few minutes to consider what I had said and to formulate his own opinions.

After I had left him, I returned to the Murder Room and found it buzzing with excitement, one cause being a telephone call from Detective Constable Staples who said that Brenda Armitage had been killed by a shot in the head, and another being a discovery in the woods near the ice house. The fatal missile had entered through Brenda's right eye, suggesting that she had been facing her killer, but the important news was that the missile appeared identical to that which had killed Edwin Drood. It was another small round ball of lead, but the pathologist agreed that it would require a ballistic expert to say whether in fact the two balls had been fired from the same weapon. None of us had any doubts that they had, but in the world of criminal investigation, one cannot presume things.

The second piece of news was that detectives searching the woods around the ice house had found a third metal pellet. It was made of lead and was rather like a large green pea. The implication was that the killer had missed with the first shot and had killed Brenda with a second or subsequent one. So three lead missiles would now be examined by the ballistics experts at the Forensic Laboratory in Nottingham — the continuing search of the grounds might reveal others and pending the return of the two fatal missiles from the hospital, we now had one which we could examine ourselves. The one thing still puzzling us was the type of weapon which had fired these missiles; our own firearms experts had expressed an opinion that the first one had come from an antique weapon.

No modern gun, rifle or pistol was known to discharge those small marble-sized or pea-sized pellets.

At this stage, it had not been thought wise to seek the advice of the Hattertons because they had not yet been wholly eliminated from the enquiry; if they had been involved in the death, even to the innocent extent to supplying the ammunition in question, they might be afraid to say so.

Among the other developments was the anticipated news that Elsinby Estate was not as financially sound as many believed. A team of detectives had asked Viscount Victor for details of the Estate, their reasoning being an interest in the future of the property, but it was quickly made clear that Viscount Elsinby was presiding over a worrying decline of income burdened by a massive overdraft at the bank. Rents from farms had not kept pace with inflation and expenditure was rising to the point of not being met from income. The Labour Government's influence had made the running of such estates extremely difficult added to which was the curse of inflation generated by socialist policies, at one point rising to almost 30 percent. Staffing levels had been reduced to ease the burden of expenditure, jobs had been lost and disposal of at least two farms had been discussed. In spite of this, no one had been prepared to confirm or deny that the estate was in serious financial difficulties, although it had emerged that all the tenant farmers and estate workers were very concerned. None could afford to purchase his own property — farm or cottage. There was talk of each tenant farmer being compulsorily retired and a manager being installed to run all the farms as one unit, a form of collective farming but no such decision had been reached. The sale of one or more of the properties had been suggested too — there were even rumours that the Hall itself might have to be sold.

One alternative was to make the Hall pay its way by renting it as an institutional building or opening it to the public. Unfortunately, these discussions, private and confidential though they were, had reached the ears of the tenants and this had caused immense distress which had not been alleviated by the estate managers. So far as the Hall itself was concerned, its maintenance and upkeep was an undoubted drain on the Estate and the family could, if necessary, occupy one of the farm houses if the tenant was evicted. If the family moved out, then the Hall could be utilised for some other fund-raising purpose. It seemed very sensible.

These were all possibilities and another was admitted by Viscount Victor; he said, quite openly, that his father had discussed the possibility of replacing him with Henry Powler. Lord Thackerston had openly said that Victor was too soft to run a tough business and that someone with the drive and initiative of Powler might succeed in securing the future of the estate. There would be no title for Powler, of course, but with Lady Violet Powler being the daughter of the Earl of Thackerston, it meant that the house and the estate would remain within the family, at least in the short term. And, Viscount Victor had said, it could be claimed that of Powler's children, Vernon aged 6, was the rightful heir due to the vital blood link. Thus in the long term, line of natural inheritance would be sustained. If the estate did pass to the Powlers, either by inheritance or through the will of Lord Thackerston, then Henry might well be its saviour, even if his methods were not altogether honest. Both the title and the Estate, plus the Hall, might be rescued. As I listened to this, I wondered if Lady Violet had known about this conjecture before coming to the party.

In my mind, she remained a suspect. Hidden grievances about the inheritance of the estate and the title did appear to present a strong motive, although I had to admit that her *modus operandi* was doubtful. If she had shot both victims, how on earth had she managed to commit the crime? Where was the gun she had used? And, I felt, the person who had conducted the killings was accustomed to handling firearms because to shoot someone in the head from even a short distance does require a considerable amount of knowledge and skill. Of all the people here present, there were many with the necessary skills, but was Lady Violet among them? A lot of country bred women were very capable of using firearms.

But would Lady Violet kill in order to inherit an estate which was sliding into financial difficulties? And if so, why kill an artist? This again presented the notion that Drood had been mistaken by the killer for Viscount Victor. Or was the Earl planning to leave the Hall to Edwin Drood, or Edwin Dickens to give him his correct name? Drood had openly boasted what he would do with the Hall if it was his, so had the possibility, however remote, produced hatred among the Thackerston relations? The Earl had refused to discuss anything about the inheritance, a fact which angered The Horse.

But in all sincerity, would the Earl of Thackerston, with a well-established family around him, even think of transferring either the whole or part of his estate to an unknown artist who used a puzzling name from Dickens' novels?

And then I remembered that Claude Jeremiah had said something important.

CHAPTER XIV

"I only ask for information."
CHARLES DICKENS, 1812–70

The snag was that I could not remember Claude's words. In the clouded recesses of my mind, I realised that he had said something of importance but couldn't bring his words to mind. I couldn't even recall when he had said the vital words or in what context they had been spoken but I now knew they had some bearing on this investigation. It was like looking into a clump of nettles and knowing that one's cricket ball is somewhere in there — but you can't find it. I knew Claude had let something slip, perhaps inadvertently, but my inability to recall his chatter was something which happens to most of us — someone says something to us which, at the time, is of little consequence but later, in the light of changed circumstances and increased information, those same words assume a great importance. It is rather like being the witness of a crime — people see something happening in the street and at the time, the full import of that occurrence is not known or even anticipated. Later, when other information comes to light, that event, however minor, assumes an importance of its own. A simple example is to see a man running along the street. That in itself is of little importance so we pay scant attention to him. Then several hours later, we discover there has been a bank raid in that very street just before we saw the running man. The raider matches the description of the man we noticed. From that moment, then the sight of that running man becomes very important indeed.

My memories of chance words used by Claude Jeremiah Greengrass fell into that category. When he had spoken them, they had raised a flicker of uncertainty in my mind even though, at the time, I had not considered them of any importance. But now, those few words had become relevant. What he had done was to use an unusual phrase, an unusual term perhaps and at the time I had overlooked it. I tried to recall the times we had met and talked since this investigation had started, and the things he had said, the questions I had asked. Or perhaps it was something he had said in one of the written statements which were now in our groaning system?

My inability to recall the words bothered me. It was like trying to recall someone's name or the answer to a quiz question when the answer is on the tip of one's tongue and yet refuses to come. What he had said at the time had registered in my mind as something unusual but I had not pursued the matter to clarify my doubts — at the time, I had not considered it important but now wished I'd checked it. Now, though, I felt that his words could be the key to the current enquiry if only they would return to my memory.

One means of reviving my memory was to re-read the statements he had made. Oblivious to the events around me, I began to sift through my massive pile of paper in an endeavour to locate those statements made by Claude Jeremiah Greengrass. I remembered my informal chat with him yesterday, when I noticed the tightness of his boots, but that interview had not been in written form. Later, that footprint had been found in the White Shrubbery and at lunchtime I had gone home for my meal but had taken time to trace Claude Jeremiah.

I'd found him at the village pub where I had quizzed him further about his presence at the Hall — and he'd admitted prowling just before 1am. He'd seen the man in evening dress and the blonde woman with her hair in a bun. In Claude's opinion, that man might have been Viscount Victor but just as easily, we knew it could have been Edwin Drood. He hadn't known the woman's identity — even though he knew Brenda Armitage, he had not recognised her because of her hair style, although he was aware that she was the Earl's solicitor. Claude had not overheard any conversation between them.

Because of that sighting, and because of Claude's footprint in the earth of the White Shrubbery, I had persuaded him to come and be interviewed by the CID. And so he had. The interview would have been most unpleasant because he would have been treated as a suspect rather than a witness, but the benefits of such an intense interrogation were that it would elicit the truth and so eliminate Claude as a suspect — which in fact had happened. Later, after Brenda's death, he had helped us to examine fences and gates at the rear of the Hall to decide whether or not an intruder had entered by that route. I had chatted to him on those occasions and now struggled to remember our conversations. I couldn't. I needed to know what he had said in his formal statement and so I began to search my files. Perhaps those important words were contained in writing? If so, this would be a bonus.

I knew Claude had been quizzed at length about his furtive presence last night, and about his old boots which had been found abandoned in the ice house; he had explained his unusual relationship with Lord Thackerston and the estate, giving his version of the authority he possessed to remove things from the Estate and the ice house. He'd grumbled that poachers were taking pot shots at "his" rabbits too. Most of his evidence would be recorded in a formal written account now filed among other papers relating to the murder investigation. In my capacity as an official statement reader, had I come across those mysterious words in Claude's formal version? I retrieved his statement without difficulty and began to study it carefully. It began in the formal manner with his name, date of birth, address and occupation, which he gave as General Dealer, and it read as follows:

"I am in business on my own account and since returning from my unit at the end of the war, I have operated a small, but highly successful general dealership with satisfied customers all over the North Riding of Yorkshire. During my military service I was driver to the Earl of Thackerston; he was my CO in the Green Howards and because I'd known him as a lad at Elsinby, we were pals. When I left the army, he said I could remove unwanted objects from his estate — discarded furniture was put in the old ice house where it was dry and I just helped myself, either to sell it or keep it. Things like old dining room chairs or even armchairs were thrown out and I could take them and sell them. I remember, when he had WCs installed in the Hall, the staff threw out thirty jerries — chamber pots — and I sold them all to collectors. Lord Thackerston let me do that, and he let me wander around to set snares for rabbits and take pheasants in season. The gamekeepers know me and in fact I protect the game on the estate — somebody's been killing rabbits recently without authority, and I told Roy Cleghorn -I think it's stopped now.

"I can almost come and go as I want, but I make sure I never exceed my welcome, I've never done a dishonest thing against Lord Thackerston or Viscount Elsinby since he took over. Young Victor let me continue like his dad had done.

"Now, on Saturday night, I came up to the Hall, well, Sunday morning it would be, in the early hours. I had my dog Alfred, with me, he's a lurcher and is trained to very high standards of obedience. I often do this — I come up to the big house to keep an eye on things, especially that rabbit shooter, protecting my own interests I suppose. Anyway, on that night it would be about one o'clock in the morning and I'd got myself felted (hidden) behind the White Shrubbery because I realised somebody was standing at the other end, not far from me. I ducked down — I think I must have put my foot on the earth because that print you have shown me is definitely from my boots — I got these boots from the ice house, by the way, and left my old ones in there, to burn them later. They'd been thrown out by somebody for me to take. I've not pinched them, like I said, I have permission to remove things that are thrown out and left in that ice house. It's the Estate's way of getting rid of stuff and helping me at the same time. When I was squatting behind the shrubs, I saw this man in evening dress just standing there. He was smoking, I could see the glow from the tip of his cigarette when he lowered it from his mouth and held it in his hand. I'd say it was a cigarette because of the smell — some of the smoke wafted over to me. It was definitely not cigar smoke. The light from the conservatory was on him, but from where I was hiding he was like a silhouette so I couldn't be sure who it was.

"I thought it was Lord Thackerston's eldest son, but couldn't swear to that. I don't know a man called Edwin Drood so I can't say if it was him. The man I saw was about thirty to thirty-five years old, I'd say, fairly heavily built with dark hair and he was wearing an evening suit. Then I saw a woman come and talk to him. She had blonde hair done up in a bun; she had no coat on but a short sleeved white blouse. They chatted a while in low voices and I couldn't hear what they were saying, and then she went back inside. I don't know who she was, it was too dark for a good look and she was facing away from me all the time. I saw other people in the conservatory, drinking and chatting, and soon after she went inside, everybody vanished into the house. There was nobody in the conservatory but the lights were on and the door was wide open.

"The man was still standing there, near the White Shrubbery and he was alone, nobody else came out to speak to him so I decided to leave. All the ground-floor lights were on, but apart from the conservatory, all the windows were covered with curtains. I saw some upstairs lights on as well.

In the big bedroom over the lounge, I saw somebody moving about, just the head and shoulders, but I have no idea who it was, I was too far away. It was a man, I can say that, and he was thickset with greying hair. It might have been the Earl, he does have grey hair. I left the shrubbery by crawling low into the darkness behind it, into the shadows, and then climbed over the boundary fence.

"This put me into the field, which is part of the estate's parkland, but I was now in total darkness. I'm very good in those conditions, then me and Alfred came home. I got in about quarter to two. Me and Alfred walked across the fields down to the road, but I never heard a shot. With my trained hearing, I think I would have heard a shot if it had been fired while I was walking down the field, and I know Alfred would have done. He never showed any sign of hearing a shot — he always tells me if other folks are about, especially other poachers. I did not kill anybody and was not in possession of a gun that night."

The statement was signed "Claude Jeremiah Greengrass" and dated with today's date. I read it several times, but the key word eluded me. What I sought was not here so it must have been something he had said to me informally. My time chart did not reveal the presence of anyone else, save Drood, Beswick and Brenda, outside the conservatory around one o'clock. At that point, everyone had gone indoors to hear the birthday speech — except Drood and his killer. Other movements that I had recorded were that Lord Thackerston had left the lounge around 12.30am to go to his room to prepare his speech; around that time, Edwin Drood had been in the front entrance hall, apparently agitated. He'd probably gone outside via the front door to walk around the building to meet his killer. At 12.45am, Ned Powler was seen creeping from the lounge, but his tale about split trousers had been verified; Aunt Felicity had also gone upstairs about one o'clock for some indigestion tablets, returning about 1.15am to hear the speech. At that time, there had been mention of fresh air circulating on the landing on the first floor — the landing window had been open with the curtains drawn back, thus providing a convenient sniper point.

My own inspection had convinced me that anyone standing at that window with a gun could have hit a victim standing near the shrubbery. It was one of several possible sniping points from the upstairs rooms, especially those facing south or west. Lord Thackerston's bedroom, above the lounge and with a large bay window, was ideal — so had someone hidden there during his speech and then killed Drood who'd been outside? Edwin had not been seen alive after one o'clock, I repeated to myself. So had Brenda shot him? And then killed herself? But if so, we had not found her weapon . . . And had anyone seen her at the speech?

In spite of the established facts, there was chipping away at my conscience that mysterious something which Claude had said. I stopped reading for a moment or two, my brow creased in thought as I tried to recollect his words. Inspector Oakland came to see how I was progressing and I informed him of my researches, my suspicions and my inability to pull that annoying piece of information from the depths of my brain.

"Why not take a break and have another word with old Greengrass?" suggested Oakland. "You've had your head in those files far too long, a break will do you good — and you are invited for dinner, remember!"

And so I left the Murder Room. Keeping an eye open for possible snipers, I jumped into my minivan and drove back into the village. I made for the untidy Greengrass ranch where I guessed the old rogue would be having his tea. I was right; when I rapped on the door, Alfred barked his warning and a voice inside growled, "Who is it?"

"PC Rhea," I said. "Can I come in?"

"Not if you've come to arrest me for that murder, no you can't."

"I've come to pick your brains again," I confessed. The door opened and he admitted me to his scruffy home where a meal of ham and eggs was sitting on a plate. Alfred had his own meal on the floor but I had no idea of its constituents. I accepted Claude's offer of tea from an old army tin mug and settled at his table.

"So, what's up?" he grinned.

I tried to explain my dilemma, struggling to explain how I was battling to resurrect some word or phrase he had said either yesterday or today but I could not make him understand what I was getting at. In the end, I said, "Claude, the sighting you told me about, the man outside the conservatory. You thought it was Viscount Victor, didn't you?"

He frowned. "No, I said I had no idea who it was. It could have been anybody, he was done up in one of those monkey suits and they all look like penguins in 'em."

"I thought you said you thought it was Lord Thackerston's son?"

"Aye, I did. But not Victor. That eldest son of his, the one he had out of wedlock. I thought it was him, I mean, he looks just like him, from the back that is, sturdy chap, dark hair worn long . . . no, Mr Rhea, I never said it was Victor."

"So this eldest son, who is that?"

"Dickens, they call him. Edwin Dickens. His mother was a cleaner, the family wouldn't let her wed His Lordship, so he kept mum about the kid for a while, then started to pay him an allowance and bring him home. He wanted to be an artist, so Lordy funded him. I thought you would have known that, being a snooper!"

"So you thought the man having a smoke outside was Dickens . . . the man we know as Edwin Drood!"

"I don't know him as Drood, constable! I told you I thought it was Thackerston's eldest son, didn't I? Like father, like son, that's what I say. It's a few years since I saw him, he used to come to the Hall as a lad. It's years since I've seen him, but yon chap standing near the shrubbery did have the family look, if you know what I mean. I knew it wasn't Victor because he was smoking, that's summat Victor never does."

It was then I recalled the mysterious phrase I'd been trying to remember. At the time, it had puzzled me because

Claude would have called him Elsinby or Viscount Victor if that's who he had really meant. But he hadn't used those terms. He'd referred to Lord Thackerston's lad — and now a similar matter puzzled me.

"You called Brenda his solicitor lass, didn't you?"

"Aye, for t'same reason. She's his, an" all, illegitimate by another woman, and so is Lady Penelope Prittleford, and Evelyn du Bartas . . . he was always a bit of a lad, was Lordy, couldn't keep his hands off working-class women, so there's umpteen little Thackerstons around the country. He had a busy social life, had Lordy, before he joined up, then he went wild and wasn't much better when he was demobbed."

"I think you'd better come and tell my boss that," I suggested.

"Oh, not again!" groaned Claude Jeremiah Greengrass.

CHAPTER XV

"A smattering of everything and a knowledge of nothing."
CHARLES DICKENS, 1R812–70

I returned to Elsinby Hall with Claude Jeremiah Greengrass in the van, along with Alfred, his dog, in the rear. We were greeted at the gate by Sergeant Blaketon who, upon seeing Claude, allowed a wide smile to brighten his face. It was evident from his demeanour that he thought Claude had been arrested. Before allowing us into the grounds, he opened the van door at Claude's side, and almost gloated,

"So it was you all along, Greengrass . . . I might have known!"

"Me, Sergeant Blaketon? What was me?"

"The villain we've been hunting, the murderer . . ."

"Now hang on a minute!" Claude spluttered. "I'm no killer, Mr Blaketon, I'm here to help enquiries, volunteering my services like a good citizen; that's typical of you, having a go at me when I'm helping to find out who's been bumping off His Lordship's kith and kin."

"Kith and kin? What are you talking about, Greengrass?"

"Helping to catch a killer, that's what, Mr Blaketon. Privy to secrets, I am. I want the killer caught. Me and Lordy are pals and I don't go around blowing holes through his rabbits like some folks have been doing. We go back a long time, me and Thackerston, we fought side by side to save our country. Been through hell together, we have . . ."

"That's right, Sergeant," I had to support Claude otherwise he might decide to jump out of my van and say nothing to the CID. "He does have permission to roam these grounds, and to take unwanted furniture and other cast-offs from the ice house; what's rubbish to these folks will fetch a few quid for Claude when he sells it. He takes rabbits and pheasants too, Sergeant, with permission I might add, and I must say that Claude's been a tower of strength during this enquiry, he's helped us a lot."

"All I can say is don't let that man con you into believing everything he says, Rhea! Don't forget he's been around the Hall in very suspicious circumstances — footprints in the shrubbery, boots in the ice house . . . that sort of evidence is enough to get you hanged by the neck on the gallows, Greengrass! I don't trust you one inch, not one solitary inch!"

As I drove to the front door of the Hall, I noticed the Wooden Horse walking round the footpath, risking snipers. I knew they'd be covered by armed detectives lurking in the bushes. Detective Sergeant Wood, with Detective Superintendent Galvin leading the way, were deep in conversation as they walked from the fountain towards the front door. Wood was carrying a gold pocket watch. The case was open to reveal a white face with Roman numerals; he was holding it carefully by the end of the chain which was also gold. The watch was dangling from the end, swinging like a pendulum. They saw me as I pulled up with Claude and headed in our direction. We climbed out of the van, leaving Alfred inside, and I noticed Claude was wearing his brown boots. And he wasn't limping now.

"Boots feel better, Claude?" I smiled.

"Aye. they are. Quality tells, Mr Rhea. It took me a while to get 'em worn in, but they're better even since yesterday.

Give 'em another week and they'll be as comfy as a pair of old slippers."

"Hello, Nick, what's this? Claude coming to confess, is he?" The Horse had a warm smile on his large face.

"No I'm not, and I've had enough of this, what with Blaketon thinking I'm the killer and you blokes making unsavoury jokes . . . all I can say is that it's a good job I can take a joke. And you lot are all a joke if you don't mind me saying so . . . fancy you not knowing Lordy has had a life of non-stop breeding just like those pedigree sheep and cows of his. He's got kids everywhere, a right old ram he was in his youth — and he's still fairly fit if you ask me."

"What's he trying to tell us, Nick?" asked The Horse.

Standing outside the front door of Elsinby Hall, I recounted Claude's exposition of the complicated and extensive breeding capabilities of the Earl of Thackerston and as I concluded my account, The Horse groaned.

"Nobody, but nobody has even hinted that!" he sounded dismayed and even shocked. "I have conducted a very searching interview of Lord Thackerston, Viscount Elsinby and the rest of them and not one of them has even hinted that there were illegitimate members of the family, let alone that some of them were right here at the party — and that two of them have been murdered."

"The family never speaks of it," said Claude, blinking furiously as he stood before the two detectives. "That's summat I learned very early on. You'd never get any of the family to admit those folks were the offspring of the Earl — it's a bit like the royal family never talking about their illegitimate members. My Alfred's a bit like that — he's from really good stock, you know, bags of breeding there, but nobody'll admit he's a dog of real quality. His dad has a pedigree a mile long."

"There's blue blood in most of us, Claude, so why have you told us all this?" asked The Horse. "Why did you suddenly see fit to reveal what I see as a family secret, you being such an old friend of Thackerston? Aren't you betraying a confidence?"

"Confidence? The whole bloody army knew what he was up to, and the whole village knows. But it wasn't quite like that, you see, was it, Constable Rhea? I mean, I thought everybody knew and I certainly thought you blokes knew. I never thought of it as breaking a confidence, I was just reminding you, Constable Rhea that is, of what everybody knew long before Mr Rhea ever found himself in Aidensfield. The village folk know all about it, well, most of them do, the older generation that is, and I thought you, the constabulary that is, would know such things . . . so, I mean, when I told Constable Rhea all about Lordy's love life, I had no idea I was revealing family secrets, did I? I had no idea he'd not levelled with you, in the circumstances, you know, his kids being bumped off by somebody. Not that I would reveal any of his real secrets. Anyroad, I just want the killer caught, Mr Galvin, that's what this is all about, isn't it?"

"It most certainly is, Claude. Thank you for volunteering this information. It alters the entire concept of our investigation and if the two murder victims were the illegitimate offspring of Lord Thackerston, then it does suggest a motive for the killing — especially if he was thinking of making changes to the Estate. So, Nick, can you take a statement from Claude? Get as much detail as you can — if it's possible, determine which of the people presently with us have emerged from His Lordship's somewhat active loins, with dates and places they were born. Be as accurate as you can. We can always make further checks if we have to. I think you'd be the best person to interview Claude — you know him better than the rest of us. I'll have to see Lord Thackerston again about all this. Now, before you leave us, Claude, any idea who this watch belongs to?"

At a signal from The Horse, Detective Sergeant Wood displayed the gold watch he was carrying, holding it high at the end of its fine gold chain. The case was open and I could see it was equipped with a stop mechanism, that the case was in plain gold and that even the hands were gold — including the tiny second hand with its own dial. I noticed that it had stopped, the pointers showing ten minutes past one. I could just read the inscription on the face, the maker's name, I thought — it said "Frères Sinderby, London".

"How old is it?" I asked.

"Eighteenth century, we think," said The Horse as Claude inspected it carefully without being allowed to handle it. "The work of Frères Sinderby dates to that period — that's something I remember from my antiques course."

"What's on the outside of the case?" asked Claude. "Close the case lid, will you?"

Wood said, "I can't close it, Claude, I don't want to touch it but I will turn it round so you can see the case lid . . ." and so he did. On the lid, etched into the gold, was a tiny depiction of a sheaf of reeds. They were tied in the middle so that the base and the top spread slightly.

"Thatching reeds," muttered Claude. "That's a family heirloom, it belonged to the Earl of Thackerston's father, the old Earl, and that watch is supposed to be handed down from father to eldest son, the eldest son receiving it when he comes of age. The father gives it to him on his twenty-first birthday. Now, I reckon it belongs to somebody who's here in the Hall now, that's what I say. Where's it been?"

"It was found in the fountain, Claude, half an hour ago. It's been there a while, we think, probably since yesterday, it's stopped as you can see. Half past one. I'm not sure whether that's from the effect of the water or whether it needs winding. Now, I wonder who's lost it?"

"Well," said Claude. "If that watch had been passed from father to son, as it should have been, then that murdered chap, Dickens or Drood or whatever he called himself, should have had it, not Viscount Victor. Dickens was the eldest of Thackerston's sons, he was born before Viscount Victor, before the war even. So what was it doing in the fountain?"

"That's what we would like to know," said The Horse. "Our search teams found it not long ago, it was missed on the first sweep because it was hidden beneath some vegetation, but the movement of the water cleared it and it was noticed not long ago. We don't think it has been in the water for very long — for one thing, we know the fountain was faulty only yesterday and that it was not working until late last night. And if the gardener had been working on the fountain, he would surely have noticed this among the vegetation before the water was turned on. He has been interviewed and agrees with us — if this watch had been lying there before he switched on the water, he would have seen it."

"So that chap I saw this morning, at one o'clockish, he must have dropped it?"

"Or perhaps the killer could have dropped it, Claude?" suggested The Horse. "Now, the Earl said Edwin's gold watch was missing, so we can assume this is it, eh? We'll have to show it to him to be sure. Maybe there's another elder son, one not even known to you? Now, there's a thought! So, Bernard," and Galvin turned to his side-kick. "Take this to the Earl to ask if it's the one that belonged to Edwin. If so, why was it thrown away, why was it in the water of the fountain?" With our allotted tasks, we turned towards the main door, walking along the south side of the Hall as afternoon turned into evening. Across the low valley, I could see a train chugging along the line towards Ashfordly, I could see the smoke rising from the chimneys of cottages and farms along the dale, I could see the white cattle and sheep grazing in fields below the mansion and in all, it was a scene of blissful peace.

But here, on the hilltop, there was murder and mystery with the reputation of a noble family about to be shattered by revelations which must surely be made public. I shuddered at the effect this would have upon not only the Elsinby family but also the estate with its complement of tenants and workers. And what was the Earl going to do about it all? I had not seen him to speak to, I could not know his reactions or his thoughts and since the news of the first murder had been revealed, he seemed to have retired to his room, being far from prominent during the last twelve hours or so.

I found myself worrying about Viscount Victor and his family... ahead of them lay nothing but trouble and distress. It would require a strong family to weather the proverbial storms which lay ahead. As we reached the front door of Elsinby Hall I stood back to allow The Horse and Wood to enter but the door opened before we reached it. Through the windows at each side of the doorway Johnson, the butler, had obviously noticed our impending arrival and was holding the heavy door open. Leaning on his thick walking stick and panting slightly, he was smiling as if we were new arrivals at some fashionable function.

"Please enter, gentlemen."

"Thank you, Johnson," acknowledged The Horse as he stepped inside, followed by Detective Sergeant Wood. I followed, but when Claude strode forward, Johnson said, "The rear entrance, if you please, Mr Greengrass." And there was disdain on his face as he scrutinised Claude's filthy old overcoat and other smelly clothing; only his boots were of top quality, even if they now required polish.

"You what?" bellowed Claude. "I'm a guest here, just like them!"

"The rear door, if you please, Mr Greengrass. His Lordship is most particular about the use of the front entrance and there is a special tradesman's door to the rear of the premises. I should deem it a pleasure if you would use that door."

"I'm here on important business, I'll have you know, I'm a vital witness in this murder carry-on, knowing the family like I do. And I'll have you know that me and Lord Thackerston are old mates," blustered Claude. "Fought side by side we did, in the war, me and him, faced enemies for worse than you, Jasper Bloody Johnson, and we beat 'em..."

"The rear door, Mr Greengrass." Johnson, the unflappable, was not to be shaken from his resolve and although we could have insisted on Claude's right to enter through this door, The Horse knew better than to antagonise a butler. We depended upon him for the smooth running of frequent cups of tea during our enquiries and the power such persons wielded within a household of this kind was awesome. The Horse nodded.

"Would you mind, Claude?" His voice showed sympathy with Claude.

I said, "I'll come with you, Claude."

As the heavy oak door closed behind the two detectives, I walked beside Claude as we strode past the dining room, now being prepared for dinner yet again, and beyond the north wing to the door which led via the yard into the passage containing the butler's room, the TV room, the secretary's office and the gun room.

"That man's a twerp!" muttered Claude. "You give folks like that a bit of power and it goes to their heads . . . he's a right Mister Jobsworth is that one."

"Has he been here long?" I asked. "I can't say I've seen him around the village."

"The one I got on with was old Hewitt," puffed Claude, my pace being rather too speedy for him. "Lovely old feller, retired five years ago. This chap's arrived since then. He doesn't get out much, that leg of his makes it hard work for him, but he does go to Ashfordly with the estate's official driver. He sings in the church choir in his off-duty time, does a bit of teaching organ music, they tell me, when he can spare the time. You won't see much of him in Elsinby or Aidensfield."

"Does Johnson object to you taking stuff from the ice house?" I asked.

"No, he never has done. Mind, the Estate let him know I had access to the grounds whenever I wanted," Claude panted. "But I don't like Johnson, Mr Rhea, I wouldn't trust him as far as I could throw him."

"Why not?" I was interested now.

"He's been shooting my rabbits just for fun," Claude grumbled. "I've found one or two shot lately, bloody great holes blown in 'em. And I've seen him hobbling about among those trees with his bloody great stick . . ."

"He does live here," I said. "And the house has a room full of guns for the staff to use. His Lordship won't want the place over-run with rabbits!"

"Aye, well, I know that. I know the gamekeepers pot 'em when they breed too fast. But they let me do that, rabbits are money for me, Mr Rhea, they're nowt to folks who live this sort of life. But this chap is different. His eyes are too close together for one thing," Claude pronounced. "You never can trust a person whose eyes are too close together. The evil eye, my old mother said. Folks with their eyes too close have got the evil eye. And worse still, his eyebrows meet. Now that is a bad sign, Mr Rhea, eyebrows that meet across the nose . . . no, I'll never trust that chap."

"But has he done anything to make you think like that?" I persisted.

"He doesn't need to," said Claude. "I'm old enough and wise enough to know who I can trust and who I can't."

My endeavours to discover whether or not Johnson the butler had actually done anything harmful to Claude came to nothing. Other than being blamed for shooting rabbits to which Claude felt he had sole rights, and refusing admittance to Claude via the front door, I could not identify any specific thing which he had done to antagonise Claude — he had never tried to stop Claude helping himself to cast-off junk and he had never tried to prevent Claude's open access to Elsinby Estate. All he'd done was to perform his butler's duties in the way he felt best.

When I entered the Hall via the rear entrance as indicated by Johnson, with Claude on my heels, Johnson was heading our way along the passage. His heavy stick was once more serving as a kind of non-slip crutch as he moved speedily in our direction along the canvas covering of the rear corridor. He smiled at me.

"I apologise to you, constable, about the business at the front door, but His Lordship's orders must be obeyed."

"Of course," I had no wish to argue. "Now, I need to interview Mr Greengrass in private. Do you know if there is a free room?"

"The secretary's office is free for the time being," he smiled at me, a cold smile I felt. "Would that be suitable?"

"Yes, perfect," I said.

"The man's a moron," muttered Claude beneath his breath as Johnson opened the door for me. I led the way inside; the desk contained a pile of official statement forms because the room had served a similar purpose many times previously during the past few hours and so I prepared for my task. Johnson asked if we'd like a cup of tea each, to which we responded positively, and then, seating Claude on a chair beside me, I began my interview. What he told me was quite remarkable.

Private Greengrass had been official driver to the Earl of Thackerston during the war when Thackerston had been CO of the unit. The Earl, who was then Viscount Elsinby, was given a wartime commission in the Green Howards, the North Riding of Yorkshire's own regiment. His father, the old Earl, was still alive and running the estate. Claude and Viscount Randy had gone everywhere together, even into France, the Channel Isles and other points overseas, Claude being his trusted friend and worthy driver. Overseas, Randy's proclivity for young servant girls, a taste he had inherited from his own father, had become evident to Claude and the nobleman had made no attempts to keep his activities secret from Claude.

He'd had a wonderful time among the ladies of foreign nations just as he'd had in England before the war. Back in England in 1943, Claude had been asked to drive him, off duty and in a civilian hired car, to a smart hotel in Syndenham. By that time, Randy's father, the Earl of Thackerston, had died and so Randy had become the new Earl of Thackerston. The occasion had been the twenty-first birthday of a private soldier at home on leave — Private Edwin Dickens. The new Earl, in civilian clothes, was attending not as the Earl of Thackerston nor indeed as an army officer, but as plain Mr Randolph Whitlock. Claude, as an old friend from the Elsinby area, had been allowed into the party and there he had been witness to the presentation of a gold watch to Edwin Dickens. It was the Thackerston watch, the heirloom, the watch which was passed from eldest son to eldest son upon their coming-of-age.

In his statement, Claude said, "I was told not to mention this to anyone at home, Lordy said it was all that Edwin would get, because he was illegitimate and because Lordy could not marry Edwin's mother, the lad would never inherit the title. He could never be a future Lord Thackerston or Viscount Elsinby, but the watch was his, and he could pass it on to his children. The snag was that lad grew up as queer as a nine bob note and never got married, so that line threatened to end, you see, Mr Rhea. Edwin often came to Elsinby Hall for holidays and visits, when Lordy was living there, that was before Viscount Victor took over, but because he was such a lot older than the others, they just thought he was a family friend. I knew him as Dickens then, I've never heard him called Drood. Nobody ever said he was a relation, I don't think the other children knew, but I knew. I watched him grow into his twenties, you see, and I thought it was him standing there, near that shrubbery last night, even though I haven't seen him for years. I reckon because Viscount Victor can't produce kids, Lordy wanted to do something about the inheritance now that the Estate's not doing very well. But I have no idea what was in Lordy's mind, I've not spoken to him for ages, you see. I can't see him passing the Estate over to a poofter, he hated 'em during the war. Subversives he called 'em. Lordy wants heirs, Mr Rhea, he wants the family to keep the Estate, all of it."

Claude then went on to detail other children he'd learned about, Lady Penelope Prittleford, Evelyn du Bartas, Brenda Armitage among them. They were all younger than Drood, younger than Viscount Victor too. Were there more, I asked. Claude thought there would be more, perhaps unknown at this stage, but other than the acknowledged members of the family, Drood, Lady Penelope, Evelyn du Bartas and Brenda

Armitage were the only illegitimate ones at present in the Hall. And two of those had died.

Lady Penelope and Evelyn du Bartas were still alive.

But for how long? I asked myself as I concluded my interview with Claude Jeremiah Greengrass.

Now that was over, it would soon be dinner time.

CHAPTER XVI

"It is called the Thorn of Anxiety."
CHARLES DICKENS, 1812–70

Before we assembled for dinner, The Horse confronted the Earl with the information Claude had provided. Under gentle but firm pressure, the Earl of Thackerston admitted paternity of the four children in question. He had not seen fit to divulge this to the police because he felt it was a confidential family matter which had no bearing on the investigation. Not even his legitimate family knew the full extent of his unofficial brood. He now accepted that his withholding of information might have hindered the investigation, but he did stress that he had not made any decision about the future of Elsinby Estate or of the Hall itself. Rumours abounded, but none had any foundation and even if he intended to make changes, he could see no reason why this should have caused the deaths of Edwin and Brenda. The Earl was as puzzled as the police, there seemed to be no motive.

The Earl did admit that Edwin was demanding and overbearing at times; he was not universally popular and he enjoyed having money. He was a genuine artist but treated his work as a business rather than an art, going off to paint in his studio just as any other person might have gone to work in an office. He seldom allowed his art to intrude upon his leisure moments. The Earl did confirm, however, that Edwin was not blackmailing him — the money he paid to Edwin was a genuine allowance, a way for the Earl to express his responsibility for fathering Edwin and it had been paid since birth, first to Edwin's mother and then to Edwin upon his coming-of-age.

In spite of Edwin being the first-born son to the Earl, there was no way he could inherit the title but the Estate, or part of it, could be willed to him. The Earl was aware of Edwin's great desire to own the Hall, but such a scheme formed no part of the Earl's plans. Under prolonged questioning by The Horse, the Earl said Edwin had long known the circumstances of his birth and it was a sore point with him that the absence of a marriage certificate for his mother had denied him the right to the Thackerston/Elsinby titles and all that went with them. All that he had, apart from a fairly generous allowance from the Estate, was the Thackerston watch, itself a valuable heirloom. The Earl had examined the gold watch found in the fountain and confirmed that it was indeed the Thackerston watch and that it had belonged to Edwin — he had no idea how it had come to be in the water.

Brenda Armitage was another of the Earl's secret offspring, the result of a liaison with Rose Armitage, a maid at a friend's country house. When Rose had drowned herself, the Earl had cared for Brenda; she had matured into a clever and beautiful young woman with an aptitude for civil law, hence her occupation. The Earl said he had appointed her his personal lawyer because of her knowledge and qualities, and not for reasons of nepotism. She had proved most capable and one of her responsibilities was the continued funding, from the Estate's income, of the Earl's family of illegitimate offspring, Edwin Drood included. All had benefited from some sort of income from the Estate, including herself; in this respect, they had been well treated. Brenda had known the family history exceedingly well, she'd known the current

Earl's history too and in all these highly delicate matters, she had been totally reliable and utterly discreet. It would be difficult to find a suitable replacement, he admitted. The Earl even went so far as to say to The Horse, "She knew more about the family than me! I wasn't too fussed about knowing of my ancestors, but she was. She ferreted about in old documents and had acquired a massive knowledge of our family history, both good and bad!"

Due to her closeness to family secrets, Brenda's death had devastated the Earl; her death had upset him far more than that of Drood. What he'd intended to be a happy occasion had been reduced to tragedy but the Earl could offer no clues as to who the killer might be. From an investigative point of view, however, the fact that Edwin and Brenda were not contenders for Elsinby Estate meant that the inheritance question was not a motive for the murders. But if that was true, what was the motive? Sexual attacks and robbery had been ruled out. Jealousy? Homosexuality? Had Brenda been a lesbian, The Horse wondered, but the Earl assured him that she was not. Drood was homosexual, that was common knowledge but had he been killed for that reason? If so, why had Brenda also been disposed of, almost certainly by the same killer?

The Horse had then asked if he could have access to the family papers, especially those upon which Brenda may have based her research, and, somewhat reluctantly, the Earl had consented. The Horse had asked if they were kept at Elsinby Hall, his concern being that someone might have gained unauthorised access, but the Earl assured him they were secure.

They were in a vault at the family bank in Ashfordly and would be made available tomorrow. The Horse did elicit from the Earl, however, that whenever he came to Yorkshire on business, he stayed at Elsinby Hall which he still regarded as his home. From time to time, he did have meetings with Brenda, always at the Hall. Sometimes, when she had required access to the papers, they had been brought to the

Hall. The Earl assured The Horse that the papers were secure while at the Hall — no one was able to obtain unauthorised access to them. There was a safe in the Viscount's private office where confidential documents were stored and the papers were stored there while temporarily out of use during their periods at the Hall — such as lunch periods. After use, they were returned immediately to the bank vaults in a sealed package. The Horse thanked him and assured the Earl that his family honour and respectability would be maintained, even in the event of a murder trial.

Upon his return to the Murder Room before dinner, The Horse told us about these developments and asked us to seek another motive. Then he outlined his plans for the meal, warning us of the possibility of another murder. To counter that, Inspector Hailstone had produced a plan which would provide security for everyone during the meal. Very simple, it was based on the fact that the dining room was not large enough to accommodate all the police officers at one sitting. There would be two sittings. The first would comprise family, guests and some police officers, while the second would consist entirely of police officers. When police officers were not dining, they would be responsible for the overall security of the people and premises, both indoors and out, especially while the meal was in progress.

To the family and guests (and therefore to the murderer), it would seem that no special security arrangements had been effected but in fact, the entire premises would be secure. The plan was to trap or unmask the killer. The police had the names of everyone in the house, whether resident or not, and they would be discreetly checked into the dining room to ensure that everyone was present. Johnson had been supplied with a list of names, ostensibly to compile a seating plan; he had no idea of its real purpose. If anyone was absent before the meal started, there would be an immediate search by armed police. Anyone not wishing to partake of the meal would be under guard during the dinner. The grounds and in particular those areas adjacent to the dining room would be under armed guard too, huge widows reaching from floor to ceiling were a feature of that superb dining room and so the diners could provide easy targets to a killer hiding near the blackthorn patch. Nonetheless, it had been thought unwise to close the curtains before dusk. Any departure from normality might alert a sniper, if indeed there was one. The curtains would be drawn just before the meal began.

To provide the best cover, armed officers would be concealed in the thick foliage around the house and they would supervise all paths, fences and gates leading from the open countryside. If this meal, this gathering of people, this last supper, was to draw the killer from his or her hiding place, it should result in a swift arrest. Of that, The Horse and Hailstone were confident.

In those final moments, it is fair to say that those of us working in the Murder Room were extremely tense. There was a tangible undercurrent of worry. It is fair to add that many believed someone was going to be murdered tonight in spite of our efforts to prevent it. If the killer had already murdered in defiance of our presence, it could happen again and we all knew it.

There was much activity in the house during the half hour before dinner. Johnson, his heavy stick tapping along the floor, was circulating with his silver tray full of drinks, maids were offering everyone an aperitif, and people were standing around in the entrance hall, the lounge, the stairwell and the library. I noticed that none had ventured into the conservatory this time; indeed, its outer door had been locked. Detectives now mingled with the guests, chatting as they would at any party of a similar kind and although the outward appearance of the prelude to dinner was one of assurance and normality, the police knew it was far from the case. Somewhere among these people there was a ruthless killer. Well briefed by The Horse, we all kept our ears and eyes open; everyone, including the police officers themselves, was under the supervision of everyone else.

Someone had placed a seating plan outside the dining room door, enabling seats to be found with ease. It was based on the plan used for last night's meal which meant the family and remaining guests occupied the same positions, with extra places being laid for the police officers. I noticed that, during the first sitting, The Horse and Detective Inspector Hailstone occupied the places which had been used by Edwin Drood and Brenda Armitage. I hoped that was not a bad omen. As I moved among the crowd, I glanced outside; I could see Sergeant Blaketon, weary but still very much on duty, parading around the exterior, chatting to his uniformed colleagues.

I knew he would be praying that no further crime would occur this evening. It had been a long day for all of us . . . another killing would be a dreadful finale.

Then, prompt at eight o'clock, the tension was broken when Johnson banged the gong to announce that dinner was served. "My Lords, Ladies and Gentlemen," he shouted above the noise of the crowd. "Please take your seats for dinner."

Slowly, we all began to filter into the dining room. The tables were a picture. White tablecloths, white crockery, silver cutlery and polished glassware beautifully set beneath burning white candles in silver candelabra exuded an aura of style and wealth and as we all sought our places, Johnson and the maids helped us to find the right tables. White flowers and foliage from the garden decorated the tables and adorned the room; a huge mirror above the fireplace, in which silver birch logs blazed, added light and space to the grand room. All the family portraits of bygone earls which lined every wall contained dashes of white — they were flowers, usually, but some were clothing and, in one case, a stunning white coach drawn by four white horses served as the background to a solemn-faced long-deceased Earl Thackerston.

There were three sprigs and a top table. The Horse and Hailstone were on the central sprig and they were seated opposite the Earl of Thackerston who was on the top table; The Horse must have agreed to this, perhaps with a view to protecting the Earl should something awful occur. The top table comprised the same grouping as for Saturday's dinner, with James Whitlock being on the end of the table to the Earl's left and the Earl of Ploatby on the extreme right. I was on the sprig opposite the Earl of Ploatby and thus nearest the door.

The fireplace with its huge mirror above the mantelpiece was behind me and opposite, across the three sprigs, were the massive windows which overlooked the drive and the white-laden bushes outside. Evelyn du Bartas had her back to those windows, she being at the head of that sprig while Lady Penelope Prittleford was at the head of the sprig upon which I was seated. Thus she was facing the big windows. As we settled down to await the signal to begin our starter (slices of chicken and asparagus terrine served with warm watercress sauce), the maids, crisp in their black dresses and white aprons and with no signs of weariness or anxiety, stood beside each table. They were awaiting the order from Johnson to commence the serving of any wine required to complement the starter.

Johnson, ram-rod straight with his faithful stick resting against the wall, stood to the left of the Earl of Thackerston with his eyes watching every move made by the girls; he was there to ensure the wine was at a peak of perfection and, now that Phyllis Catchpole had gone home, he was also supervising the meal. I got the impression he would be a hard taskmaster, wanting everything to be absolutely right. Outside, dusk was darkening the grounds but inside, the brilliant lighting from both ceiling and wall lights made the event a glittering occasion. I could see that my police colleagues were mesmerised by the splendour — under normal circumstances, they'd have been having fish-and-chips tonight but were eager to sample something from the rich man's table.

I saw the Earl raise a hand before Johnson; Johnson muttered "Yes, m'lord," and he raised his hand towards one of the maids.

She went across to the windows and began to close the huge white velvet curtains. The curtains in the rest of the house would also be closed. We now seemed secure from outside influences and the Earl began to eat. This was the signal for us all to begin and the chatter ceased as the sound of human voices was replaced by the noise of busy cutlery clattering upon expensive china.

From my position, I could see everyone. High on the wall above the top table were the portraits of ancestors in dark oils and below sat members of the present family. Having demolished my starter I studied them. The Earl of Thackerston, red faced with thick grey hair and a big nose was the image of his ancestor on the wall above; Viscount Victor was a younger version of the same fellow with the younger James carrying the same characteristics. Not quite like peas in a pod, the family resemblance did emanate from that table with surprising force, perhaps due in some respect to the portraits which graced the walls. I could see the likeness in others too — Evelyn du Bartas, in spite of being feminine and very attractive, did have recognisable facial features, as did Lady Penelope Prittleford, although in their cases, the likeness was rather more slight. It was the sort of likeness which might elude one's notice unless one was seeking it. I now began to seek similar likenesses among the others, wondering who among them the randy Earl Randy had fathered.

The Countess of Ploatby, a cousin of the Whitlock family, also boasted the characteristics, but she was a legitimate member from the Earl's side . . . my eyes ranged across the gathering. I was now fascinated by this curious family — a maid cleared my empty plate without me realising because the soup course was due.

She was asking if I required a white bread bun or a brown one while I was alternatively studying the ancient portraits and the people around me. On the wall, directly above James Whitlock was the last Earl, Earl Randy's own father and I wondered if he had been such a libertine as his son. And as I gazed into that aristocratic face, a face turned slightly to the left in the portrait and highlighted by shadows beneath the chin and eyes, I wondered what secrets that mind contained.

In the background was a miniaturised version of the White Shrubbery, also in contrasting light and shadow and as I turned my attention, I saw Johnson turn to his left and nod his head to indicate that the soup course should now be served. I smiled as I thought how like his superiors he was; that same sturdy stance, dark well-tended hair, round red face and bulbous nose . . . I knew that some dog owners looked like their dogs, some husbands and wives grew to have similar appearances, but a master and servant?

I watched Johnson very closely. The stick was at his side, dispensed with and propped against the wall now that he was not mobile, but his movements, his demeanour, his facial characteristics . . . they were just like the others! But he was not another son of Earl Randy — he was too old for that! Then I remembered another comment by Claude Jeremiah Greengrass. Like father like son, he'd said. So was the most recently deceased Earl just as prolific a breeder as his son, the current Earl? Looking at Johnson I could well believe that he and the Earl of Thackerston were related by blood . . . half-brothers even?

"Your soup, sir," said a voice in my ear.

"Thank you." I'd heard somewhere that one should not thank servants at occasions of this sort, but the young lady was not a servant of mine. So I thanked her.

Taking my soup spoon, I found myself thinking of Edwin Drood, the real Edwin Drood from Dickens' novels; his uncle, John Jasper was suspected of murdering Drood and here, in this house, we had a man called Jasper Johnson who might be no less an uncle, albeit via illegitimate means, of Edwin Drood.

So was the butler the murderer? He seemed to know the family well — he'd known of the Dowager Lady Ploatby's preference in flowers at table. I smiled to myself at the thought — that sort of thing only happened in crime fiction — but then, as I began to sip the hot mushroom soup, I thought of other things that had transpired this weekend. I was concentrating so hard that I was not chatting to my colleagues, but they did not notice — they were re-living the excitement of

England's victory in the World Cup. I realised that, of all the people here, Johnson could have had the opportunity to kill. On Saturday night, he could have asked Drood to meet him near the White Shrubbery after he, Johnson, had ushered everyone else into the lounge for the birthday speech. And being Johnson, always around the place, no one would have noticed either his presence or his absence.

Johnson was part of the scenery, part of the ambience of the Hall, and if he had stood at the back of the lounge during the speech, who would have known? Or if he'd been absent, who would have commented? He had been seen chatting to lots of people, ostensibly asking if they required a drink.

If Johnson had been seen in the Viscount's office, or in the kitchen, or on the stairs, no one would think it odd. Likewise, no one would think it odd if he'd been absent from anywhere. Most certainly, they would not regard his presence, anywhere in the house or grounds, as suspicious. He'd be almost invisible — they'd fail to notice him. And in Brenda's case, he did know his way around the exterior of the building, he would know about the ice house, he would know how to dodge the police to arrive there unseen and he could have persuaded Brenda to meet him there . . .

I then recalled something else Claude Jeremiah had mentioned. He'd accused Johnson of shooting rabbits in the grounds, just for fun. Then, in a flash of the obvious, I knew why Johnson had been doing that! He'd been practising — he'd been practising with the rabbits as targets . . . and that's why that ball of lead shot had been found near the ice house! The shot had not missed Brenda — it had not been intended for her. Some time beforehand, it had been aimed at a rabbit and it had gone right through the rabbit, as Claude had said, to blow a bloody great hole through it! The rabbit's carcass would have disappeared due to foxes, scavenging birds like magpies or sexton beetles, allowing the pellet to remain on the ground.

But Claude hadn't said anything about Johnson carrying a gun. He merely said he'd seen Johnson in the woods with a huge walking stick . . .

Claude had worried about poachers. It had been a poacher's gun. A secret gun. A walking stick gun! God! I now knew — I *knew* Johnson was the killer. That walking stick of his was a poacher's gun, a high powered, very sophisticated air weapon, one whose missiles were lethal over more than a mile.

Missiles from such a gun could penetrate an inch of solid oak. That explained why no shots had been heard — those guns, operated with compressed air under very high pressure, were silent and as I thought about that possibility, I realised that Johnson must have used two sticks this weekend. Sometimes, I'd heard him tap-tapping along the floor but at other times the stick sounded like a crutch — and most crutches had a rubber tip so that they would not slip on smooth floors. I realised I'd heard two distinct sounds from Johnson's stick . . . because one of them was a gun and it would have a metal ferrule at the end of a rod which was inserted and which acted as a cleaner.

The gun would be primed by pumping the handle, just like any other pump, and, by removing the ferrule and the rod, it revealed a smooth barrel. A few lead shots could be held in the handle, probably with a screw-on lid . . . and blackthorn, that spiky tough wood which was used for shillelaghs, was ideal for such a weapon. And once it was made, it would be hidden among all the other sticks kept at the Hall, or used by Johnson as his own walking stick.

I looked at his stick now. It was at his side, reclining against the wall of the dining room. But which stick was it? Was it the one he used as a gun, or a real stick? I found myself in a dilemma. Was I being stupid? Had I convinced myself of his guilt, just as, at one stage I thought Lady Violet might be the killer or even, God forbid, the Earl himself?

Even so, why would Johnson want to kill Edwin Drood and Brenda Armitage?

Both were older than Viscount Victor, of that I was certain having studied all the statements but neither could inherit the title. So had they been scheming to acquire the Estate, or part of it — the Hall for example? Lady Penelope

Prittleford and Evelyn du Bartas were both younger than Victor and they could never be considered as heirs. So was there another likely heir in the family, someone older than Victor? Johnson himself even? What was his true pedigree? Or had Johnson fallen in love with either Edwin or Brenda, and lost both of them to each other? Had Johnson regarded Edwin and Brenda as a threat to the status quo of Elsinby Estate? Maybe he'd overheard them plotting together? Maybe he'd seen confidential papers after creeping around on silent soles? He was known to suddenly appear on cue . . .

As I sipped my soup, now with no real enjoyment, I was struggling to decide how to tackle the problem I had created for myself. It occurred to me that the only real way to determine the guilt or innocence of Johnson was to examine his walking stick, either the one at his side or the other one I believe he used. I looked around the room for a member of the firearms team but there was none here. They were currently guarding the house and grounds. I decided I must leave the room, a rude gesture at such a grand meal, but one which must be excused. Finishing my soup, I whispered to the detective next to me, "I've got to go . . . back in a minute!"

"It's all that wine!" he chortled.

Being so close to the door, which was standing ajar to allow a circulation of air, I was able to slip out, hopefully without anyone noticing.

Once outside, I padded across the bare floorboards of the entrance hall towards the carpeted section and felt sure I had not been missed. I saw a detective at the lounge door and he acknowledged me. I said I was having a breath of fresh air. He smiled and indicated he was ready for his meal as I continued towards the stick collection. I saw all the walking sticks adorning the walls and corners and began to seek one which was identical to that carried by Johnson, a black stick of large proportions made from the wood of the blackthorn. There were hundreds of sticks of assorted styles.

Many could be immediately disregarded because of their appearance but I reasoned that if Johnson was exchanging sticks on a swift basis, the twin of his own would be very accessible. If the blackthorn stick occupied a regular place among the others, no one would imagine that a replacement, albeit of a temporary nature, would be a gun in disguise. And if Johnson always walked around with a stick, who would think that his stick was in fact a gun — and a murder weapon?

And then I found it.

In a metal umbrella stand at the foot of the stairs, standing almost out of sight behind the beautiful white grand piano, was a black walking stick which looked exactly the same as the one carried by Johnson. It was among dozens of others, all of different styles and in differing species of wood. I lifted it from the stand to examine it, concentrating upon the task in hand as a maid walked past carrying an empty wine carafe. She smiled at me, clearly puzzled at my interest in the sticks, and disappeared into the Z shaped passage which I knew took her into the dining room.

Wondering if she would report my presence to anyone, I carried the stick towards a wall light to gain a better look and began to feel it, seeking moveable sections. It was difficult to see it properly here so I took it into the rear passage, the one which led to the Viscount's office because the light was better. I twisted and pulled at the stick and concluded that this was indeed nothing more than a very heavy walking stick made from the wood of the blackthorn, complete with knots and rough bark.

It was not a secret firearm, and I saw that the tip bore a rubber ferrule, very similar to those used on crutches. If my surmise was correct, therefore, the one currently with Johnson in the dining room was the gun. Now I had to return and somehow warn The Horse.

But the tap-tapping of a walking stick immediately behind me made the hairs on the nape of my neck stand on end.

"I think you and I need to talk, PC Rhea," said the menacing voice of Jasper Johnson.

CHAPTER XVII

> "His face looks so wicked and menacing as he
> stands leaning against the sundial."
> CHARLES DICKENS, 1812–70

"Into the conservatory, Mr Rhea," Johnson ordered. He had the walking stick gun pointing directly at me and I could see it was ready for use, the brass ferrule having been removed. He was walking with the aid of his free hand against the wall. His lameness was quite genuine, I noted. In the conservatory, which was deserted, he pushed past me, unlocked the door and said, "Outside, constable, to the shrubbery. And do not try to stop me . . ."

"But why?" I asked. "Why do this?"

"For family honour," he said. "I have never sought to capitalise upon my birthright, I was born out of wedlock and I have no claims to any inheritance. I was content with my life Mr Rhea, not like awful Drood and that scheming woman. I do not wish to have any claims on the title or the estate, but they were plotting Mr Rhea, plotting to get this fine house. Not the title, not the entire estate, just the Hall. They would have ruined it, Mr Rhea, they intended to turn it into an art college and conference centre for homosexuals and lesbians, Mr Rhea . . . imagine that . . . our home, the family house! Someone had to stop them, Mr Rhea, I had to stop them, I had to dispose of them, so that the rightful heirs could keep it in the family. I succeeded Mr Rhea, with their deaths, the threat has ended. No one else would have died, Mr Rhea, if you had not poked your nose in — like Brenda, you know too much and so you must join them.

"I'm sorry. This was never intended, but go over there, against the shrubbery, into the shadows. I am afraid you will have to die because, like Brenda, you know too much. Afterwards, I shall return to His Lordship with a bottle of finest claret after locking the conservatory door and no one will know I have been here. You were just a little too clever, Mr Rhea, which I find very sad. All I wanted to do was to secure the rightful heritage of Elsinby Hall in the face of those who would destroy it . . . I am a firm believer in tradition, Mr Rhea, of continuity of family even though I cannot claim one of my own . . . now, stand over there; there, against the shrubbery . . ." and the pitch of his voice began to rise. It contained the distinctive sounds of madness, the sounds of a man with whom reasoning would be impossible.

In the darkness which had descended, I moved across the grass, wondering where everybody was . . . where were the detectives? Where were the men who were supposed to be guarding the house and grounds? I stared about myself in bewilderment and desperation as that dreadful gun with the gleaming brass muzzle followed my every move. With the ferrule removed, I knew the gun was primed. I was the target — I thought of those rabbits which had been earlier targets, I thought of running but running would be futile. If Johnson could hit a moving rabbit, he could hit me.

I needed assistance. I needed my colleagues and friends. I daren't shout, in his present state of excitement, that might precipitate his action so I was playing for time, desperately playing for time. I saw the upper rooms were all in darkness, no one seemed to be watching from there.

And downstairs, just like last night, all the curtains were closed. I was alone with this madman. Alone in the garden with no one to share my fate . . . I had to keep him talking.

"Why, Jasper, why? Why kill Brenda?"

"She knew too much, she couldn't keep her nose out of things, couldn't stop researching the family . . . she discovered that the seventh earl's orders allowed an illegitimate son to inherit the Hall. Not the title or the Estate, just the Hall. He had written "eldest son" not "eldest legitimate son" and for that reason she maintained Edwin should have the Hall . . . she said he would make it pay its way, that Victor should move into one of the farm houses and that income from Edwin's work would secure the Estate's future . . . but I ask you, Mr Rhea! Can you imagine what future generations would think? Well, if you can't, I can. I cannot bear to think of Elsinby Hall as anything but the family home of the Whitlocks. But those considerations didn't concern her . . . she was a lawyer, a clever one, and she only thought in terms of what the law said, not what families wanted . . . now, stand over there . . ." He directed me towards the very place that Drood must have stood. Then, painfully I felt, he moved towards the sundial, resting his rear against it.

His leg bothered him — with the stick being held as a gun and trained on me, he needed some support but at the moment, the gun lowered. I was safe, if only for a few seconds longer. I had to persuade him to talk.

"But did the Earl know this? Had he any idea of their plans?"

"Of course he had. But he couldn't tell you, could he? Not when you were investigating a murder. He'd have looked the guilty party, he'd have had the motive for murder, on top of which he was determined not to let them get the Hall."

"So while he refused, they could not proceed with their plans, surely?"

"They were going to take the case to the High Court, Mr Rhea. She said they were prepared to let a court decide upon the validity of the disputed papers, and that would mean national publicity about the Earl's behaviour. That was their threat — I have saved him and the family from that embarrassment."

"But the killings, Jasper? Does anyone know your part in them?"

"Of course not, constable. This is my doing, it is my contribution to the family, my secret help. Now, it is time . . ."

"But the watch? The Thackerston watch?" I was struggling to find something else to ask him. "You threw it away?"

"Edwin had no right to it, he was illegitimate. I took it off the corpse and got rid of it. I threw it in the fountain. It has been rendered valueless."

"But he was your nephew!" I shouted.

"And that is something I'm not proud of. I hate men like that, constable, can you imagine Elsinby Hall going to a man like that? I was his uncle, their uncle, I suppose, but I'm the uncle of Vernon too, remember. I am his blood relation but one who can never inherit. The house, along with the title, will surely pass down to Vernon. It makes it a real family enterprise . . . now, I must return to the meal, constable, otherwise I shall be missed. So farewell. I am sorry, but . . ."

And he raised the gun.

At that moment, I heard a whispered voice in the shrubbery behind me and immediately a furry, noisy, snarling grey blur bolted from the shadows. Something which was growling and snarling seized the good leg of this madman; unbalanced, he crashed to the ground as I heard Claude Jeremiah Greengrass say, "That'll teach you to shoot my rabbits, Jasper Johnson. Come on, Alfred, leave him be . . ."

I was already picking up the fallen gun as The Horse materialised from the darkness with three armed policemen.

"Alfred got there first," grinned The Horse. "Sorry for the delay, Nick, but we had to hear his confession. Well done for abstracting it from him. I saw you leave the room. I heard the maid tell Johnson you were looking at walking sticks and saw him leave . . . then I knew! You should have told me, you know. Anyway, we heard everything he said, we had him in our sights, but Claude's dog got there first. Well done, Claude!"

"Ay, well, a feller has to protect his rabbits," muttered Claude as the armed officers were hauling the distraught struggling Johnson to his feet. Claude looked at me and blinked, "By gum, Mr Rhea, I thought he'd got you but Alfred got there just in time. Mind, I said Johnson was no good, his eyebrows were too close together, like I said. Come on, Alfred, time to go home. This chap'll not shoot any more of our rabbits."

"I don't know what you were doing here, Claude, but thanks," I shouted after him as I followed The Horse, the detectives and Jasper Johnson into Elsinby Hall.

"Don't thank me, thank that white rabbit," Claude chuckled as he ambled off.

"What white rabbit?" I called after him, but he just winked and made no reply.

Jasper Johnson said nothing further about his reasons for killing Edwin Drood and Brenda Armitage. Later, when the Earl was asked the truth of his allegations about Drood and Brenda, the Earl said that Edwin would never have got his hands on Elsinby Hall in spite of the contents of any earlier agreements. The Earl felt sure that any court of law, in determining such cases, would consider "son" meant legitimate son. He was not afraid of letting a court decide the issue.

That being so, why did Jasper kill him? The mystery of Edwin Drood remains.

THE END

ALSO BY NICHOLAS RHEA

CONSTABLE NICK MYSTERIES
Book 1: CONSTABLE ON THE HILL
Book 2: CONSTABLE ON THE PROWL
Book 3: CONSTABLE AROUND THE VILLAGE
Book 4: CONSTABLE ACROSS THE MOORS
Book 5: CONSTABLE IN THE DALE
Book 6: CONSTABLE BY THE SEA
Book 7: CONSTABLE ALONG THE LANE
Book 8: CONSTABLE THROUGH THE MEADOW
Book 9: CONSTABLE IN DISGUISE
Book 10: CONSTABLE AMONG THE HEATHER
Book 11: CONSTABLE BY THE STREAM
Book 12: CONSTABLE AROUND THE GREEN
Book 13: CONSTABLE BENEATH THE TREES
Book 14: CONSTABLE IN CONTROL
Book 15: CONSTABLE IN THE SHRUBBERY
Book 16: CONSTABLE VERSUS GREENGRASS
Book 17: CONSTABLE ABOUT THE PARISH
Book 18: CONSTABLE AT THE GATE
Book 19: CONSTABLE AT THE DAM
Book 20: CONSTABLE OVER THE STILE
Book 21: CONSTABLE UNDER THE GOOSEBERRY BUSH
Book 22: CONSTABLE IN THE FARMYARD
Book 23: CONSTABLE AROUND THE HOUSES
Book 24: CONSTABLE ALONG THE HIGHWAY
Book 25: CONSTABLE OVER THE BRIDGE
Book 26: CONSTABLE GOES TO MARKET
Book 27: CONSTABLE ALONG THE RIVERBANK
Book 28: CONSTABLE IN THE WILDERNESS
Book 29: CONSTABLE AROUND THE PARK
Book 30: CONSTABLE ALONG THE TRAIL
Book 31: CONSTABLE IN THE COUNTRY
Book 32: CONSTABLE ON THE COAST
Book 33: CONSTABLE ON VIEW

Book 34: CONSTABLE BEATS THE BOUNDS
Book 35: CONSTABLE AT THE FAIR
Book 36: CONSTABLE OVER THE HILL
Book 37: CONSTABLE ON TRIAL

MORE COMING SOON

Gorgeous new Kindle editions of the Constable Nick books soon to be released by Joffe Books.

Don't miss a book in the series — join our mailing list:

www.joffebooks.com

FREE KINDLE BOOKS

Do you love mysteries, historical fiction and romance? Join 1,000s of readers enjoying great books through our mailing list. You'll get new releases and great deals every week from one of the UK's leading independent publishers.

Join today, and you'll get your first bargain book this month!

www.joffebooks.com

Follow us on Facebook, Twitter and Instagram
@joffebooks

Thank you for reading this book. If you enjoyed it please leave feedback on Amazon or Goodreads, and if there is anything we missed or you have a question about, then please get in touch. The author and publishing team appreciate your feedback and time reading this book.

We're very grateful to eagle-eyed readers who take the time to contact us. Please send any errors you find to corrections@joffebooks.com. We'll get them fixed ASAP.

Made in the USA
Coppell, TX
12 February 2021